Raider's Oath

Chronicles of Alcabaza Book 2

Morgan Lee Clasper

Published by Morgan Lee Clasper. For any inquiries, please contact:

morgan@morganclasperauthor.com

or visit: https://www.morganclasperauthor.com/

Cover Design by Fabrice Bertolotto

Illustrations by Marina Baskakova

Edited by Darcy Werkman at The Bearded Book Editor

Proofread by Darcy Werkman

ISBN: 978-0-473-59375-9

Books also by Morgan Lee Clasper

The Frostwing Quadrilogy

Frostwing: Dragonbond

Frostwing: Firebreath

Frostwing: Permafrost

Frostwing: Reaver's War

The Chronicles of Alcabaza

Dragon's Mark

Raider's Oath

Nomad's Ruin

Alchemist's Order

Contents

Oath-Breaker

THE STEADY THUMP OF WINGBEATS ECHOED in the night air. The wind ruffled the eagles' feathers, tugging at the cloaks of the Raiders perched atop them. Keegan pressed himself against the saddle, hunkering his shoulders against the night's chill.

"Not much further, lads," he said.

Around him, several other Raiders flew as dark silhouettes in the night. The rugged crests and mesas of the Badlands swept past below, broken only by a few faint lights from nomad camps nestled among the rocks.

"Keep it down," another Raider replied.

"Relax," Keegan said. "We're far enough from Alcabaza now that nobody will hear us."

The other Raider shot a glance over his shoulder. "Do you really want to risk that chance? It'll be a miracle if nobody has got to that ruin first and claimed it for themselves."

"Hey," Keegan said, "the Oath has been broken. Who says we can't give them a little *persuasion*?"

The eagles fell into a tight formation, gliding over the Badlands. Keegan leaned forward, peering over his bird's massive wingspan to scour the land below. He'd sent one of his Raiders forward to light a torch to signal them, but the Badlands remained shrouded in darkness.

"Where's our scout?" the Raider asked. "We should be there by now."

Keegan shrugged. "The moon is weak tonight. Maybe he hasn't seen us yet."

His eagle twitched its head. The huge feathers adorning its wings—each one as long as his arm—caught the wind and stabilized it against the air currents. Nearby, another eagle flexed and unflexed its talons in anticipation.

"Someone's jumpy," Keegan said. He patted his eagle's neck. His other hand fell to the polished hilt of his sabre. "If it's a nomad or pack of gorgons who get there first, we'll show them who's boss."

Faint moonlight reflected off his eagle's harness. It flickered for a moment as a shadow passed above. It only lasted a second, but Keegan's muscles tensed. He opened his mouth to warn the others, but an ear-splitting screech cut him off.

A flurry of wingbeats sounded as a pack of eagles erupted from the darkness. Keegan's eagle let out a cry of alarm and jolted aside as another bird ripped past. Keegan fumbled with the reins and twisted his body around, trying to get a glimpse of their attacker.

One of his Raiders screamed as his eagle collided with another bird. Talons flashed and the pair spiralled out of view. The glint of sabres reflected the moonlight.

"What do we do?" one of his Raiders yelled.

Keegan forced himself to focus. "Split up!" He yanked on his eagle's reins and put the bird into a dive.

They pivoted away from the chaos with a burst of wingbeats. The pained screeches of eagles cut through Keegan's ears. Metal clashed as sabres met, and the panicked voices of his comrades rose above the fray.

"I can't get a good look at them!"

"Head for the gullies! We'll lose them there!"

The wind whipped Keegan's face. He gripped his sabre and wrenched the blade free. A glance over his shoulder revealed a pair of eagles gaining on him. He scanned their riders for any sign of their identity. Black material covered their faces, topped with wide turbans. Keegan suppressed the panic rising in his chest.

His eagle twisted aside as one of his pursuers attacked. Wingbeats echoed in Keegan's eardrums. He straightened his eagle's course and the Badlands whipped past below. Twisted spires and buttes materialized from the darkness. One wrong move and they'd smash right into them. Keegan smiled. "Let's see how well you fly."

He spurred his eagle on. His pursuers fell into file behind him. They grappled with their eagles' reins as they flew low to the ground, weaving past boulders and cliffs. Keegan hunched over his saddle, reins pulled close to his chest. His eagle's head darted side to side as it scanned for a safe passage. One of his pursuers swore and fell back to avoid a boulder.

Keegan laughed. "Nice try, Oath-breakers," he spat.

A cliff appeared in front of him.

His eagle screeched in alarm and tried to pull away, but they were travelling too fast. Keegan braced himself as the bird slammed into the rock. A sickening crunch rang out and a force ripped Keegan from the harness. His sabre flew from his hand and the entire world spun.

3

A jolt of pain exploded through his ribs. Keegan gritted his teeth as he bounced across the ground. Thorny bushes snagged at his clothes and sliced his skin. He skidded to a halt in a pile of bushes.

Silence descended. Keegan coughed. Flecks of blood stained the dry earth. He wiped his mouth and then clutched a hand to his ribs. He winced—broken.

Keegan scanned his surroundings for his eagle. He clawed at the ground, struggling to pull himself free of the foliage. A few feathers spiralled in the air above.

Wingbeats sounded, and Keegan stopped crawling and lay still. A dark shape passed overhead. Keegan spat a curse, then wrenched a knife free from his belt. The shape landed and one of his pursuers climbed off. Up close, Keegan made out the dark material adorning his body and his eagle's harness, camouflaging them against the night. The bird ruffled its feathers. A moment later, the second one landed.

"That was a bad collision," the first one said. "No eagle could survive that."

"And the Raider?" the second one asked.

The first one studied the ground. "He must have been thrown. He could be anywhere."

"As long as he's dead."

Keegan clenched the knife tighter. His nostrils flared. He tried to pull himself to his feet, but the pain in his ribs made him stop.

Don't be stupid, he thought.

One of his pursuers climbed atop his eagle. "We'll look for the body in the morning—if the gorgons don't find it first."

The pair erupted into the sky. Keegan waited until the wingbeats faded, before dragging himself out of the bushes and staggering to his feet. The sticky sensation of blood crept down his skin from dozens of thorns. He shrugged off the stinging pain and turned back the way he had come.

Being stranded alone at night is suicide. He knew this place was gorgon country. He tore up a nearby sapling and stripped its leaves to form a walking stick. Leaning his weight against it, he gritted his teeth and began to walk.

He just had to make it to Alcabaza before the killers found him.

Aegon

"AND IF YOU LEAN TO THE SIDE LIKE THIS," Isiah told Tessa as he braced himself against Aegon's scaly flank, "you tell her to turn."

The Badlands sprawled below, illuminated by the vivid hue of the blue-white sun overhead. The light reflected off his dragon's scales in a dazzling display, forcing him to squint.

"And what about when you want to go down?" Tessa asked. Her arms were wrapped around Isiah's middle. "I still don't understand how you do it without reins."

"It goes deeper than that," Isiah said. "Ward always said that after you bond, they can sense what you want them to do."

"So it's like magic, huh?" Tessa asked.

Isiah shrugged. "I guess so."

Aegon turned on her wing, spiralling around a rock formation. Isiah shifted his weight, settling into the swell of her wingbeats. Without Ward or any of the Royal Guards to train him, he'd spent weeks figuring out how to fly with her.

"Well, we need to land," Tessa said. "My legs are getting sore."

Isiah guided Aegon into the safety of the rocky spires that had become her home. The cave appeared and he braced himself as she landed. Tessa let go of his waist and slipped off the dragon's back. She winced and stretched her lower back.

"You need a saddle," she said. "It's nothing like riding an eagle."

"You just have to get used to it," Isiah replied. He gave her a nudge. "*You* were the one who wanted to go flying today."

Tessa rolled her eyes. "You can walk back to Alcabaza with that attitude, wise guy."

She ran her hand down Aegon's flank. A shimmering mix of silver scales adorned the dragon's body, giving way to intense blue and purple where the sun touched her. Thick hind legs supported her weight, while her wings doubled as arms with long talons. Aegon let out a plume of hot breath and gave Isiah a knowing look.

"Hey, I've got to deal with her all day," Isiah said. Tessa folded her arms, and Isiah raised his hands in mock surrender. "Kidding, kidding."

She smiled. "You've got the Raider spirit," she said. "I'll give you that."

Isiah laughed. Ever since they'd defeated Enrik and his gang of Raiders, he and Tessa had grown closer. Getting away from Lazaro's house and the stuffiness of the city let him relax and lower his guard. Due to the risk of Raiders spotting them, they often went out to fly Aegon across the Badlands under the cover of night.

Tessa sighed after a moment. "Lazaro will probably be wondering where we've got to."

Isiah groaned. "Lazaro would come with us if he could."

Since Aron had told the Raiders the truth about Enrik's plan to sell the oasis water to the nobles at Paradon, the Raider groups had allowed Lazaro to remain in Alcabaza. Isiah knew the Raiders hadn't apologized for arresting them and trashing their house, but he was thankful for their unspoken truce.

"At least Lazaro is looking out for us," Tessa replied.

Isiah feigned offence. "Does he still not trust me?"

Tessa winked at him. "He doesn't trust you not to get up to no good." She turned and beckoned him. Her dark hair swished behind her, and her colourful robes matched the reds and oranges of the Badlands.

Isiah gave her a sly grin. "So I need a chaperone now, do I?"

He said goodbye to Aegon and took off after Tessa. They exited the cave and followed a narrow, rocky path to a nearby spring, where Vyrro sat waiting. The giant eagle perked up when he saw them. He ruffled his feathers and marched over.

"There you are," Tessa said. She patted his scaly leg. "How about we head back to Alcabaza?"

Isiah stopped by the pool and filled his waterskin, before clambering up behind Tessa. Vyrro kicked off and took to the air with a series of wingbeats. Isiah took one last look over his shoulder at Aegon's cave, before the rocky landscape stole it from view.

The Badlands fell away and the city of Alcabaza came into view. Isiah raised a hand to shield his eyes from the sun as the massive mountain materialized. A grassy plain, coated in a sea of maize, sprawled around the mountain's feet. Its flat peak, squared off as if cut by a huge knife, broke the skyline. Eagles, no more than dark silhouettes, spiralled around it.

8

Vyrro lowered his head and picked up speed, sensing their home was near. The city hugged the mountainside, divided into three terraces cut into the rock. Hundreds of squat, flat-roofed buildings sat piled atop one another, fighting for space and spilling over the edges. Near the foot of the mountain, a lattice of beams and scaffolding supported wooden elevators that lifted merchants into the city.

Vyrro folded his wings and dropped onto a landing pad near the mountain's peak. Beyond, Raiders streamed past the eagle pens, heading further into the roosts.

"What's going on there?" Isiah asked.

Tessa furrowed her brow. "I don't know."

Luca emerged from the crowd. He bounded toward them, his golden hair flapping wildly.

"I'll take Vyrro for you," he said. He grabbed hold of the eagle's harness as Isiah and Tessa slipped off.

"What's with the commotion?" Tessa asked.

"A Raider meeting," Luca replied. "You know how well Lazaro gets on with the other Raiders. He skipped it and sent me here instead."

Tessa smiled. "That's like him alright." She cocked her head. "What's it about?"

"Nothing important, yet," Luca said. He started leading Vyrro away. "I'll let you know if anything interesting happens."

The pair bid Luca goodbye, then Tessa led Isiah away from the mountaintop and down a staircase into the city itself. Isiah pushed through the crowd to keep up with her. No matter how long he spent in the city, he was sure he'd never find his way around.

Streams of people jostled him back and forth through the narrow streets. Some ducked into twisting alleyways, while others crowded around merchant stalls. Dust spiralled into the air from hundreds of shuffling feet. Occasionally the sound of a donkey rose above the chatter.

Isiah tightened his cloak and hastened after Tessa. They passed a bazaar with its brightly coloured tarps and suffocating incense, then past a row of houses with clotheslines strung over their flat, walled roofs. Isiah caught glimpses of the plain far below.

"Is it me, or has it got busier here?" he asked.

Tessa mulled it over. "It's a good season for merchants. Nobody stays in Alcabaza for long." She paused. "Except us Raiders."

They made it down to the lowest terrace. The streets here were wider, and the steady grumble of machinery sounded in the direction of the elevators. Wooden platforms extended off the mountainside, with staircases disappearing to meet the elevators. Caravans of merchants and nomads entered the city, their mules straining under the weight of goods. Taverns, carved into the mountain itself, stood open to receive them. It reminded Isiah of when he'd first arrived at the city with the nomad Reuben.

They passed the entrance and navigated to the edge of the terrace, where Lazaro's house sat alongside a row of others, jutting over the edge. Windows—a few boarded up—looked out over the street, while a sturdy door was set into its dusty sandstone walls. Tessa produced a key from her cloak and let them both in.

The bright colours and deafening sounds of the city faded as Isiah ducked inside. A cool shadow washed over his skin, driving away the heat from the searing midday sun. Tessa poked her head into the dining room that jutted off the entryway.

"Lazaro, we're back," she called.

"Lazaro went out," Aron said. "He's avoiding the meeting. Told me to keep an eye out for you." He wandered into the hall and cracked a mischievous smile. "I thought you'd invite me flying with you."

"Hey, Aron." Isiah nodded at the boy.

Aron clapped Isiah on the shoulder. "How did training go?"

"We're getting somewhere," he replied. "It would go faster if Ward was still alive to teach me."

Tessa pushed past them and dumped her gear on the dining room table. Lazaro had managed to replace most of what had been destroyed in Enrik's raid with the money they'd earned from the ruin. A few windows remained boarded-up, but the place was almost back to normal.

"At least you have something to fly," Aron said. "I don't know the first thing about *eagles*, never mind dragons."

While Aron fell into a conversation with Tessa, Isiah climbed the creaky staircase to the cramped storeroom that he slept in. Lazaro had moved a few of the barrels and crates out to make room for a second bed. Aron's gear lay in a pile nearby. Isiah stepped over the mess and placed his sabre on his bed.

He cast another look at Aron's side of the room. Ever since Enrik died and his Raiders had scattered, Aron had been without a home. Tessa had offered to let him stay with them—a proposition that Isiah was beginning to have second thoughts about.

A small window let a shaft of sunlight into the storeroom. The heat from outside made Isiah's skin itch. He wandered to the washroom and studied his reflection in the small, cracked mirror. He peeled back his cloak to reveal his warped, disfigured skin. The scarring stretched from his chest over his right shoulder and upper back—the sign of being Marked.

Isiah gave the rusty hand pump a push and waited until water appeared. Cupping it in his hands, he doused his Mark to relieve some of the redness and itching. It sapped the heat away, giving him momentary relief.

Isiah let the pump run dry, then readjusted his cloak to cover his Mark. It felt bumpy to the touch—like a melted candle. He pushed the thought out of his mind and exited the washroom. When he returned downstairs, Aron was leaning against the table, still chatting with Tessa.

"Have you been keeping tabs on the other Raiders?" Tessa asked.

Aron nodded. "Nobody has a clue about Aegon. If anyone starts spreading word of a dragon, I'll be the first one to know."

"Good," Isiah said. "It feels wrong leaving her on her own like this. She must be lonely."

"She'll be fine." Tessa put a hand on his arm. "She's in a good hiding place. No Raiders ever fly near there."

"Unless they find a ruin or something," Aron said.

Isiah shifted his footing. "Then let's hope they don't."

"If I hear any whispers from the Scavengers, I'll tell you," Aron said. "But keeping a dragon hidden isn't an easy job, you know."

Tessa tilted her head and peered out the window. "I think I see Lazaro."

She broke away from the table. Isiah went after her, relieved for the distraction. Tessa opened the door and Lazaro stepped in.

"You're back, are you?" He nodded at Isiah. "You're supposed to tell me before you run off."

Tessa rolled her eyes. "Relax. We had Vyrro with us."

Lazaro ran a hand through his short-cropped hair. Stubble clung to his tan skin, and his nose slanted to the side from an old scuffle. "Then maybe you can put him to use and find a ruin for us." His nose shrivelled as he looked around their still-damaged house. "Those damn Raiders trashed everything."

Lazaro filed inside, followed by the twins Darla and Antony. Tessa started to close the door, but Isiah caught someone running down the street.

"Hold on," he said.

Luca pushed through the crowd. He skidded to a halt in the doorway, doubled over.

"Luca!" Tessa's brow crinkled. "What's wrong?"

"Something is going on at the meeting," he said between panting breaths. "You guys should see this."

Lazaro stepped into view. "How serious is it?"

"I ran as fast as I could." Luca beckoned them. "Come on. We'll miss it."

Lazaro adjusted his sabre. "This better be good."

They followed Luca deeper into the city. As they ran, Isiah fought the welling unease in his gut. They ran up the terraces and reached the eagle roosts. Isiah's lungs strained at the thinning air. As they drew closer, a commotion reached his ears. It came from the direction of the Raider meeting he'd seen earlier.

He ran past the eagle pens and their colourful tarps, then skidded to a halt on the edge of the group. Lazaro craned his neck to see into the ring. Shouting erupted from inside.

"Get in there." He gave Isiah a push. "See what's going on."

Isiah put his head down and shoved his way into the crowd. Tessa and Aron came after him. He neared the front of the crowd where he could get a look at the source of the noise.

"My eagle crashed in the Badlands," a Raider said. Bandages covered his torso, and his clothes were torn at the edges. Cuts crisscrossed his exposed arms. "The gorgons almost found me before I could get here."

Frenzied conversation rippled around the crowd. Raiders shifted their footing and cast suspicious glances at one another.

"What are they saying?" Isiah asked.

"Shh," Tessa replied. She craned her neck to try and get a closer look.

"Did you see who they were, Keegan?" another Raider asked. "Even a small glimpse?"

Keegan shook his head. "It was too dark—and they were wearing masks. They didn't want to be identified."

The frenzy grew louder. Isiah spotted Lazaro and Darla pushing into the crowd.

"They weren't Royal Guards," Keegan replied. "They had eagles."

One of the Raiders narrowed his eyes. "So you're saying we've got Oath-breakers among us?"

"Nobody has ever committed such a blatant attack," one of the Raiders said. A few strands of grey hair poked through his beard. He lowered his voice. "Except maybe for Lazaro's gang. They've always been a wild card."

Isiah glanced over his shoulder at Lazaro. He saw the man's fists tighten. Darla grabbed Lazaro's arm.

"Whoever it was, they clearly planned it," Keegan said. "Who says they won't do it again?" He spread out his arms, then winced at the pain. "It could be any of you."

Several Raiders dropped hands to their weapons. Groups huddled closer together. Lazaro broke away from the crowd, and Tessa pulled Isiah after her. They made it out of the crowd and reunited with Lazaro and the others.

"Someone else broke the Oath?" Isiah said. "Why would they do that?"

"To deal with a rivalry, perhaps," Tessa replied. "There are more than a few feuds that have fallen short of blood because of the Oath. But now that Enrik broke it . . ."

Lazaro scowled at the Raiders. "The nerve of them to accuse us. I should have given him a piece of my mind."

"Not here," Antony said under his breath. "We don't need another fight."

They wandered away from the group, back in the direction of their house. Isiah let the sounds of the crowd fade to the edge of his awareness. The Raider's Oath was the only thing stopping anarchy. "What happens if someone else decides to break it?" he asked, but he already knew the answer.

"Then the whole of Alcabaza could fall apart," Tessa said.

"Do you see why I called you?" Luca asked. "The Raiders are scared. I hear it from the handlers when I'm caring for the eagles. They figure if someone as popular and influential as Enrik could be a traitor, secretly working with Paradon, who else could be hiding secrets?"

Isiah tightened his cloak. He tried to ignore the ever-present feeling of his Mark. Whenever he was in the city, he could feel people's eyes washing over him. All it took was for one Raider to get too suspicious.

They left the roosts and entered the lower levels of the city.

"What do we do now?" Darla asked.

"Nothing, yet," Lazaro replied. He slammed his fist into his palm. "If they think they can pin this on us, they've got another thing coming."

"We're just an easy target," she said. "After what happened with Enrik and all. The Raiders realized their mistake. We're not Oath-breakers."

"There are still more than a few of them who want to see us hanged," Antony replied. He turned to Tessa. "I don't know about Lazaro, but I don't like the idea of you flying Aegon at night with these attacks going on."

Isiah faltered. "What do you mean?"

"I mean if you keep sneaking off at night, you're going to end up running into trouble," Antony replied.

Tessa folded her arms. "It was only one group. For all we know, Keegan got into a scuffle with another gang and they wanted revenge."

"Antony's right," Lazaro said. "You know how I feel about you associating with dragons. I won't have you endangering yourself like that, Tess."

"Then we'll be careful," she shot back. She glanced at Isiah. "Right?"

"No nocturnal flights," Lazaro repeated. "If whoever is out there wants our blood, then they'll have to go through me."

Tessa huffed.

"He's only doing what's best," Antony said.

"What about scouting, then?" Tessa asked.

Lazaro's nose crinkled. "Scouting is different."

"Oh yeah, how?"

"Nobody is being attacked in the day, for starters," Darla cut in. "Just hold off on your nocturnal escapades, okay?"

They reached their house and Lazaro ducked inside. Isiah's head swam. The sight of Keegan and his injuries was burned into his mind. The idea of rogue Raiders hunting the Badlands made his skin crawl.

"We'll sneak out," Tessa said under her breath. "We can look after ourselves."

Isiah shook his head to clear the thoughts. "Maybe flying at night isn't such a great idea."

Tessa rolled her eyes.

"You know he means well," Isiah said.

She sighed. "I know, you're right." She checked that nobody else was listening. "But sometimes I wish he'd leave us alone."

Keegan's Ruin

Isiah adjusted himself on Vyrro's saddle for the hundredth time. Tessa's body pressed against his front, and Aron clung to his back. Isiah squirmed as the straps of Vyrro's harness cut into his legs.

"Vyrro isn't designed for three people," Tessa said. "They should know that."

Antony had insisted the three of them go out when scouting for ruins. *For extra security*, he'd said. Lazaro had forbidden them from travelling close to the area Keegan had been attacked.

"You know, it makes me wonder what Keegan was after that was so important," Aron said. "I mean, why did those mystery Raiders attack *him*?"

"I told you," Tessa replied. "It must have been a rivalry."

"But to go to all that trouble? Why not attack him inside Alcabaza? It would take much less effort."

"Are you saying we should go and check it out?" Isiah asked.

"Well," Aron said, "I don't want Lazaro to kick me out, so *technically* no. But all I'm saying is Keegan must have been going somewhere."

"Or he was scouting," Tessa replied.

"At night? Come on, Tessa. You don't scout for ruins at night." Aron leaned closer, further squishing Isiah. "You *raid* them at night, so nobody can see where you went and follow you." He pointed to the horizon. "I recognize the place where the attack happened. I reckon I can guide you there."

Tessa dug her leg into Vyrro's side. The eagle responded by pivoting on his wing. His tail feathers opened to act as a rudder. Isiah shielded his gaze from the twin suns above. The blue-white sun baked the Badlands in heat, while its reddish cousin sat off to the side.

"Lazaro doesn't trust us," Aron said. "You know we won't find any good ruins unless we push the boundaries a bit." He nudged Isiah. "What do you say?"

Isiah tore his eyes away from the Badlands below. "He has a point."

"And if we get there first, we can clear out any good stuff before Keegan is the wiser."

"Fine," Tessa replied. "We'll take a look." She spurred Vyrro on. "Nobody can ambush us in the day. You can see for miles here."

"Exactly." Aron grinned. "I thought *you* were the adventurous one."

Tessa spurred Vyrro on toward the area where Keegan had been attacked. The spires that sheltered Aegon's home sat on the horizon.

"I want to check on Aegon," Isiah said.

"What about the ruin?" Aron asked.

"We can do that after." He craned his neck to get a better look at the spires. "We could even use her for protection."

"You know flying her in the day is a bad idea," Tessa replied.

Isiah wrung his hands. "I know that. It's just . . . I feel bad for leaving her so much."

Vyrro flew toward the spires. After a few minutes, he entered their shadows and neared the cave where Aegon lived. A rocky trail led up to her cave, which was carved halfway up the side of the spire. Vyrro flapped his wings and landed on an outcrop with a cry of greeting. Isiah slipped off as Aegon's serpentine head emerged from the cave.

Isiah's Mark gave a twinge as the dragon laid eyes on him. He brushed it off.

Aegon unfolded her wings and glided down to meet them. The dragon dwarfed Vyrro. She lowered her wing for Isiah to climb on.

"How about we go flying?" he asked her.

"Stay low," Tessa told him. "The landscape will make you harder to spot."

Aron scanned the sky. "Do you see anyone around here? Raiders never visit this place."

"You're right, Tessa." Isiah settled into the dip between Aegon's shoulders, and she prepared to launch herself. "I'll be careful."

The dragon and eagle took off and cleared the spires, soaring toward the place where Keegan was attacked. Aegon hung close to the ground as Tessa had suggested, weaving between mesas and over flat patches of scrub.

Around them, craggy rocks and boulders concealed dark hollows and caves. A dead eagle, no more than a pile of feathers and picked-clean bones, lay where it had fallen. A couple of fat vultures turned their heads to watch Vyrro drift overhead.

Tessa's nose crinkled. "He was right about the gorgons."

A patch of stone caught Isiah's eye, almost invisible against the rocky backdrop of cliffs. "There's the ruin."

Aron rubbed his hands together. "See? I knew we were onto something."

Tessa pulled on the reins and Vyrro slowed, circling around the site in a wide arc. Aegon tailed the bird. Tessa leaned over his flank and studied it. "That's a ruin, alright."

"Maybe we should check it out," Isiah suggested.

"We'll tell Lazaro," she replied. "We can raid it together."

"If he doesn't flip out on us for disobeying him," Aron said. "We're not supposed to be here, remember?"

Tessa fidgeted in her seat. Aegon flew closer to the ruin, giving Isiah a better view. Sandstone bricks were cut into the rock, forming a doorway that disappeared into darkness. A rocky overhang shielded the ruin from above, making it near-impossible to see from the sky.

"Looks like a good one," Isiah said.

"Look at you," Aron replied. "We've got an expert on ruins here." He gave Isiah a playful grin. "You've only been a Scavenger for a few months."

Isiah ignored the embarrassment. "I mean, nobody will have found it before us, right? We should go before any other Raiders come looking."

"The Oath is broken," Aron said. "The other Raiders might not respect Lazaro's claim. Keegan might have even got here first, for all we know. That means it's technically *his* ruin to loot. We'll miss out."

"Alright." Tessa pulled on Vyrro's reins. "Then let's be quick."

Vyrro descended into the shadow of the cliffs and landed with a thud. Isiah braced himself as Aegon did the same, coming to rest on a patch of bare ground. Isiah climbed off and stretched his legs.

Tessa approached the ruin. "We don't have any torches—or rope, or anything."

Isiah scanned their surroundings. Low, dry bushes hugged the sandbanks and dried-up ponds around them. "We can use these."

He collected a stick and, after carefully splitting the top with his sabre, stuffed it with grasses and foliage. "A few of these will give us enough time to check it out, right?"

Tessa put her hands on her hips. "It might be empty for all we know."

"Then we'll have saved Lazaro coming out here to be disappointed."

As Isiah and Aron made the torches, Tessa led Vyrro away and hid him behind a rock formation. "Just in case anyone else is flying by," she said. "You should hide Aegon too. There's an overhang nearby."

Aron scoffed. "Good luck hiding anything that big."

Isiah ignored him. He put his hand on Aegon's neck and willed her to follow him. He took her around a corner to a rocky overhang.

"Wait here," he instructed. Aegon let out a puff of hot air from her nostrils and nuzzled him.

Tessa grabbed an empty bag from Vyrro's saddle. "We don't have much room for loot."

"Then we'll take the best stuff and leave," Isiah replied.

They returned to the ruin and, after lighting their torches with a fire-starter, cautiously ventured inside.

"Scavengers first." Aron stepped aside.

"We're *both* Scavengers," Isiah said.

They descended into the tunnel. Sand and dust coated the floor, and cracks riddled the stonework from earthquakes. As they went, the air grew colder. It clung to Isiah's skin, making his hair stand on end. When Tessa coughed, the sound echoed into the darkness.

The passageway began to narrow, forcing them to duck. Isiah saw that Tessa's breathing was quickening. He lowered his voice. "Are you sure you're going to be alright?" He remembered her claustrophobia at being trapped inside a ruin once before.

"I'll be fine," she replied. After a moment she reached down and squeezed his hand. "But thank you."

After a minute, the passageway widened into a room. Their torches pushed away the shadows, revealing old pillars and piles of rubble. Isiah kept his free hand on the hilt of his sabre.

"Stick together," Tessa said. "In case we run into a gorgon den."

They ventured deeper into the ruin. Isiah broke away from the others and raised his torch to survey the walls. Murals, faded and covered in sand, stared back at him.

"What do you think this place was?" Aron asked. His voice bounced off the walls.

"It looks like a tomb," Isiah replied. "Remember those murals in the ruin Enrik was excavating?" He abandoned the murals and tentatively checked one of the many branching passageways. The dust, disturbed by his footsteps, swirled in the air and tickled his nose.

"You were right," Tessa said. She motioned to a row of stone coffins stacked atop one another. "It's like a burial ground or something."

Aron rubbed his hands together. "I wonder if there's any magic. There's usually magic in tombs."

They picked a tunnel and started down it. Isiah scanned for the faint glimmer of gold. A few low stone tables sat in alcoves, along with more coffins.

"Maybe we've got to find the rich people's burial chambers," Aron suggested.

Tessa's nose crinkled. "Or it's already been looted."

Isiah beckoned them. "Come on. Let's look a bit further."

Tessa and Aron hastened after him. Isiah checked a few more small rooms that branched off, but nothing of value presented itself. His heart sank when he spotted another table. Wooden cups and goblets were scattered across the floor around it.

"Somebody has been here," Tessa said, echoing his thoughts.

Isiah wiped his fingers across the surface of the table. The dust was disturbed, as if somebody had haphazardly swept things off the table. "Maybe they were in a hurry. There might be something left behind."

Tessa tugged on Isiah's arm. "Then we'll come back with Lazaro. We'll get lost if we stay down here for long."

Isiah glanced at his torch. It had begun to burn low. He sighed. "You're right."

He went after Tessa and Aron. They navigated their way back to the ruin entrance and began up the sloping tunnel to the outside. After a moment, a glimmer of light appeared ahead. Isiah hastened toward it, but Tessa caught his arm.

"Wait," she said.

Isiah paused. Over the sound of their breathing, they could hear a noise from beyond the entrance.

Wingbeats.

They backed away from the entrance. The wingbeats grew louder, followed by a few thuds as eagles landed. Muffled talking reached Isiah's ears.

"Get those eagles unloaded. Who knows if we'll find something good."

Tessa swore under her breath. She grabbed Isiah and Aron's arms and pulled them after her. "Don't let them see your torches," she said.

Isiah pressed himself against the wall of the main cavern. "They're blocking the entrance."

"Who are they?" Aron hissed.

"Someone must have had the same idea you did." Tessa craned her neck to peer down the tunnel. "They'll be here in a minute."

"What if we make a lot of noise?" Isiah asked. "It could scare them off if they know there are already Raiders here."

"Or they could mistake us for nomads," Tessa replied. "I hid Vyrro. We've got no eagles to prove we're Raiders." She lowered her voice. "And we can't let them know about Aegon."

Isiah racked his brains. The Raiders' voices grew louder. "What if we confront them?" he asked.

Tessa shook her head. "It's too risky. Without the Oath, who knows what they'll do if they know we're alone down here."

"We have to do *something*," Aron said.

Tessa broke away from the wall. "We can hide." She nodded to herself. "We'll wait for them to start exploring and we can slip out while nobody is looking."

Without waiting for their reply, she took off. Isiah stumbled after her. His torch faded to a bundle of glowing embers, casting barely enough light for him to see the way ahead. "If we don't get lost in here," he said.

From behind them, the Raiders filed into the main entryway. Their voices climbed above the hammering of Isiah's own heart.

"Fancy Keegan thinking he could sneak off at night like that. There must be something good down here for him to do that," one said.

"Keep your wits about you," another replied. "Who knows if those rogues aren't lying in wait for us. Do you think they've got the guts to show their faces around Alcabaza after what they did?"

Isiah rounded a corner. He skidded to a halt to avoid bumping into Tessa. She looked around and swore. "Where are those rooms we found?" she asked.

"You must have taken a wrong turn," he replied.

The voices sounded again. "Split up, groups of three. Holler if you see anything strange."

Isiah wrung his hands. "Keep going."

They followed the tunnel for a minute longer, before the tunnel came to an end. The floor dropped into darkness. Isiah raised his dying torch to illuminate an empty chasm.

"It's a ravine," he started.

"And a dead end," Tessa replied.

Aron pointed to the ground. "Look at that."

A metal pole protruded from the earth, with the end of a rope tied around it. Isiah and Tessa exchanged glances.

"It's the only way," Aron said. "Unless you want to risk going back and running into them."

Tessa gave the rope an experimental tug. "It's recent. It must be from the same Raiders who looted it."

"You're the lightest," Aron said. "You go first."

Tessa clenched the handle of her dying torch between her teeth and grabbed the rope. She carefully lowered herself off the edge and, gripping the rope, began to climb down. Isiah leaned over the edge to watch her.

The seconds ticked past. Aron cast a nervous glance behind him. "She's taking too long."

Tessa's torch flickered across sheer rock walls. Beyond its faint glow, darkness extended. The voices behind them grew louder. Isiah prayed she'd make it to the bottom soon.

The rope snapped.

Isiah's heart flew into his throat. The metal pole lurched as the rope tore free and flew into the darkness. Tessa's torch went out. Aron grabbed Isiah's arm and pulled him away from the edge.

"We have to hide," he hissed. At the far end of the passageway, light peeked around the corner. Aron threw his torch into the chasm and crouched behind one of the many stone coffins.

Isiah hesitated. His muscles were locked. He snapped himself out of his trance and quickly followed Aron's lead. He crouched in the darkness behind a coffin, trying to ignore the image of Tessa's light snuffing out. She hadn't even had time to scream.

The Raider's torch flooded the tunnel in firelight. Shadows danced across the walls as three figures marched past. Isiah caught glimpses of them, but he didn't dare raise his head over the lid of the coffin.

One of the Raiders swore. "What is this supposed to be?" she asked.

"Looks like a ravine," another replied. "Or a fissure from an earthquake, maybe?"

"Or whoever built it couldn't be bothered to make a bridge."

Isiah risked peering out to see one of the Raiders lean over the edge.

"Nothing," he said. "Waste of time." He broke away. "Come on. There's nothing down here but bones and dried corpses."

Isiah waited until their footsteps had faded, before crawling out of cover to the edge of the chasm. He squinted, searching for any sign of Tessa. As the light from the Raiders faded, darkness swept in until it was impossible to see.

Aron grabbed Isiah's cloak. "Careful. You'll fall in."

"We have to find her," Isiah said. He fought the urge to call Tessa's name. "What if she's hurt?"

"We can't do it in the dark," Aron replied. "We need more torches. Come on—we can't help her if we can't see."

Fighting every fibre in his body, Isiah tore himself away from the chasm and then felt his way along the wall. With every step, nausea gnawed at his gut. Tessa was down there somewhere.

And the Raiders were still blocking their escape.

Chasm

TESSA'S BODY JOLTED AS THE ROPE SNAPPED. Her stomach lurched as a feeling of weightlessness seized her, before she plummeted into the chasm. She opened her mouth to scream and her torch flew into the darkness. She braced herself to hit the ground.

A couple of seconds passed until her feet connected with the earth and a bolt of pain coursed through her ankle. Her foot twisted and she collapsed onto her side. The torch clattered and went out, plunging her into darkness.

Tessa clutched her ankle, gritting her teeth as a throbbing pain coursed through her leg. She choked back the urge to make a sound in case the Raiders heard her. She probed her ankle, searching for any breaks.

Nothing. Tessa breathed a sigh. It was only twisted. She suppressed the icy panic and tried to survey her surroundings. A shallow layer of sand had broken her fall. Beneath it, smooth rock formed the bottom of the chasm. She felt about and found the rope lying in a pile nearby where it had fallen—but no torch.

Calm down. She forced herself to take a deep breath. The familiar sensation of being unable to breathe began to creep up on her, but she expelled it. *Not now.*

Tessa crawled about, searching for the torch. Her ankle hurt to move, but she ignored it. The torch had to be nearby. If she could light it again . . .

She paused. A faint glow caught the corner of her eye. Cautiously, she crawled toward the source. As she went, the rock beneath her palms turned to sandstone bricks. The light grew stronger, emanating from the far end of the chasm.

Tessa looked up at the darkness above. Isiah and Aron's torches had gone dark. She hoped the Raiders hadn't found them.

They'll find Lazaro, she told herself. *He'll know what to do.*

The light grew brighter. It shone with a faint purple hue, seeming to beckon her. Tessa dragged herself to her feet and hobbled over.

Sandstone bricks covered the floor and walls, stretching into darkness. A few doorways disappeared into the rock. In the centre of the space, looking out across the floor of the chasm, stood an altar.

Tessa's breath escaped her in a rush. She'd heard stories from Lazaro about the things Raiders found in tombs. Her mind raced, and for a moment she forgot her pain.

Could it be some kind of magic?

Tessa tentatively reached out and touched it. A totem, its features worn away until it was no more than a vague shape, sat in the centre of the altar. Coloured rocks formed its eyes, radiating the soft light she had seen.

A plaque sat beneath the figure. She leaned over and blew on the inscription, trying to clear the dust and sand. She squinted in the dim light. *Still illegible.*

Tessa glanced around. Shadows shrouded the chasm. Without her torch, she knew she'd never find a way out. Her gaze returned to the totem.

She swallowed to clear her throat. "You don't mind being moved, do you?" Her voice came out shaky. Lazaro had warned her not to mess with things in ruins—and after she'd seen the power the oasis had . . .

Tessa took the totem in both hands. She gave it an experimental tug. The scrape of stone echoed as it budged. Gritting her teeth, Tessa placed one foot against the altar and pulled.

The totem came free with a jolt. An electrical shock erupted through her body like a bolt of lightning. A flash of pain stabbed Tessa's palms. She gasped and dropped the totem. It hit the floor and split apart. Tessa clutched her hands to her chest as the totem's eyes grew brighter. They split the darkness, flashing across the chasm walls.

Tessa stumbled away. She raised an arm to shield her eyes. The light seemed to stab her, shining through her eyelids and piercing at her brain. It washed over her skin, pricking her with heat. Her injured ankle gave way and she collapsed.

The totem exploded into dust. Its eyes bounced across the sandstone. Tessa lay motionless, arm still clamped across her eyes. The shock faded, leaving a weird nauseating sensation in her gut. She rolled onto her side and fought the urge to throw up.

The totem's twin eyes lay in the sand. Their light dimmed, before they went dull. Dust from the totem swirled in the air, making Tessa's eyes water. She staggered to her feet and leaned against the wall. Her mind spun.

Calm down, she told herself. Her throat tightened in panic, and the familiar suffocating weight of the earth seemed to close in on her from all sides. She sucked in a deep breath and tried to focus on Isiah. Her pulse began to slow.

Isiah's face flickered in front of her. Tessa paused. She could have sworn she saw his messy hair and bright eyes. She squeezed her eyes shut.

Get a grip, she scolded. *Now you're imagining things.*

The twin stones still gave off a glimmer of light. Tessa scooped them up and placed them on the altar in front of the inscription. The language was too old for her to understand. She cracked open her bag and carefully placed the plaque with the inscription inside.

Helen will know, she thought. Helen was good at reading old stuff.

Beyond the altar stood two doorways, bordered by sandstone bricks. Holding the twin stones ahead of her, Tessa inched her way toward them. The darkness swirled around her. She prayed the faint light wouldn't go out and plunge her into pitch-black.

If they go out, I'll never find my way back.

One of the doorways led to an old staircase, its steps rounded and chipped by time. With one hand on the wall to keep her balance, Tessa began to climb. Her shallow breathing bounced off the passageway, deafening in the silence. The air, thick and filled with dust, tickled her nose and made it hard to draw breath.

The minutes ticked past. The staircase continued to climb, unending. Tessa clutched the stones to her chest, squinting in the shadows to make out each step. She strained her ears for any sign of Isiah and Aron.

Or the Raiders.

The staircase ended at another doorway. A tunnel intersected it. Tessa tried to get her bearings.

I must still be in the ruin, she thought. *I can't have gone far.* She hoped she was right.

The plaque with the inscription seemed to weigh her down. She still felt the dim stinging sensation in her palms. Her gut churned at the thought of what she'd found.

Movement sounded ahead. A stone clattered. Tessa heard Aron curse.

"Aron?" she whispered. She didn't dare raise her voice in case any of the Raiders were within earshot. "Isiah?"

"Tessa?" Isiah asked.

Despite herself, a wave of relief washed over her. She hurried to the source of the noise and bumped head-first into Isiah. Their foreheads met and he grunted in pain.

Tessa rubbed her head. "How did you find me?"

"We were looking for another way down," Isiah replied. "The Raiders almost found us, but we slipped away."

"Are they still around?" she asked.

"I don't know."

"They must be distracted by now," Aron said. "We should make a run for it."

Tessa bit her lip. "Do you remember the way back?"

"I think so," Isiah said. "But we don't have any light."

"Use this." Tessa pressed one of the stones into Isiah's palm.

He furrowed his brow. "Where'd you get this from?"

"I found it," she lied. "At the bottom of the chasm. It doesn't matter."

Tessa followed the boys as they retraced their steps towards the exit. Part of her wanted to tell them about the altar, but she kept her mouth shut. Whatever magic she'd found, telling Isiah would only worry him. She rubbed her palms against her clothes to ease the throbbing sensation.

I'll tell Helen first. She'll know what to do.

After a few minutes, they neared the exit. A glimmer of daylight, only visible because of the near-total darkness, beckoned them. They paused at the entrance to the main room and waited.

"I don't hear anyone," Aron said. "Do you think they left already?"

"Maybe," Tessa replied. "Let's not push our luck."

They broke from cover and ran toward the tunnel. No Raiders confronted them as they jogged toward the daylight and finally emerged in the open. The bright sunlight stabbed Tessa's eyes, forcing her to raise a hand to shield them. Further off, the Raiders' eagles stood waiting.

Aron laughed. "Made it! Those Raiders will be none the wiser." He clapped Tessa on the shoulder. "For a moment there I thought we'd lost you."

Isiah turned to Tessa. "Are you hurt?"

She forced a smile. "No. It'll take more than that to do me in."

Her smile faded as boots crunched on stone. The subtle sound of a sabre being drawn met her ears.

"What do we have here?" a gruff voice asked.

Lazaro's Lot

Isiah's hand flew to his sabre. He wrenched it free and spun in the direction of the noise. A Raider stood atop a pile of rock, sabre in hand. A pipe poked between two rows of yellowed teeth.

"Fancied stealing someone else's ruin, did you?" he asked.

Tessa and Aron drew their blades. Isiah took a few steps back as the Raider jumped down from his perch. His colourful robes flapped in the breeze, camouflaging him against the rock.

"It's a good thing I stayed behind to watch the eagles," he said. He nodded to the trio. "Empty your bags."

"Cool it," Aron replied. "We only flew out here to see what Keegan was after. We're all Raiders here."

"Really?" The man looked over his shoulder and whistled. A second Raider trudged over a crest. "Then where are your eagles?"

"We hid him," Tessa cut in. Her eyes darted between the pair. "To stop anyone from stealing him."

The second Raider waltzed over. "I know you," he said slowly. He wagged a finger at Tessa. "You're Lazaro's lot."

The first Raider's mouth twisted into a sly smile. "Then nobody will notice if they go missing."

Tessa adjusted her grip on her sabre. "The Oath still stands."

"That's up for debate," the Raider replied.

Isiah cast a look in the direction they had taken Vyrro and Aegon. The two Raiders were close, but if he could reach his dragon in time . . .

Aron raised his hands. "Look," he said, "we're all not supposed to be here. This is Keegan's claim. How about we all agree to look the other way?"

The Raider's smile dropped. "Keegan's a friend of mine." His voice took on a hard edge. "He even sent me over here to look out for thieving rats like you."

Isiah caught Tessa's eye. She nodded in the direction of Vyrro. His muscles coiled, ready for a fight. The handle of his sabre felt slick with sweat.

"Here's what's gonna happen," the Raider said. He and his friend circled them, like predators waiting to strike. "You'll give us your valuables and we'll march you into Alcabaza to face the Raiders for violating Keegan's claim. Or"—he lowered his voice—"I call for the rest of my group and we bury you inside the ruin."

Isiah and Aron took a step back. The Raiders pressed in, cornering them against the cliff near the ruin entrance. Their sabres gleamed with a cruel light. Isiah fought the urge to make a break for it. He knew Aegon was painfully close. He could almost feel her presence.

"This ain't a fight you want to take," the Raider snarled. He tapped his blade against the tip of Tessa's sabre. The metallic ring made Isiah's skin crawl. "Because the Oath ain't going to protect you no more."

An ear-splitting bellow cut him off. The Raider's heads snapped around to see a glittering shape erupt from the Badlands. Isiah's heart flew into his throat as he realized what it was.

36

Tessa seized her chance. She swung her sabre and batted away the closest Raider's blade as Aegon closed in. The dragon's enormous wingspan stirred the dust and surrounded her in a billowing cloud. The Raiders' eagles screeched in panic and pulled at their binds.

The Raiders swore and stumbled away. One of them fumbled with a whistle. An eagle broke free of its ropes and launched itself into the air.

Tessa grabbed Isiah's hand and yanked him away from the chaos. "Come on!"

Isiah recovered his senses and stumbled after her. "What are we doing?"

"They can't know the dragon belongs to us," she replied. She leapt over a pile of rocks and ducked through a crop of scraggy bushes. Isiah hastened after her, raising his hands to shield his face from the foliage. Behind him, panicked cries broke out as Aegon closed in on the Raiders.

Isiah's foot caught on a root and he was sent sprawling. He clutched his throbbing knees and peered out at the dragon.

The Raiders slashed the ropes to their eagles and the birds scrambled away. A smouldering heat welled in Aegon's silvery chest, before she cracked open her jaws and spat a trail of fire after them. The flames fell short as the eagles spiralled into the air.

"How did she know we needed help?" Aron asked. "Did she hear us?"

Isiah swallowed. "I don't know." He waited for his heartbeat to slow. Aegon glared at the retreating Raiders, before breaking away and slithering in their direction. Tessa made sure the coast was clear, then stepped out.

"That wasn't good." She folded her arms. "Who knows what those Raiders will tell the others."

Isiah pushed out of the bushes and reunited with Aegon. A blast of hot air baked his face. He stroked her opal flank. "They can't prove it had anything to do with us."

"That doesn't mean they won't tell stories about a wild dragon hunting in the Badlands," she replied. "Maybe they'll even try to blame Keegan's attackers on it."

Isiah's mind flashed back to when he first met Tessa while travelling with nomads. She'd been hunting wild dragons then.

"I *knew* we shouldn't have visited the ruin," Tessa said. "But *someone* thought it would be a good idea."

Aron raised his hands. "Now, now, let's not be too hasty here. How about we fly back to the dragon's hiding spot? We'll talk about this in Alcabaza."

Isiah cast a nervous glance at the tunnel entrance. "Good idea."

Aegon lowered her wing to allow Isiah to clamber on. As Tessa and Aron ran off to recover Vyrro, he guided Aegon to take flight. She kicked off and drifted low to the ground, taking shelter behind crags of rock. He stroked her flank and she returned it with a reassuring rumble.

"Thanks for helping us back there," he said, unsure if she could understand him. The dragon turned in the direction of the spires that marked her hidden home.

Isiah hoped they hadn't blown her cover.

Magician's Tricks

THEY FLEW BACK TO ALCABAZA IN SILENCE. TESSA KEPT her eyes glued to the horizon, waiting for the mountain that the city was built into to materialize. When it came into view, she spurred Vyrro toward it and the eagle glided toward the roosts. As they landed, she narrowed her eyes and surveyed the Raiders. She didn't spot the ones that Aegon had scared away.

"Do you think they'll say anything?" Isiah asked.

"They're bound to," she replied.

"No," he said, "I mean about us."

She mulled it over. "I don't know. I'll tell Luca to listen to the handlers. They always know what the Raiders are up to."

As she spoke, a couple of boys scurried up and offered to take Vyrro. Tessa slid off the bird, patted his flank, and nodded to the handlers. She led Isiah and Aron away from the roosts as the handlers took her bird away.

They navigated through the cramped, bustling streets of the city toward their home. After a while, they reached the house and Tessa let herself in.

Antony sat at the table, stitching a Raider harness. He looked up as they entered. "Did you find anything?"

"No," Tessa lied. She exchanged looks with Isiah and Aron. "We decided we needed some air, is all." She hugged the bag with the plaque tight and hid it from Antony's view.

Isiah and Aron excused themselves, leaving Tessa alone with Antony. She wandered to the table. "Is Helen home?" she asked.

"I think I saw her upstairs, on the roof," Antony replied.

Tessa thanked him, then hurried to the second floor. She passed Isiah and Aron's room, then turned at the end of the hall and took a narrow, rickety staircase to the roof. She found Helen there, hanging a bundle of robes on a clothesline.

Tessa wandered over. She clutched the bag with the plaque to her chest. The woman turned as she approached.

"Tessa," she exclaimed. "Good timing. Help me with this, will you?"

Tessa obeyed. Helen was a tall woman, with arms thicker than half the Raiders in Alcabaza.

"What brings you up here?" she asked.

"I found something while flying in the Badlands," Tessa explained. "I wanted you to take a look at it."

"Out there?" Helen laughed. "The only things to find out there are scorpions and gorgon dens." She put out a burly hand. "Let's have a look."

Tessa lowered her voice. "Don't tell Lazaro, okay?"

The woman furrowed her brow. "Just what have you been doing out there that requires so much secrecy?"

Tessa opened the bag. "We found a ruin earlier."

Helen put her hands on her hips. "A ruin? Why didn't you come back here and tell us? You know how dangerous it is alone."

"It wasn't my idea." Tessa started to protest, then stopped herself. "We only went inside for a moment. I think—I think I found some magic."

Helen's stern expression flickered for a moment. "What kind of magic?"

"It was an altar," Tessa explained. She recounted the story of finding the altar at the bottom of the chasm. She left out the part about falling while hiding from the other Raiders. She pulled the plaque out. "I remember you learned how to read stuff in tombs."

Helen took the plaque from her and squinted at it. She moved away from the low wall and the busy street beyond so that nobody could overhear them. "I've seen stuff like this before."

Tessa fumbled with her pocket. "I also found these." She pulled out the twin stones.

"Those look like they're used for rituals," Helen replied. "A lot of tomb relics have them. Merchants like to hawk them to nomads as protection charms." She scoffed. "Merchants are conmen." She patted the inscription. "But this . . . it's different."

Tessa wrung her hands. The memory of being hit by the magic made her insides roll. Ever since finding the totem, something had felt . . . off. She put a hand on her stomach to quell it.

Helen squinted at the inscription. "It's archaic," she said. "And faded. I'll have to take it to my room to study."

Tessa's shoulders slumped. "Can't you make out anything?"

The woman brought it close to her face and blew on it. Tessa coughed at the shower of dust. Helen scrunched up her nose.

"It says something about a mirage, I think. Like those ones nomads see when they get lost and wither away to dehydration."

Tessa pulled a face. "What sort of magic does that?"

The woman ignored her. "Then there's a word for a trick. No—deception." She traced her finger across it. "Then an old word for *eye*—or is it a sun?" She muttered to herself. "No, I was right. Maybe it's some old shaman's plaque." She grinned. "Or a magician's tricks. Does this help?"

Tessa forced a smile. "It does."

Before Helen could rope her into a job, she scurried away. She needed time to think.

She retreated to her room and slipped inside, closing the door behind her. It was next to Lazaro's room, with a raised bed beneath a window overlooking the plains. She hung her sabre on a rack and collapsed onto the bed. Part of her felt guilty about Lazaro forcing Isiah and Aron to share the cramped storeroom.

"Mirage, deception, eye," she repeated. She stared at the ceiling, where a few cracks in the plaster snaked across it. "What's that supposed to mean?" She lifted her hands and inspected her palms. Despite the burns, no sign of damage was visible. "And how is it supposed to even work?"

Tessa scrunched up her face and turned her hands over in front of her. *What do all these things have in common?* After a moment, she gave up and let her hands flop onto the bed.

"Maybe it *is* just some magician's tricks," she said. "An illusionist's spell, maybe." Something clicked in Tessa's head. She sat up. "What if . . ."

A knock sounded at the door. "Are you alright?" Isiah said.

Tessa stood and opened the door to find Isiah holding a half-eaten apple.

"You were acting kind of weird on the way back," he said.

Tessa stepped aside to let him in. "It's fine," she said. Her mind flashed back to when she had seen the image of Isiah's face in the ruin. "I want to try something."

She plucked the apple from Isiah's hand and placed it on her bed-side table.

"What are you doing?" he asked.

"I found something when I fell," she replied. She sat on her bed and focused on the apple. "Give me a moment."

Tessa let Isiah's presence fade to the back of her mind. She furrowed her brow, concentrating on the apple. A small part of her felt like an idiot. She tried to recreate the feeling of being trapped in the chasm.

Slowly, a nauseating feeling welled inside her, the same gut-churning shock that she'd felt when she picked up the totem. The apple began to flicker. Tessa imagined it whole. For a moment, the bite marks disappeared.

"Tessa." Isiah's eyes widened. "How did you . . ."

Tessa's breath escaped her. She deflated and the apple returned to its former shape. She waited for the nausea to subside. "I found magic," she said. "I think it lets me cast illusions."

Isiah sat on the bed. He watched the apple as if expecting it to change again. "When did you discover this?"

"Just now," she replied. "Helen helped me." She hesitated. "Don't tell Lazaro, okay?"

"Why?" Isiah asked. He scooped up the apple and poked the part where the illusion had been. No trace of it remained. "That's so cool."

"I don't want to worry him," she replied. "And I don't want him knowing we snuck out."

"Okay." Isiah's gaze fell to his lap. "I'm worried about Aegon."

"She'll be fine," Tessa said. She put a hand on his knee. "She's a dragon, remember?"

Isiah's mouth flickered into a smile. "I guess. But I hope we haven't blown her cover. If the Raiders go looking—"

"They won't find her," she said. "The Badlands is a big place. There are so many ways to hide. Luca can keep an eye on the Raiders. We'll know if they're planning anything."

Isiah sighed. "You're right." He started to the door. "What are you going to do about your magic?"

"I don't know. Helen's looking at the inscriptions I found. Maybe she'll figure out how to make it work better." Her smile dropped. "But don't tell anyone, okay? Not even Aron."

Isiah gave her a reassuring smile. "Got it."

Her bedroom door creaked shut and he was gone.

Wild Card

ISIAH SAT AT THE DINING ROOM TABLE. SOFT CANDLELIGHT flickered across the faces of the Raiders around him. Lazaro sat at the head of the table, his expression shrouded in shadow. Aron sat next to him, alongside Antony, Darla, and Helen. Only Luca was missing.

"Something's wrong." Tessa stepped away from the window and let the curtain fall back into place. "They're up to something. Where's Luca?"

Isiah wrung his hands. Several days had passed since their close shave at the ruin. They hadn't ventured out again, and he was beginning to miss his nocturnal flights with Aegon. That evening, he'd spotted the Raiders setting up torches. As night fell, Lazaro had grown increasingly twitchy.

Lazaro stood. "Let me have a look." He walked over to the window Tessa was standing at and pulled aside the curtain. Torchlight from the streets filtered through, making their shadows dance across the walls like twisted stick figures.

"What does it mean?" Isiah joined the pair at the window. Torches, their flames whipped by the wind, lined the streets. Darkness shrouded the plains, wrapping the Badlands in a thick blanket. Clouds churned above, threatening rainfall.

"There are no celebrations on our calendar," Tessa said. "I checked. Do you think the Raiders are up to something again?"

Lazaro cocked his head. Outside, clusters of people navigated the streets, hunched together for safety. The shadowy figures of beggars were slumped in doorways and inside alleys. "Nobody told *me* anything."

Tessa caught Isiah's eye. He knew what she was thinking. *What if somebody found Aegon?*

A thud at the door made them jump. Lazaro crossed the room in three paces and ducked into the hall. Tessa and Isiah ran to the spot where Lazaro had disappeared and listened.

"Luca," Lazaro said. "What's the word from the roosts?"

"There's a meeting," Luca replied.

"Another?" Lazaro asked. "They had one not even a week ago."

"It's a big one," he said. "This ain't a small get-together."

Isiah could almost hear Lazaro scowl. "What is it this time?"

"They didn't say," Luca replied. "But every Raider in the city has been ordered to attend."

Lazaro scoffed. "Ordered? They don't boss us around. That's not how Raiders work."

"They weren't joking," Luca said. "They mean business."

An eternity seemed to pass. At last, Lazaro sighed. "Fine." He called over his shoulder, "Get your sabres. We have business to attend to."

Antony and Darla slipped from the table. Isiah tried to read their expressions, but their stony faces revealed nothing.

"A surprise meeting?" Helen said. "At this hour? Who do they think they are?"

Lazaro returned to the dining room. He adjusted his scabbard. "I don't know, but I'm keen to give them a piece of my mind."

"Keep your cool, Lazaro," Antony warned. "There's no need for us to make a scene. Let's tag along and see what the other Raiders have to say."

Isiah hurried to his room with Aron to grab their sabres. As they went, he fought the growing unease.

"What do you think it could be about?" he whispered.

"I don't know," Aron replied. "I've never heard of a meeting being called at night like this. Something's serious."

They collected their gear and rejoined the others at the front door. The Raiders were ready to leave. They spilled out of the house and began following the torch-lit road up to the eagle roosts.

Silence cloaked the city. A cold wind whistled through the streets, stirring the torchlight and tugging at the edges of their clothes. The alleyways and side streets were deserted, save for a few beggars huddled together to fend off the cold.

"I've never seen the place so deserted," Tessa said. Their footsteps crunched on the dusty stone street. Their breath formed a faint mist. Tessa's hand found Isiah's and slipped around it.

They climbed to the eagle roosts. As they went, the torches grew brighter, fighting against the relentless wind and leading toward a large building off to the side. Handlers scurried about the eagle pens. None turned to look as they passed.

"Where are we going?" Isiah asked.

"It's a tavern," Aron replied. "Enrik's gang used to practically live out of it. Raiders don't like mingling with the nomads on the lower levels."

Isiah's mind went back to the dark, cramped tavern he found while travelling with Reuben. As they drew closer, the Raiders' tavern appeared. A wooden façade covered the front of the structure, with a foundation of thick stone blocks. The structure melted into the mountainside, overshadowed by the eagle pens and landing platforms of the roosts.

Talking reached Isiah's ears from within. Firelight lit up the building's windows, and a few Raiders loitered in the entryway. Lazaro nodded at them as he passed.

"You're late," one of them drawled.

"We had better things to do," Lazaro replied. He pushed through the doorway and disappeared inside. Antony and Darla went after him. Taking a deep breath, Isiah followed.

The lights and sounds of the tavern washed over him, clearing away the night's chill. A roaring fire bathed the interior, and Raider groups sat clustered around the many tables. A bar stood on the far side, along with a small stage for hosting entertainment. A couple of stray dogs darted between tables, hunting for scraps.

"This doesn't look like a meeting," Tessa said.

"It is," Aron replied. He pointed to their empty tables. "Nobody's bought anything, see? They're here for something else."

Isiah rounded his shoulders, aware of the many pairs of eyes on him. He scurried after Lazaro and slipped into a seat. Despite the din of talking, the tension in the air made his skin prickle. He sensed it in his gut, like the deadly calm before a storm. Behind the Raiders' bright eyes and fake laughs were cold, calculating stares.

"Listen up, you lot," a voice yelled. Something slammed against wood. The Raiders' heads turned to the stage, where a female Raider was waving her arms. Keegan sat in the front row, his limbs still bandaged. A walking stick leaned against his chair. The two men Aegon had chased sat nearby.

"You might be wondering why we brought you here on such short notice," the Raider stated, "and at this time of night, too. It's not to celebrate." She turned her head, surveying the crowd. Isiah shrank down in his seat as the woman's eyes passed over him. Her voice took on a serious tone. "Another group was attacked yesterday."

Her words rippled across the crowd. Some Raiders swore and slammed their fists. Others listened in silence.

"It was my brother and his gang, attacked near the outskirts of Alcabaza," the woman continued. Her dreadlocks, studded with eagle talons and trinkets, bobbed as she talked. A curved sabre swung at her side, its handle rounded and shaped like an eagle's foot. "I was scouting when I saw it. A black-clad group descended on them, felling their eagles and killing them all. My brother died before I could fly him back to Alcabaza."

A few pained cries rose from one corner of the room. Raiders muttered among each other.

"The Oath is dead," the woman said, "unless we root out the killer."

"We should raid Edward's house," one man shouted, pointing at his rival. "If we find the black outfits, then his gang is guilty!"

"Shut your mouth," Edward yelled. "This is all Enrik's fault. If he hadn't broken the Oath, none of this would have happened."

"You have a good point," the Raider with the dreadlocks said. She tilted her head back to peer into the far side of the tavern. "And somehow, Lazaro's group always manages to find themselves in the middle of it."

Lazaro pressed his palm against the table. "Don't try and pin this on us, Mauriel," he hissed. He ignored Antony's stern expression. "We have nothing to do with the killers."

Mauriel raised her hands. "I'm not pinning this on you," she said innocently. "But I do find it curious how you've fallen out with nearly every Raider gang in Alcabaza at one time or another."

A few Raider groups devolved into frenzied muttering. Chairs squealed as several men stood and started a shoving match.

Mauriel spun on them. "Keep your heads on straight! Let's not do the killer's work for him."

The Raiders ignored her. Isiah caught their suspicious glances. The stray dogs bolted from the room as the chattering grew more frantic.

Mauriel stepped down from the stage and waltzed toward Isiah's table. "And how do you explain your escape from our prison?" she asked. "You miraculously made it out of the city after being arrested on charges of Oath-breaking—and who can forget the time one of your Scavengers released a dragon that slaughtered a bunch of Raiders?"

Lazaro stood. Darla caught his arm. "That had nothing to do with me."

"Cool it," Antony warned.

"No," Mauriel said, "of course not. It just so happened that you found the one Scavenger who was secretly a spy for Paradon!" She turned her attention to Isiah, Tessa, and Aron.

"Leave them out of this," Lazaro ordered. Several Raiders looked up from their arguments as Mauriel's words caught their attention.

"But that spy escaped back to Paradon, so Aron told us," Mauriel said. "You broke out of prison on your own, fought Enrik, foiled his plan, and the dragon's escape was a mere coincidence."

Isiah squirmed in his seat. His Mark itched. He kept his head down so none of the Raiders could look too closely at him.

"How convenient it all was," she said. "It's also convenient that your Scavengers were present when a wild dragon chased some Raiders near the place Keegan was attacked."

Isiah saw the flash of surprise behind Lazaro's eyes. The pair of Raiders Aegon had attacked wandered over. One rolled up a sleeve. Behind the cover of the table, Darla's hand crept toward her sabre.

"We had nothing to do with that," Lazaro snapped. "We hate dragons as much as you do. Wild dragons are nothing new."

Mauriel twirled one of her dreadlocks. "It's only a coincidence, Lazaro," she replied. "Perhaps one coincidence too many."

The Raiders drew closer. Darla let go of Lazaro's arm and he rose to his full height. His nostrils flared. "I resent being accused of breaking the Raider's Oath." His spittle landed on Mauriel's forehead.

The woman slowly wiped her brow. "Oath-breaker or not, I think we can all agree that you and your gang have caused more trouble in Alcabaza than you're worth."

One of the Raiders made a grab for Lazaro. Lazaro shoved the table aside and swung a fist at the Raider. A sickening crunch sounded and the man spun away.

The Raiders burst into motion. Darla yanked on her sabre, but Mauriel grabbed her arms before she could free the blade. Shouting erupted as the Raiders closed in. Isiah staggered to his feet as his chair fell over. Lazaro slammed his fist into the man who had attacked him, but the other Raiders closed in.

Isiah wobbled, trying to keep his balance. His body was crushed against Tessa and Aron. Tessa fumbled with her sabre hilt, but the crush of people made it impossible to draw her weapon. She screamed and bit a Raider's hand as he grabbed her.

"Arrest them!" Mauriel ordered. She grappled with Darla. The woman lunged forward and slammed her forehead against Mauriel's nose, making her reel away.

Hands grabbed at Lazaro, catching his arms and wrestling him away. He grunted in pain as the bloodied Raider landed a punch to his gut.

A hand caught hold of Isiah's arm. He tried to wrench himself free, but the crush of people hemmed him in on all sides. Tessa cried out as more hands dragged her away. Isiah tried to reach her, but she was too far.

Something slammed into Isiah's back. A shock of pain ricocheted through his shoulder blades. He fell to his knees and the hands pinned his arms behind him. Somebody pulled his sabre free and confiscated it.

The crowd began to disperse. Chairs lay strewn across the floor. The Raider Lazaro had punched held a rag to his bleeding head. Mauriel wiped her bloody nose and spat on the ground.

"You've always walked a thin line, Lazaro," she said. "But the Oath tied our hands."

Lazaro glared up at the woman. He tried to wrench himself free, but the other Raiders held him tight. "You've got nothing on us," he snarled. "You need proof."

"Not to exile you," Mauriel replied. "I'm not going to throw you in prison to rot, or execute you for Oath-breaking." She pushed her hair out of her face. "The Raiders will hold a vote on your banishment. Until then, you can stay locked up."

A chorus of approval went around the Raiders. They began to drag Lazaro and the others away. The crowd parted to reveal Tessa and Aron. Tessa watched with wide, fearful eyes as Lazaro was pushed around by his captors.

"Troublemakers are thrown out of the city," Mauriel said. "And that doesn't only apply to sleazy merchants or drunken nomads." Her lips parted as she turned to Isiah, revealing a predatory grin. "But I know of a better way to use Scavengers."

The Raiders yanked Isiah to his feet. His arms were forced against his back, making his shoulders burn. Tessa called out to Lazaro, but the Raiders pulled her and Aron away.

"Put them in the cellar," Mauriel ordered. "We can't do anything with them right now."

An elbow in Isiah's back made him walk. Tessa writhed beneath her captors' grip, but her struggling achieved nothing. Isiah's captors forced him through a doorway and Lazaro disappeared from view.

"I'll deal with the Scavengers in the morning," Mauriel announced. She paused. "And after that, we have a dragon to hunt!"

Isiah's blood turned to ice. The Raiders pushed him down a flight of stairs and swung open a wooden door. A shove sent him sprawling. He landed in a pile next to Tessa and Aron. The door slammed shut, plunging him into darkness.

"See you in the morning, Scavenger," a gruff voice said. "Oh, and don't mind the rats."

Goose Chase

Isiah groaned and rubbed his aching arms. The muffled sound of Raiders talking filtered down from somewhere above, but he couldn't make out any words. He shifted his weight on the hard floor.

Tessa stood and stumbled to the door. She rattled on the handle. It didn't budge. She pounded it with her fist. Each bang echoed across the space.

"Are you alright?" Isiah asked. A lump formed in his throat.

"We need to get out of here," Tessa replied, rattling the door harder. She spun around. "Did you see if they had a key?"

Isiah cautiously stood, leaning against the wall for balance. In the shadows, he made out large wine barrels. The soft scamper of a rat emanated from somewhere beyond.

"They're taking Lazaro somewhere," Tessa said. "We have to break him out."

"You heard what Mauriel said," Aron replied. "They're holding a vote. Lazaro will be fine until the morning."

Tessa ignored him. She felt the door, probing the lock. "See if you can find anything that can help us." Her voice grew higher with each word.

Isiah leaned against the barrels, trying to collect himself. His shoulders still ached where the Raiders had pinned him. He steadied his breathing. "They're going to hunt Aegon," he managed to say.

"We'll worry about that later," Tessa replied. "We need to find a way out of here first."

"It's a cellar," Aron replied. "In a mountainside. There's not even a window to climb through."

"Then look for a bit of wire or something," she snapped. "We must be able to make a lockpick."

"And then what? Waltz out while every Raider in Alcabaza is sitting up there?" Aron's voice grew louder. He stopped himself. "We need time to plan."

Tessa stopped. She sank to the floor, her back against the door. "You're right." She slammed her hand against the stone. "I knew we shouldn't have come here. Lazaro was right to avoid meetings."

Isiah sat next to her. The cold stone sapped his body heat away. When he put his hand on Tessa's leg, she was shivering. "We have until morning," he said. "There'll be plenty of opportunities to get away."

"You don't know that," she replied.

"Lazaro can look after himself," Isiah said, more to himself than to her. "And so can we." His words hung in the air.

"He's right," Aron said after a moment.

Tessa sighed. She shuffled closer to Isiah and rested her head on his shoulder. "It's cold down here."

Isiah bit his lip at the thought of Aegon, blissfully asleep in her cave. She had no idea what the Raiders were about to do. "Once we get out of here and find Aegon, we'll be fine," he said. "We can reunite with Lazaro and we'll be safe."

Even as he said the words, a nagging voice in the back of his mind told him he was wrong.

* * *

"Good morning!" Mauriel's sing-song voice called.

The door lurched, knocking Isiah forward. He and Tessa scrambled away as light flooded the cellar. His limbs were stiff from the cold, and goosebumps riddled his skin.

Mauriel stood in the doorway with several Raiders. They marched into the cellar and dragged Isiah to his feet. One of the Raiders grabbed Tessa, but she pulled her arm away and stood herself. Further back, Aron rubbed the sleep from his eyes.

"Did you have a good night?" Mauriel asked.

Tessa glared at her. "Where's Lazaro?"

"I wouldn't worry about that," Mauriel said. "I told you I had a plan for you." She motioned to the Raiders, who grabbed Isiah's hands and pinned them behind him. The familiar bite of rope cut into his wrists.

"Remove their harnesses," Mauriel said. "We can't have them looking like Raiders where we're going."

One of the Raiders produced a knife and cut away the straps that pinned Isiah's robes to his body. The material hung loose, reminding him of the merchants and nomads who inhabited the city.

"Tie them together," Mauriel said, "and follow me."

The Raiders obeyed. Isiah found himself at the front of the line, being led up the stairs and through the tavern. The room stood deserted. There was no sign of the previous night's brawl. Mauriel led him out of the building and into the bright Badlands sun.

"Where are you taking us?" Tessa snapped. She was behind Isiah, with Aron in the rear.

"You're not in a position to ask questions," Mauriel replied. Her dreadlocks swung as she walked.

The eagle roosts faded behind them. Mauriel fell into stride beside Isiah. She grabbed his hood and yanked it up over his head. His robes hung loose, concealing the binds around his wrists. The other Raiders closed in to form a tight-knit group.

"Let's not make a scene," Mauriel hissed. "We're just a normal Raider group out for a walk." As she spoke the words, Isiah felt the prick of a knife in his back. "You got that?"

Isiah nodded.

Mauriel beamed. "Good."

They walked further into the city, before making a sharp turn into a long, covered structure packed with colourful market stalls. Isiah's nose crinkled as the aroma of incense hit him in the face. Merchants hawked their wares as streams of nomads and city-dwellers funnelled past.

It's a bazaar, Isiah thought. Bright tarps and rugs coloured in deep red and purple hung from the rafters, and an arched roof protected them from the harsh sun. A donkey wandered past, led by a couple of merchants. Voices bartering and children laughing filled Isiah's ears.

Mauriel scrunched up her face. After a moment she exclaimed, "There."

The Raiders pushed Isiah and his friends in the direction of a merchant group. They loitered to one side, surrounding a band of a dozen people. Despite the dim light, Isiah made out the ropes connecting the people's wrists. Isiah's heart sank.

"The city-dwellers don't like the sight of labourers," Mauriel said. "They couldn't care the least about beggars, but how *terrible* it is for them to be reminded of slavery." She waved at the merchants as they approached. "But these bazaars give us the perfect cover from prying eyes."

Tessa gasped. "You're smuggling us out of the city."

"You're a smart one," Mauriel said sarcastically. She patted Tessa on the head. "And you'll be far away before Lazaro and his gang are set loose. What better way to rid him from Alcabaza than to send him on a wild goose chase to find his sister?"

"You're sick," Tessa spat.

Mauriel laughed. She reached the merchants and engaged in a hushed conversation. One of the men tapped his foot. Isiah strained to hear them.

"You kept us waiting," the merchant said. "What's so special about these ones, anyway?"

"They're Scavengers," Mauriel replied. "We caught them pickpocketing from their group."

"And you can't just disown them?"

Mauriel shook her head. "They know the city too well—and our roosts. They'll forever be a pest. Why not offload them and get them out of our hair for good?"

The merchant shrugged. "Fair enough." He produced a pouch of coins. "Our usual rate?"

"Hey!" Tessa cut in. "You can't sell us! I'm a Raider, not a Scavenger. We're with Lazaro. Ask around and you'll see for yourself."

Mauriel laughed. "You'll have to gag this one," she said. "She's such a convincing liar."

Mauriel collected the pouch and the Raiders pushed Isiah toward the group of labourers. The merchant—a short, bearded man with a dust-stained face—secured him to the rest of the convoy.

"Right, you lot," he ordered, "start walking. We're already late. I expect to reach our camp by noon."

Several labourers lurched forward and the chain began to move. Isiah found himself being dragged along with the crowd. Part of him urged him to resist, but he knew it would do no good. One of the other labourers was too slow, and a merchant repaid him with a strike from a long stick.

Mauriel gave them a little wave. The rest of the bazaar stole her from view. The merchants marched Isiah and his friends out and through the city. He kept watch for any sign of Lazaro, but deep down he knew it was hopeless. Tessa walked behind him, her head bowed.

The crowd parted to let the merchants pass. A flicker of pity crossed the faces of some, while others averted their eyes and hurried in a different direction. As they neared the edge of the city, the grumble of machinery became audible.

Isiah mustered the courage to speak. "Where are we going?"

The bearded merchant grunted. "For processing."

The machinery grew louder. The stone streets of the city gave way to wooden platforms that jutted over the distant plains below. A ramp led down to one of the elevators. Isiah remembered arriving with Reuben. He'd seen merchants with a crowd of labourers then.

"What does processing mean?" he asked.

The merchant scowled. "Keep walking."

Isiah flexed his wrists. The ropes cut into his skin, making his fingers numb. He mentally groped for a plan. "These binds are too tight."

The merchant brandished his stick. "You'll learn pretty fast to stop talking if you keep up like that."

Isiah fell silent. Pulleys squealed and ropes creaked as one of the elevators was lifted to the ramp. The labourers piled on. The elevator—no more than a wooden platform with waist-high sides—swayed as they boarded. A voice gave the all-clear and the elevator lurched into motion.

As it descended, the lattice of beams and supports that made up the city's underbelly drifted past. Pulley-boys, no more than shadows, darted between the ropes and winches, operating their elevator. Several other elevators lifted merchants and nomads to the city.

The elevator hit the ground with a jolt and one of the walls fell, forming a ramp. The merchants herded the labourers off.

"Get a move on," the bearded merchant ordered. He grabbed Isiah's collar and pushed him off the elevator. "Scavengers like you might be used to flying eagles, but the rest of us don't have that luxury. You'd better get used to walking."

A wide dirt path led through the plain. Run-down fences, separating fields of maize and wheat, bordered it. Farmers worked in the fields, tilling the ground with hand tools.

"Eyes on the path," the merchant snapped. Isiah winced as the stick connected with his shoulder. "Unless you want to be put to work alongside them."

The path led away from Alcabaza, cutting through the plain and then splitting off and winding into the Badlands. Isiah shot a glance over his shoulder at the city. A few silhouettes of eagles circled above it.

The labourers left the plain and climbed the steep bank into the mesas and gullies of the Badlands. Merchants bordered the line, guiding them through the terrain. *And making sure nobody tries to escape*, Isiah thought.

The merchant beside him fell back to bring up the rear. Isiah risked talking to Tessa.

"Where do you think we're going?" he whispered.

"It must be a merchant camp," she replied. "They spring up near the big cities." She crinkled her nose. "That's where they sort the labourers before they get marched off to different parts of the Badlands."

Isiah swallowed. His mouth, already parched from spending the night in the cellar, felt shrivelled. The lump in his throat had returned—but not from dehydration.

Aegon, he thought. He willed his thoughts to travel to her, but he knew it would do nothing. *Where are you?*

The line of labourers snaked through a gulley and passed into the shadow of overhangs. Fallen rocks and loose scree littered the ground. Sheer, painted walls of stone hemmed them in. Beyond, a thin coil of smoke curled into the clear air.

Isiah rounded a corner and the merchant camp materialized. A palisade wall bridged the gap between the cliffs, each log sharpened into a crude point. Beyond, a series of tents stood, their peaks poking higher than the walls that surrounded them. A few more merchants stood near the gate, alongside mules laden with bags.

"Took your time," one of them said. "We were worried we'd have to set off without you."

"And risk our labourers dying on the trip?" the bearded merchant replied. "Pack your things. We'll depart at dawn."

The merchants ushered Isiah and the labourers through the crude palisade gates and into the camp. A large, white tent dominated the entryway, with tarps to shield the hard earth from the scorching sun. The cliffs around them provided shelter, protecting them from the wind—and the gaze of eagles who might happen to fly above.

Merchants, wielding their sticks, began untying the ropes that linked the labourers. One stopped in front of Isiah.

"And don't even think about making a run for it," he said. "We have ways of dealing with runaways."

Another merchant leaned in, grinning as he flashed a knife. "If you see anybody missing a few fingers or an ear, you know what happened."

The merchants began dividing the labourers into groups. Isiah strained his neck to keep sight of Tessa, but she disappeared into the crowd. Isiah ended up with Aron and the men on one side, with Tessa and the female labourers on the other.

"Get this lot processed," the bearded merchant said. "Then let them into the yard with the others. Everyone else can rest up and go over our planned route through the Badlands."

Wood creaked as the palisade gate shut, sealing them inside. Isiah eyed the sheer walls surrounding them. He'd never be able to climb those. But he didn't have time to think about escape.

The merchants began herding the women toward the tent. One gave Tessa a shove. She twisted around and met Isiah's gaze, before she was gone.

'New Life'

TESSA STUMBLED AS THE MERCHANT PUSHED HER. She gritted her teeth to keep from spitting an insult. Her binds cut into her wrists, making them ache, and the crush of bodies carried her into the large tent. The tent flaps closed behind her—the shadow of merchants betraying the guards.

"Line up," a female merchant snapped. She wore long, colourful robes that shielded her from the harsh sun and dust of the Badlands. Several other merchants stood around tables covered in rags.

The labourers all lined up against the far tent wall. Tessa poked the fabric with her foot, probing for a loose tent peg or any weaknesses. If only she could make it out of the camp . . .

The merchants stopped by each labourer and untied their binds. Unlike the labourers she usually saw, the people around her wore the robes of nomads and city-dwellers. The merchants paused whenever they found a gold earring or a ring.

"You won't need these where you're going," the merchant said. "You're labourers now, and it's time you got that into your heads."

Tessa waited as the merchants moved down the line. She tried to imagine punching one and causing a distraction. Her empty sabre scabbard bounced against her leg, seeming to mock her.

"Whether you're prisoners from the border, swallowed up by your debts, or you're petty criminals not worthy of living in Alcabaza, you're all here for a new life—whether you like it or not," the merchant said, strutting in front of the line. "We'll march you to the nearest city and put you to work. There's no shortage of ways for a labourer to be useful." A faint smile crossed her lips. "And for some of us to get rich in the process."

Tessa tensed as the merchants reached her. They inspected her for jewellery, then untied her hands.

"This one's got nothing," one of her captors said. She grabbed Tessa's scabbard. "But this is a fancy scabbard. Worth a pretty penny, by my reckoning."

The woman in charge grunted in satisfaction. She scooped up a bundle of rags from the table and dumped them in Tessa's arms. "Take it off."

Tessa clutched her hands to her chest protectively. "What?"

The merchant gestured to her robes. "We can sell those clothes of yours." She leaned in. "You're a labourer now, remember?"

Around her, the other merchants started handing out rags. Heat welled in Tessa's chest, but she swallowed her pride and slipped off her robes. The other merchants collected their shoes and bagged everything up.

Tessa pulled on her new rags and grimaced. The worn, rough material made her skin itch.

"Better," the woman said. She gestured to the tent flap on the far side. "Proceed to the yard. If you're lucky, we'll feed you before we depart."

The line of labourers marched into motion. Tessa wrapped her arms around herself and shuffled along with them. The Badland sun greeted her. She blinked, adjusting her eyes to it. The wall of palisade wrapped around, forming an open space littered with a couple of tarps and a few logs as makeshift benches. Labourers, all clad in the same faded clothes, sat huddled in the shade and against the walls. A few merchants patrolled between them and stood guard.

The female merchant and her cronies exited the tent and made their way to another structure. A voice called out from the other side of the tent. Tessa's stomach dropped as she realized Isiah was among them.

His Mark, a voice in her head told her.

Tessa scanned the yard. A low bench sat against the tent wall. She quickly took a seat next to a line of labourers. She racked her brain for some kind of plan. If the merchants saw Isiah's Mark, she dreaded to think what would happen.

A few holes pitted the tent wall. Blending in with the other labourers, Tessa pressed her eye against one. It gave her a view of the interior of the tent. Isiah and Aron were marched in alongside their group. The merchants began untying them and checking them for valuables.

"You haven't earned the right to wear anything more than rags," a merchant said. He passed out the same moth-eaten cloth she'd been forced to wear. "Time to swap."

The merchant stopped in front of Isiah. Tessa saw him falter.

"What do you mean?" he asked.

"I mean, give us those fancy robes of yours," the merchant replied. Isiah swallowed. "Now?"

The merchant sighed. "Yes, now." He pushed the robes against Isiah's chest. "Like everyone else."

"I—I can't," Isiah stammered.

"Why not?" the merchant said. "Are you squeamish?"

"I—I've got a skin condition," Isiah lied. His eyes darted about. "These robes were made special."

"I don't care if your head is falling off," the merchant replied. "Either you get changed now or I'll beat you within an inch of your life."

Tessa's pulse quickened. Her mind raced as she desperately tried to find a plan.

"Hey, you," a voice snapped. Tessa pulled away from the hole to see a merchant staring at her. "Stop spying."

A few of the other labourers laughed. Tessa waited until the merchant wasn't paying attention, then put her eye back to the hole. Isiah fumbled with his collar. Many of the other labourers were already done. The remaining merchants closed in on him.

Tessa held her breath. She focused on Isiah's Mark, willing it to change. She conjured up the image of the apple in her room. A familiar unsettling feeling welled inside her. Isiah pulled his robes off.

"See?" the merchant said. "Was that so hard?"

Isiah studied his shoulders with wide eyes. Tessa gritted her teeth, willing the illusion to last. He hurriedly pulled on the rags and dusted himself off.

Tessa pulled away from the hold and slumped against the material with a sigh. A minute later, Isiah's group filed out of the tent. She caught his arm as he passed and pulled him toward her.

"Isiah," she said.

He collapsed on the bench next to her. "Tessa." She caught the slight tremble in his voice. "You won't believe what happened."

"I know," she replied. She leaned in and lowered her voice. "I used my magic."

Isiah faltered. He pulled up his collar and inspected his Mark. "How did you—"

"Like in my room, remember?" she asked. "I was watching you."

Isiah nodded slowly. His expression dropped. "Wait, does that mean you saw me . . ."

Tessa covered her mouth so he couldn't see her smile. "It worked though, didn't it?"

"Guys." Aron sat opposite them. "I overheard those merchants say where they're gonna take us. They say we're marching at dawn for some salt mines on the other side of the Badlands. It'll be a week before we even reach the halfway point."

"Damn Mauriel." Tessa kicked the ground. "She must have had this all planned out from the beginning."

"They're stopping at a couple of settlements along the way," Aron added. "Maybe we'll be dropped off there." He put a hand to his mouth and leaned in. "Or we can escape on the way."

"What about Lazaro?" Isiah asked. "Won't he come after us?"

"There are tons of merchant trails that stretch all over the Badlands," Aron replied. "How will he know which one we followed?"

"And he won't recognize us," Tessa added. She bit her lip. "Without our robes, we'll be impossible to spot from the air."

Aron stood. "I'm sick of sitting about and waiting," he said. "I'm gonna take a look around. Maybe I can learn something useful." He turned to Isiah. "You coming?"

Isiah joined him. He adjusted his rags to make sure his Mark was covered.

"Be careful," Tessa warned.

The pair melted into the crowd of labourers. Tessa stayed put, watching the merchants as they patrolled around the camp. She tried to count the number of guards and what weapons they had.

"Who's Lazaro?" a voice asked.

Tessa jumped. She turned to see a girl on the edge of the yard. She peered out from beneath a makeshift hood that shielded her from the sun.

"Oh," Tessa said. "He's a friend." A nagging voice told her to keep quiet.

The girl shuffled over. She brushed a few loose strands of hair from her face. "I thought labourers didn't have friends."

Tessa sighed. "It sure looks that way."

"Are you from Alcabaza?" she asked.

"How did you guess?"

"I saw your robes when you came in with the others. You were a Scavenger, right?"

Tessa checked that none of the merchants were listening. The nearest labourers were engaged in their own hushed conversations, or staring aimlessly at the ground. She leaned in. "I'm a Raider."

The girl frowned. "You can't be a Raider. How'd you end up here?"

"It's complicated," she replied. "What about you?"

The girl drew her knees to her chest. "I don't want to talk about it."

Tessa shrugged and let the matter drop. She resumed watching the guards, trying to figure out when they changed shifts. A few mules leaned against the palisade wall. She wondered if she could spook them and cause a commotion.

There has to be a way out, she thought. *All I have to do is find it.*

∗ ∗ ∗

"Get up!" a merchant barked.

Tessa shifted and opened her eyes. The twin suns peered over the horizon, casting long shadows across the camp. Despite how early it was, the Badlands was already beginning to heat up.

Tessa propped herself up on her elbows and took a moment to collect herself. Her face fell as she remembered where she was.

The other labourers woke up and then ordered themselves into a line. A few merchants passed out wooden bowls. Tessa brushed the dust off her rags and hurried to join them. She strained her neck to spot Isiah and Aron.

"Eat quickly," the bearded merchant ordered. "Either we make good ground this morning, or you'll be marching under the midday sun."

Tessa collected her bowl. It contained a watery broth, but her aching stomach didn't complain—not that the merchants would listen to her protests, anyway.

The girl she'd spoken to the previous day stood off to the side, on the far end of the line. The merchants finished handing out the bowls and then several departed to load their mules for the journey ahead. As soon as the labourers had finished, the merchants re-bound their wrists and connected their ankles with ropes.

To stop us from running, Tessa realized.

Beyond the white tent the merchants used for processing, the palisade gates creaked open. The merchants spurred their mules and began herding the labourers toward it.

Tessa caught sight of a few large, hulking beasts beyond. Scaly flanks protected their large bodies, and saddles laden with bags hung from their hump-like backs. They had short, stumpy heads tipped with beak-like mouths and short tails that wobbled as they walked. She recognized the creatures as some of the pack-beasts that the nomads often used.

The line lurched into motion. Slowly, they trekked out of the camp and into the Badlands beyond. The merchants rode their mules at intervals, keeping the labourers in order and brandishing long sticks at anybody who lagged behind.

Tessa winced as her bare feet met the hard, rocky terrain. The ropes around her ankles restricted her movement so that she couldn't take a full stride. The bright, shimmering blue sun above warmed the rock. She knew that by midday it would be blistering.

They rejoined the trail and left the camp behind. The steady trotting of mules' hooves and the thud of the pack-beasts' heavy feet broke the morning stillness. A couple of merchants fell into quiet conversation. Tessa strained her ears, but they were too far for her to hear.

As the twin suns crept higher into the sky, Tessa settled into a mindless shuffle. It let her mind wander. She flexed her wrists, probing her binds for weakness. Merchants weren't good fighters. Not like Raiders. If she got a sabre in her hands, she'd have a shot at escaping.

The sun beat down on her shoulders, the thin rags doing little to protect her. She tried to spot Isiah in the line, but everybody looked the same. She hoped his Mark wasn't giving him trouble. Further back, one of the labourers stumbled, and a merchant swooped in with his stick.

"Get a move on," he snapped. "We have to make good time. We're already behind schedule!"

Tessa winced as they crossed a patch of sharp rocks. The sun neared its midday point, scorching the earth with its unrelenting glare. She remembered when she was a kid, when her parents would fry food on the rocks when scouting.

The labourer in front of her stumbled. Without arms to steady them, they collapsed to their knees. Tessa heard a girl gasp in pain.

"You!" the merchant barked. "You're slowing the whole line down."

The labourer twisted around. Tessa recognized the same girl she'd met in the camp. The merchant marched over, stick in hand. He grabbed the girl and yanked her to her feet.

"It was my fault," Tessa said quickly. "I bumped into her."

The merchant whirled on her. "Then don't be so clumsy."

He shoved Tessa forward and whacked her with his stick. Tessa clenched her jaw against the sting of the impact. She refused to give the merchant the satisfaction of a response. She blinked back the tears and kept walking.

When Lazaro finds me, she thought, *they'll wish they never crossed us.*

Mauriel

MAURIEL HUNCHED HER SHOULDERS AND HURRIED through the alleyway. She ducked from shadow to shadow, stepping over the unmoving forms of beggars and slipping past the closed shutters of houses. She neared the edge of the city, where the stone turned to wooden platforms and houses spilled out over the empty air.

She stopped at a dead end. Her hand hovered above the hilt of her sabre. She'd taken a risk leaving the roosts without her Raiders at night. Every shadow appeared to conceal a half-starved beggar with a knife or a gang of thieving nomads waiting for their next victim. She strained her ears, listening for any sign of movement. Boots crunched on stone.

"Did it go according to plan?" a voice asked.

Mauriel jumped and her sabre flashed into her hand. She sighed as she recognized the voice. "It went off without a hitch."

A figure stepped out of an alleyway. Black robes clad his body and a mask obscured his face—a necessary precaution, he'd told her. Mauriel was sure his eagle wasn't far away.

"You could have sent someone to the roosts," she said. "Instead of having me walk all the way out here. If anyone sees me with you, I'll be hauled off and killed as an Oath-breaker."

"Relax," the man replied. He gestured to the roosts. The faint moonlight played across his crooked metal hand. "The other Raiders are none the wiser, and soon I'll be out of your hair. I wanted to speak to you personally."

Mauriel folded her arms. "You killed my brother."

"He got in the way," the man said. "It was unfortunate, yes. But as soon as you've finished helping me, the killings will stop and your precious Oath can go back to the way it was." He paused. "Where is Lazaro?"

"He's cooling off with the rest of his gang in the prison," Mauriel replied. "I convinced the Raiders to vote against him. He'll be exiled and his house seized tomorrow morning."

"And Isiah?" the figure asked.

"Sold to the merchants, along with Lazaro's brat of a sister and that traitorous Scavenger, Aron. They'll be miles away by the time Lazaro is released. He'll be kept busy looking for them."

"Good work," the man said. "I should have dealt with Aron earlier. I always did question his friendship with Tessa." The man waved his hand. "But that doesn't matter now. What about the dragon?"

"The one that chased Keegan's friend? We're assembling a hunting party to find it."

"Make sure you do," the man replied.

Mauriel grunted. "I don't see why it's such a big deal. Dragons cross the border all the time. Why is this one so special?"

The man dropped his voice. "Because Isiah is the boy who freed the dragon from our arena."

Mauriel paused. "But Aron said—"

"Aron lied to you all," the man said, cutting her off. "Isiah was from Paradon all along. I saw it for myself. He's Marked." He stepped forward. "You have to kill the dragon. My Raiders don't have the numbers on our own."

"We've got the situation under control," Mauriel said.

"Don't underestimate it. The dragon didn't kill Isiah like it should have. I'll sleep easier once I know it's dead and there's one more loose end tied up."

"Alright." Mauriel rubbed her hands together. "A good old-fashioned dragon hunt. It'll be easy."

"See that you take care of it." He paused. "I'll return with your reward once this whole *situation* is cleared up."

Mauriel gave him a mock salute. "See you around, Enrik."

Enrik marched into the shadows. Mauriel waited a few moments until wingbeats echoed and a shape erupted from behind a row of houses. An eagle glided into the night sky and soared toward the Badlands. She watched him go, then turned and marched back to the roosts.

Gorgon Territory

DARKNESS CLOAKED THE BADLANDS. The last of the sun's rays dipped beneath the horizon and the scorching heat dissipated. The labourers sat huddled on the cooling earth, sheltered inside a winding riverbed. The merchant's fire crackled. The light danced across their hunched forms, casting distorted shadows on the ground behind them.

Tessa rubbed her aching feet. Her legs were sore from a day of walking, and her calves were caked in dust. The merchants had unbound her wrists, but she still wore the ropes around her ankles. Her sweat-drenched clothes stuck to her skin, chilling her as the warmth from the sun leeched away.

One of the merchants stood and waltzed over. "For some of you, it's your first night on the trail," she said. Tessa recognized her as the woman from the tent. "You might be wondering why you can't just loosen those binds on your ankles and make a break for it."

Among the crowd, Tessa caught Isiah's eye. The possibility had crossed her mind the moment the merchants had stopped to set up camp.

"But this is gorgon territory," the woman continued. "And you should know the stories of gorgon packs stumbling upon lost travellers and tearing them to shreds."

Tessa shivered—and not from the cold. She'd faced off with gorgons before.

"We're miles from the nearest settlement, deep in an arid and unforgiving wilderness," the woman said. "So keep that in mind next time you think about escaping. You wouldn't last a day out there."

She returned to the fire. A cool wind stirred Tessa's hair, bringing with it the aroma of whatever the merchants were cooking. Her stomach groaned in protest. Nearby, the merchant's mules and pack-beasts grazed on a patch of bushes.

The night grew longer, and as it did, the fire dimmed and the merchants drifted off to sleep. Several sat on watch. The labourers huddled together and leaned against boulders. Somewhere, soft sobbing reached Tessa's ears.

"Thank you for helping me," a voice said.

Tessa turned to see the same girl from before. She sat with her knees drawn to her chest, peering out from beneath her hood.

"Oh—it was nothing," Tessa replied.

"You distracted the merchant," she said. "You didn't need to." She hesitated. "Did you really mean it when you said you were a Raider?"

"I did—but they betrayed me." Part of her told her to keep quiet, but she found herself recounting the story of their capture by Mauriel.

The girl gasped. "But the Oath . . ."

Tessa scowled. "I guess they don't play by the rules anymore." She paused. "What's your name?"

"Marie," the girl replied.

They sat in silence. Marie twirled a lock of her hair. Despite the merchant's warnings, Tessa probed the knots that bound her ankles.

"I'm not from Alcabaza," Marie said suddenly. "I've been a labourer for a while. They picked me up from a farming village."

Tessa stopped tugging her binds. "What happened?"

"It was a bad year," Marie replied. "The crops failed and the families couldn't feed us. So when the merchants came in with an offer . . ." She trailed off. "They think I'm an apprentice somewhere."

Tessa shifted her weight. "I'm sorry that happened to you."

Marie motioned to Tessa's binds. "I gave up trying to escape."

"Well, I won't," Tessa replied. "Neither will my friends." She managed a smile. "And once Lazaro finds us, we'll free the rest of you, too."

Marie returned her smile. "I hope he does."

Tessa scooped up a pebble. "Do you want to see something?"

Marie nodded.

"Promise you won't tell anyone."

Tessa placed the pebble on the ground between them and focused. She tried to imagine what she did to help Isiah. A familiar sensation welled inside her—strange and nauseating. The pebble took on a shiny, black appearance. Tiny legs appeared, then a pair of antenna. It began to scuttle around.

Marie's eyes widened. "How did you do that?"

Tessa relaxed and the image of the beetle disintegrated, revealing the pebble. "It's an illusion," she explained. "Pretty neat, huh?"

"What else can you do?" Marie asked.

"I don't know," she admitted. "I'm not sure how it works."

"Well, I think it's pretty cool." Marie crawled closer.

Tessa spied Isiah and Aron on the opposite side of the camp with the male labourers. Part of her told her to sneak over and check on them.

"Do you mind if I sleep here?" Marie asked.

Tessa shifted to let Marie sit next to her. "Just keep what I showed you a secret, okay?"

Marie nodded. "You can count on me."

Merchant Den

"ALMOST THERE!" A MERCHANT CALLED. He spurred his mule across the arid terrain. "Don't stop now or we'll drag you the rest of the way."

Isiah forced his weary legs to keep moving. He lowered his head against the relentless heat and tried to keep his mind off his parched, swollen throat. The line of labourers cut through a dry river valley, heading toward a distant cluster of smoke on the horizon.

Loose, jagged rocks littered the earth, stabbing his feet. He stepped over streaks of blood where labourers had cut themselves. A thick layer of dust coated his calves and clung to the edges of his rags. His hair, drenched with sweat, stuck to his forehead.

The merchants had herded the labourers for several days, driving them through the unforgiving terrain to reach a distant camp. He'd had few chances to speak to Tessa during their journey. The thought of escape played on his mind, but the merchants always had someone keeping watch.

"I don't like this place," a merchant said. Isiah kept his eyes glued to the ground to avoid attracting their attention.

"What's so wrong about it?" a female merchant asked.

"I've heard the highlands are cursed," he replied. "Gorgons roam these hills every night. If you sit around the campfire and listen closely, you can hear their calls."

"We've got nothing to worry about," the woman said. "Gorgons don't attack groups as big as ours. They like hunting loners and small clans."

"Too many merchants have gone missing here for my liking." The merchant shivered. "Whole groups of labourers, too. They disappear into the hills, never to be seen again."

"Stop being so superstitious," she replied. "It's nothing more than a bunch of stories the older merchants like to use to scare you."

"Oh yeah?" the man said. "Then how come so many labourers go missing in these parts? It's cursed. I know it."

The woman sighed and spurred her mule on. Their words gave Isiah a flicker of hope—but he knew exchanging the merchants for a gorgon pack would be a sorry trade-off.

A few merchants headed to the front of the line, where they climbed over the ridge of the dried river and disappeared beyond. The smoke grew closer, coiling into the air from multiple sources. Flat-topped mesas and smooth boulders gave the landscape a strange, almost alien appearance. One of the merchants beckoned.

"Hurry those labourers along," he called. "A few more minutes and we'll be out of the sun."

Isiah pushed on with renewed vigour. The hope of rest and a drink gave him a new burst of energy. The sharp rock beneath his feet changed to sand and dusty earth as he climbed the riverbed and pushed into new terrain.

A merchant camp appeared ahead of them. An assortment of large tents and tarps huddled together in the barren landscape. As they drew closer, Isiah made out other groups of merchants. Their mules were tied to palisade fences nearby, alongside more hulking reptilian pack-beasts, and people in brightly coloured robes milled about inside the camp. A watering hole, brown and cloudy, let a few skeletal acacia trees grow nearby.

"There's our rest," a merchant said. "This has to be the most remote merchant den in the entire Badlands."

"Enjoy it while it lasts," the woman replied. "The boss wants us out of here tomorrow morning."

Isiah counted two dozen tents, all large enough to house multiple people. The merchants herded him into the shadow of tarps that were strung over the path. Several merchants broke off to tend to their donkeys.

"Over there," the bearded merchant barked. He pointed the labourers to a bare hillside on the edge of camp. "You can wait here."

Isiah's aching knees gave way and he collapsed on the hillside. As the rest of the labourers joined him, he made out several other groups in different parts of the camp.

"Watch them," the bearded merchant said to his companion. "Make sure they don't cause any trouble."

Part of Isiah urged him to ask for a drink, but he knew he'd only be rewarded by a strike from the merchant's stick. He resigned to sit in silence with the others.

"Isiah." Tessa's voice caught his attention. She crawled over to where he was sitting.

"Hey, Tessa." Isiah winced at the hoarseness of his voice. His tongue felt too big for his throat.

"Did you see Aron?" Tessa asked. She was with another girl, one he hadn't seen before.

"I lost him after we stopped last," he replied. "Did you have a plan?"

"Not yet," Tessa said. She paused. "Maybe we can do something tonight."

Isiah lowered his voice. "What about your magic? Can't you use an illusion or something?"

"I don't know," she replied. "It doesn't work like that."

One of the labourers swore. Isiah heard Aron apologize. He turned to see the boy crawling over.

"This is a big camp," he said. "There's a lot of trade going on. Maybe we'll get lucky and the merchants will get drunk."

Frenzied talking erupted from a nearby tent. A bunch of merchants sat around a low table. One shook a pair of dice in his hand and cast it across the table.

"No way," one of the men boomed. "You're cheating! Let me see those dice."

"I'm lucky, is all," his opponent replied. "Now, are we going again or what?"

One of the merchants stood. "I'm running out of coin to gamble," he said. "But I've got more than a few labourers to enter."

The merchants stood and wandered over to Isiah's group.

"What do I want with a bunch of labourers?" one of the merchants asked. A potbelly protruded from his robes, and his bare arms were awash with tattoos.

"You can sell them," his opponent replied. "You know there's a huge market for labourers all over the Badlands."

The potbellied man scoffed. He crossed his arms. "If they don't die on the journey." He waded into the group. "But I *could* accept them as payment."

He stopped in front of Tessa and leaned over. "This one would make a good maid for the nobles in the city we're headed to," he said. He grabbed her arm and squeezed it. "And she's in good shape, too." Tessa glared at the man. The man laughed. "But not broken in yet, I take it." He turned his attention to Isiah and Aron. "And these ones would make good gorgon hunters, by my reckoning. We get too many of them, where I'm from."

"Then I'll put them on my ledger," the other merchant replied. "If you win, you can have them."

The potbellied man grunted in satisfaction and the merchants returned to their gambling tent.

"What if we're separated?" Aron asked. "I don't like the look of all this."

"Don't worry," Tessa replied. "We'll be out of here before that happens."

As the merchants returned to their games, one of Isiah's captors came around with a waterskin and he took a swig. He didn't even care that the water was lukewarm and full of sand.

"Take it easy," the merchant said. "This has to be shared with all of you."

The merchants gambled and traded long into the afternoon. Isiah anxiously awaited the moment the twin suns would dip beneath the horizon and they could plan their escape. The merchants kept a close eye on them to avoid any escapees.

"Here they are," a voice said. Isiah's stomach dropped as the bearded merchant wandered over with a group of others. The potbellied man was with them.

"Grab the ones I pointed out earlier," he said. "They'll put on a good show."

The other merchants began selecting labourers and dragging them off. Isiah tensed as the bearded merchant approached him.

"Get up," he ordered.

"What's going on?" Isiah asked.

"What have I told you about asking questions?" He grabbed Isiah's arm. "Do as you're told."

Isiah awkwardly pulled himself to his feet and the merchant marched him over to the other group. He found himself alongside Aron and a group of other similar-aged boys.

"They'll do good, alright," the potbellied man said. "I'll take them—if they can prove their worth."

"Then you'd better do it now," the bearded merchant replied. "I'm leaving at dawn, and I'm taking them with me unless you buy them."

"So be it." The potbellied man gestured to his companions and they began leading the labourers into the camp.

Isiah's mind raced. The merchants marched him into a new part of the camp, out of view of the hillside. Several tents stood around a hole in the ground. As they approached, nearby merchants poked their heads out of tents to see the source of the commotion.

"Stop there," the potbellied man instructed. He stooped and cut Isiah's ankle binds. He then untied Isiah's wrists and jabbed a thumb in the direction of the hole. "Get in the pit."

Isiah inched toward it. A large rectangle stood at the bottom on one side. Tarps covered it, obscuring its contents. At intervals around the pit's rim, sharpened wooden stakes protruded from the earth. Isiah hesitated. "What's in there?"

"Don't talk back to me." The potbellied man shoved him. "Either you go down there or I'll throw you in myself." He freed Aron and a couple of the other labourers.

Isiah sat on the edge of the pit and slid inside. He landed on the hard, cracked earth. The rim of the pit stood a dozen feet over his head—too high to reach. One by one, the other labourers joined him. With a sinking feeling, Isiah realized what was going on.

The potbellied man collected an armful of spears and chucked them into the pit. The labourers took one each. Isiah counted half a dozen of them in total, him and Aron included. He gripped the rough wooden shaft of his spear and held it close. Its crude, flattened iron head was shaped like a leaf. On the opposite side of the pit, a ladder descended and a merchant climbed in with them.

Something inside the cage lurched. A throaty growl sounded. The merchant grabbed the edge of the tarp and pulled it free. Isiah gulped as his worst fears were confirmed.

Three gorgons paced about the cage. They snapped at the merchant with their long jaws. Strings of saliva hung from their four sabre-like fangs. The merchant carefully undid the latch to their cage and then retreated from the pit.

The gorgons spilled into the arena. They snarled and paced about, as if unsure of their surroundings. Their short, dark fur stood on end, and their ribs protruded from their sides.

"Gorgons don't like the sunlight," the potbellied man said. Around him, a growing crowd of merchants peered over the edge into the pit. "But that doesn't make them any less dangerous."

The gorgons' beady eyes fixed on Isiah and the labourers. Their muscles, weak from starvation but still limber and strong, rippled beneath their thick skin. Short tails trailed behind them, and pairs of long claws protruded from their feet.

Isiah levelled his spear at them. He adjusted his grip on the shaft. He'd faced gorgons once before with Tessa, inside a ruin. The labourers huddled together, spears outstretched.

"They pick off stragglers," the potbellied man continued. "They like to hunt in packs. Their jaws are strong enough to snap bones, and their fangs can impale a man."

The gorgons advanced. Patches of fur were missing from their flanks, and their stomachs were hollowed, but that made them no less threatening. One made a mock lunge at Aron. Isiah forced himself to control his breathing. The crowd around the pit grew larger.

"And when they're desperate," the potbellied man said, "they become more aggressive."

The gorgons charged. The labourers broke form and fled in panic. Isiah stumbled aside as a gorgon flew past him. Its hot breath blasted his skin. One of the labourers fell and the beast clamped its jaws around his leg.

The labourer screamed and dropped his spear. The gorgon shook its head, dragging him across the floor. The other two closed in to finish him. The labourer writhed in pain and beat his fists against the gorgon's snout. The merchants gasped and pushed each other to get a better look.

Isiah forced himself into motion. He raised his spear and thrust it at the gorgon's neck. The blade sliced through its tough skin and a shockwave reverberated through Isiah's arms. The gorgon barked in pain and wheeled away. Isiah dug his heels into the ground to avoid the spear being wrenched from his grip.

The other labourers collected themselves. The injured boy scrambled backwards and Aron caught his arm. The gorgon that had bitten him snapped at Isiah. Its head was level with his chest. Isiah kept his spear trained on its face.

The other gorgons circled, like wolves closing in for the kill. The labourers waved their spears, but the tremble in their hands gave them away. The injured boy gasped in pain and clutched his bleeding leg.

The lead gorgon charged Isiah. He jabbed his spear forward and stepped aside. The gorgon wheeled away at the last moment. Isiah re-adjusted his footing. He scanned for some kind of escape. The walls were too sheer for him to climb, and the stakes prevented the gorgons from escaping too.

"You'll never be gorgon hunters if you keep up like this," the pot-bellied man called. He stood with his boot-toes poking over the edge of the arena. "Get in there! Work as a team to corner one."

The injured boy leaned on his spear. Blood seeped from puncture wounds in his calf and stained the earth a deep red. Isiah swallowed. The gorgons pinned the boy with their gaze. He opened his mouth to call a warning, but it was too late.

The lead gorgon leapt at him. The boy screamed as the weight of the beast collided with him and bore him to the ground. The other labourers scattered as the gorgons closed in. The snap of jaws made Isiah's insides churn. The boy's screams fell to pained gurgles.

The merchants hollered. The potbellied man folded his arms and shook his head. Heat burned in Isiah's chest. A plan flashed into his head.

He pulled back his arm and threw his spear.

The potbellied man's eyes widened. The spear arced through the air and buried itself into his stomach. He screamed and clutched the shaft as he toppled into the arena. He landed on the stakes jutting from the wall and snapped them, before hitting the floor and driving the spear further into his gut.

The gorgons whirled on the screaming man. Isiah yelled and waved his arms at them, trying to appear as big as possible. Aron understood what he was trying to do and joined in.

The gorgons ran from the yelling boys. The screams of merchants spooked them. One leapt at the wall and scaled it.

Merchants scattered. The three gorgons crawled through the gap in the spikes and sprinted into the camp. Isiah and the surviving labourers sprinted to the wall.

"That was a brilliant plan!" Aron exclaimed. The potbellied man lay writhing on the ground. Aron kicked dust over him.

"We still need to get out," Isiah replied.

Aron knelt and cupped his hands. "I'll give you a boost."

Isiah stepped into Aron's hands and he jumped toward the stakes. Grabbing one, he clambered over the edge of the pit. One by one, the other labourers followed. The last one turned and caught Aron's arms, pulling him up.

"Come on," Isiah said. "We need to help Tessa."

The screams of merchants echoed through the camp. With it came something else. Isiah's breath caught in his throat as the shrill call of eagles split the air.

The labourers ducked as shapes blasted overhead. Voices yelled battle cries as eagles spread out their wings and circled the camp. Aron pumped his fist in the air and cheered. Isiah squinted at the birds, trying to make out their riders. *Could it be Lazaro?*

Several eagles landed among the tents. The power of their wing-beats made the structures collapse. Merchants struggled under the material, desperately trying to free themselves. Nearby labourers charged their guards and overpowered them.

Isiah took off running. He ducked beneath an eagle's outstretched wing and ran in the direction he'd left Tessa. He rounded a corner to find the bearded merchant on the floor, clutching his sword arm. The labourers cheered as a pair of Raiders untied them.

Merchants fled into the surrounding wilderness. One of the gorgons chased after them. Isiah reached Tessa's side and doubled over, breathing heavily.

"Isiah!" Tessa's eyes lit up. "I knew Raiders would come help us!"

"Secure the camp," a Raider called. His companions finished freeing the labourers and rounded up the last of the merchants. They bound their wrists and forced them to their knees. One stood guard, sabre in hand. His companion came over.

"Did Lazaro send you?" Tessa asked. "Where is he?"

The Raider raised his hands. "Hold on, there. I don't know of any Lazaro."

Tessa's smile dropped. "What do you mean? Then who are you?"

"Save your questions," he said with a laugh. "We'll answer them in good time." He pulled a sack from his eagle's saddle and tossed it to her. "Pass out some water, will you? It's still a trek to our home base."

The labourers crowded around to get their fill from the water-skins. The Raiders sorted through the merchants' collapsed tents and carried out anything of value. Isiah approached the man who had spoken to them.

"You're Raiders, right?" he asked.

The man smiled. "Indeed we are." He extended a hand. "We're here to save you."

Lazaro

"GATHER YOUR VALUABLES AND THEN HAND over the key," the Raider barked.

Lazaro stood in front of his house. Darla and Antony waited beside him, sacks slung over their shoulders. Helen and Luca filed through the door with their own.

"We, the collective Raiders, hereby declare that Lazaro and his Raider gang are to be exiled from Alcabaza," a Raider said. He held out a yellowed scroll in front of him. Several others, all armed, stood around.

"Cut the speech," Lazaro snapped. "I've heard it before."

The Raider scowled and folded the scroll. "Get out, Lazaro. You're not welcome here anymore."

Helen adjusted the sack over her shoulder and produced the key to the house—his house. The Raider pocketed it.

A fire burned inside Lazaro's gut. How dare the Raiders throw him out of his own home? He'd worked for years with Tessa to afford that place. The shutters were loose and the mortar was cracking, but it was *their* place to live.

"We'll escort you to your eagles and then confiscate your pens," the Raider said. "If you return to Alcabaza after today, you'll be executed."

"I'd like to see you try," Lazaro spat.

The Raider stepped forward. "You're lucky we don't have a dragon to feed you to." The pair stood forehead-to-forehead. "And if you can't find anyone to fly your sister's eagle, we'll take him off your hands."

Lazaro shoved the man. He stumbled a few steps, then replied with a shove of his own. Lazaro lowered his head and charged him. His shoulder connected with the Raider's chest and sent him sprawling. Before either could do anything else, Antony grabbed Lazaro and pulled him away.

The Raider stood and dusted himself off. "I defended you from Enrik too many times," he said. "No matter how many fistfights you got into, I was always there to apologise on your behalf." He spat on the ground at Lazaro's feet. "Now get out of our city."

The Raiders marched away. Lazaro gritted his teeth and waited until they were out of sight, then kicked the ground.

"Who do they think they are?" he snapped. "They don't own this city. That house is *ours*."

"We can worry about that later," Helen said. "We need to get our eagles and go after Tessa. If we're quick, we can catch up to them. She can't have been taken far."

"I have every right mind to cut off Mauriel's head," Lazaro replied. "She thinks we're Oath-breakers? Then why don't we prove them right?"

Antony swore. "Give it a rest, Lazaro!" He dumped his sack on the ground. "Your hot-headedness is what got us here to begin with. I *told* you to keep it cool before the meeting, and what did you do?" He threw up his hands. "You got into a fight that cost us our home!"

Darla and the others went silent. Lazaro's eyes flitted over their empty expressions. "Then what do you suppose we do about it?"

"I suppose we get our eagles and leave without causing another scene," Antony replied. He took a deep breath. "We find Tessa, Isiah, and Aron, and we figure out what to do from there."

"What about Aegon?" Darla asked. "You heard Mauriel say they wanted to hunt it. Isiah will be heartbroken if anything happens to her."

"I don't care about the dragon," Lazaro replied. "I care about finding my sister."

"The Raiders are setting off to Keegan's ruin soon," she said. "If we don't go now, we'll miss our chance."

"And what about Tess?" he exclaimed. "Are we supposed to leave her at the mercy of some filthy slavers?"

Darla's expression softened. "I want to find her as much as you do, but think about this."

"We don't know what way she's been taken," Antony said. "And I doubt any of the Raiders will be so kind as to tell us. It could take us weeks to track her down."

"Then we should start now," Lazaro replied.

Helen put her hands on her hips. "Darla has a point, you know. If we get Aegon, maybe she can help us."

Lazaro frowned. "How?"

"We'll be strong enough to fight any Raiders who get in our way, for starters," Darla cut in. "You know how strong dragons are. Isiah bonded with her. How hard can it be?"

"And maybe she can even help us track him and Tessa down," Helen said.

Lazaro mulled it over. He'd never wanted to let Tessa fly with Isiah on that dragon. The very thought had filled him with dread. But now . . .

"On one condition," he said. "If we find Mauriel, we take her out."

Darla grinned. "Deal."

She took off running in the direction of the eagle roosts. Lazaro took one last look at their deserted, lifeless house, then went after her.

Hidden Citadel

TOWERING ROCKY SPIRES AND BUTTES CAST long lines of shadow across the Badlands. Narrow gullies and ravines snaked off, cutting through the terrain and forming a natural labyrinth. Eagles soared overhead, guiding them toward their destination.

The chatter of excited labourers filled Isiah's ears. A flicker of hope bubbled in his insides. He quickened his pace, hurrying to the front of the line, where a couple of Raiders led the column.

"The highlands give us natural protection," the Raider said, speaking to another labourer. His calm, soothing voice put Isiah at ease. "The terrain here is so rocky and gorgon-infested that no merchants ever bother us. They don't even know we're here."

Painted cliffs, their surfaces decorated with rings of red and purple, hemmed the labourers in. The faint trickle of water from a Badlands stream emanated from somewhere among the mass of rock. Bushes, their leaves bright and lush, burst from cracks in the earth and stretched out from rocky ledges, their branches hanging over the open air.

Isiah fell into stride with Tessa and the new girl, who had introduced herself as Marie. Tessa flashed him a smile.

"Few Raiders ever fly this way," the man continued. Flowing robes covered his shoulders and snaked down his back, while a criss-cross of a harness covered his chest and pinned a knife and waterskin to his body. "There are too few ruins out this way for them to bother. The land is unforgiving—unless you know where to look."

He reached out a hand and touched a damp patch of rock. "There's water out here. And where there's water, there's life."

"Why do you live so far from everyone?" Tessa asked.

"You'll see soon enough," the man replied.

The eagles flew on ahead, disappearing beyond the rocky skyline. Isiah quickened his pace, a new burst of energy powering him on. At the back of the column, the merchants were driven on by a pair of Raiders.

"What are you going to do with the merchants?" Isiah asked.

"Oh, don't you worry about that," the Raider said. "We'll see they get their punishment for what they put you through."

Tessa furrowed her brow. "You don't approve of labourers?"

"I think it's an evil practice," the man said. "Peddled by swindlers who exploit the vulnerable to line their pockets. There's enough natural wealth in the Badlands for everyone to survive if you know where to look."

"That's why you helped us, isn't it?" Isiah asked.

"Exactly," the man replied. "We give the merchants a taste of their own medicine—and pick up any valuables while we're at it. This was our biggest raid ever." He extended a hand. "The people here call me Solomon."

Isiah shook it. The man had a firm grip, and his dark eyes sparked with life. His arms were muscular and he sported a close-cropped buzz cut. Isiah told Solomon about their capture at Alcabaza and sale to the merchants.

Solomon narrowed his eyes. "Seems you can't even trust Raiders, anymore. What has the world come to?" He paused. "We're almost there."

A towering rocky archway framed the way ahead. The spires and cliffs that hemmed them in formed one last tight passageway, then fell away. Isiah's breath caught in his throat.

A wide basin sprawled before him, ringed by walls of red rock. In the centre, a glistening pool of turquoise water sat, bursting with lush trees and vegetation. A town, packed with colourful tents and squat houses, wrapped around one half of the pool, with a single tower that loomed over its surroundings.

"Welcome to the Hidden Citadel," Solomon said.

An uncontrollable grin spread across Isiah's face. "How did you find this place?"

"Years ago, while flying," he replied. "We settled here. It's a place for outsiders and outcasts to live in peace."

Isiah struggled to keep his balance as several labourers pushed past him and ran toward the town. The eagles circled the cliffs and landed atop them, watching over the basin like feathered sentinels.

"Take a look for yourself," Solomon said.

Isiah and Tessa took off at a run, with Aron and Marie close behind. Sand kicked up behind them as they sprinted down the trail toward the colourful town. Rows of tents sat on the outskirts, with sandstone buildings clustered in the centre.

Isiah skidded to a halt in front of the lake. The ground formed a ledge, dropping a foot to a surface of clear water. He squinted into the water. It faded to a deep azure blue as it descended, making the lake seem bottomless.

Tessa's breath escaped her. "I've never seen anything like this place."

Isiah suppressed the urge to jump and cheer. The other labourers flooded into the town. Raiders handed out new clothes and set up additional tents.

"Do you understand what I was saying?" Solomon asked, appearing behind them.

"This can't be real," Isiah managed to say.

"We do our best to make everyone welcome here," he replied. "May I show you something?"

Isiah nodded. Solomon called over a couple of other Raiders.

"We settled here because we're rejects ourselves," he said. "I wasn't born a Raider, nor were many of the others."

Solomon and the other Raiders pulled down their robes to expose their chests. Tessa gasped.

"We're Marked," he said. "The dragons rejected us, Paradon cast us out of their kingdom, and, well, we all know what happens if anyone from the Badlands discovers you're Marked." He nodded to Isiah. "Right, Isiah?"

Isiah clutched his hands to his chest defensively. "How do you know—"

"I can spot somebody who's Marked from a mile away," Solomon said. "But you're in good company here."

Scars snaked across Solomon's chest and shoulders, shaped like tongues of flame. His skin was bronze, but his Mark was pale and lumpy—and smoother than the candle-wax appearance of Isiah's own.

"It looks so . . . normal," Isiah said. "At least compared to mine."

Solomon smiled. "Time is a good healer. I was Marked over a decade ago." He readjusted his robes and put an arm around Isiah's shoulders. "The people are accepting here. I'll give you and your friends a tent and you can get settled in."

Isiah followed the man to the edge of the town and toward a tent adorned with deep-red fabric, shining under the sun like a ruby. Raiders carried armfuls of robes and gear toward it.

"We salvaged the things the merchants took from you all," Solomon said. "I'm sure you'll be happy to get them back."

"And some," Aron replied. He grabbed his stuff from a Raider and disappeared inside the tent. Isiah and Tessa collected their things, then they thanked Solomon.

"No need to thank me," the man replied. "You must have had a terrible time trying to live out there with your Mark."

"You get used to it," Isiah said.

"I'll leave you to settle in." Solomon turned to go. "Speak to my Raiders if you need anything."

Solomon departed. Isiah clutched his robes to his chest and ducked into the tent. The thick material stole the sunlight away, leaving the interior awash with cool shadows. Where the sun shone through, it bathed the tent in a warm reddish light.

Tessa and Marie filed in after him. Cloth walls divided the tent into sections. They both disappeared into one and drew the curtain.

Isiah changed out of the rags and back into his robes. He breathed a sigh of relief. He never thought he'd miss them that much.

He paused to inspect his Mark. The warped, lumpy skin rippled over his right shoulder and down both sides of his torso. He grimaced.

It would take a long time for any hope of it healing. Tessa emerged a few minutes later with the rags over her arm.

"We should burn these," she said. "I don't ever want to see them again." Her colourful robes flowed around her body. The Raiders hadn't yet given her a harness to pin them flat. Despite the dust streaking her face and the tangles in her hair, the sight of her still made him pause.

"This is a nice place, huh?" Aron appeared from the back of the tent. "I could get used to this."

"We still need to find Lazaro," Tessa replied. "He'll be worried sick about us."

"Relax." Aron waved her away. "After everything we've been through, who says we don't deserve a rest?"

Isiah set down his rags. "Is there something wrong, Tessa?"

Tessa turned away. "It's nothing."

"It doesn't sound like nothing."

Tessa sighed. "I just don't like how they're from Paradon."

Aron rolled his eyes. "Not this again."

"They're Marked," she replied. "That means they were in line to be nobility, or Royal Guards." She tossed her hair. "You know how I feel about them."

"Their Marks don't mean anything," Isiah said. "How could they have any bad feelings toward Raiders? They *are* Raiders."

"I didn't say they weren't. I just said I don't trust them much."

"What about me, then?" he asked. "I'm Marked."

Tessa looked at her feet. "You're different."

"Hey." Aron put his arms around the pair. "How about we take a look around and see what it's like here. Solomon seemed nice enough." He beckoned Marie. "What about you?"

"Uh . . ." Marie's eyes darted to Tessa. "I like it here."

"Okay," Tessa said. "You win. I guess I *did* want to take another look at that lake again."

"That's the spirit!" Aron laughed. "I'll race you to it."

No Easy Burden

ISIAH WANDERED THROUGH THE DUSTY STREETS of the Hidden Citadel with Tessa, Aron, and Marie. The lake sat to their right, glistening under the sun. Greenery gave way to stacks of sandstone houses that nestled against the cliffs and jutted over the streets. Tarps in vibrant red and purple cast wide triangles of shade across the people that milled about.

They passed a small market, packed with stalls. A few children ran between them. Isiah caught sight of some of the labourers that had been in the merchant camp.

Beyond the tents and houses, the tower Isiah had seen earlier loomed. It climbed four stories high, the stone giving way to scaffolding and a wooden crane. A brick archway connected it to the nearby cliff. A cluster of houses stood under its shadow.

"Isiah!" a voice called. Solomon emerged from the crowd. "I see you're settling in. Did you find your tent alright?"

"It's great," Isiah replied. "We're grateful for your hospitality."

"It's not often that we stumble upon another person who's Marked," Solomon said. "With the whole world against us, I feel we share a connection of sorts, don't you agree?"

Tessa caught Isiah's eye. He looked for something to change the conversation. "How does this place work?"

"The lake is our lifeblood," Solomon replied. "Without it, we die. Our Raiders tend to the community, rearing our eagles and hunting in the Badlands for supplies. We ration out what we find to the people here who keep the place running."

"And you don't fight?" Aron asked. "Do you follow the Raider's Oath?"

"We don't need an Oath here," Solomon replied. "We're like family. We understand that as outsiders, it's our duty to look out for each other. I often thought that if only other cities were like that, the Badlands would be a better place."

Tessa crossed her arms. "It's not so easy with Royal Guards attacking us."

"I'm no fan of Paradon's activity, neither," Solomon replied. He gave her a warm smile. "I left that land behind a long time ago."

"Speaking of Raiders," Isiah cut in, "our friends are looking for us." He told Solomon about Lazaro.

"We need to search for him," Tessa said.

"Surely you're not thinking of leaving so soon?" Solomon stepped around a group of children playing on the dusty earth. A gap in the houses revealed the lake again. "I'll tell you what," he said, "I'll talk to my Raiders and send some eagles scouting for him. The highlands is no place for you to be wandering alone."

"That's what I was trying to tell her," Aron added.

"I have an eagle, too," Tessa said. Her expression flickered. "I'm worried about what will happen to him."

"I'll tell my Raiders about him, too." Solomon paused. "In the meantime, I have something that might take your minds off it. Some eagle chicks recently hatched on the cliffs. How about you go up and tend to them?"

Tessa mulled it over. "I've never handled eagle chicks before."

"Then why not take the opportunity?" Solomon waved over some handlers as they neared the edge of the town. He spoke to them in a hushed voice. One of the handlers—a girl wearing dust-covered overalls—gave him a thumbs-up.

"Myla has agreed to take you," Solomon said, breaking away.

Isiah thanked Solomon, then he and his friends followed Myla away from the town.

"The eagles nest on the cliffs and ledges nearby," she said. Her curly hair bounced as she walked. "It helps keep the chicks safe from gorgons."

She led them to the cliffside, where a narrow trail snaked up to the top. As they climbed, they came level with the tower.

"How long has this place existed for?" Isiah asked.

Myla shrugged. "I don't know. I was a labourer when Solomon rescued me a few years back."

"And you never left?" Tessa asked.

"Why would I? There's nobody else to look out for us out there." She gestured to the cliffs. "Beyond these natural walls, there's nothing but death and enslavement. We're safe here. Solomon took me in like a daughter."

The top of the cliff formed a ring of flat ground, studded with spires and buttes that provided perches for the Raiders' many eagles. Handlers, like the ones at Alcabaza, tended to the birds.

"I hope you're not scared of heights," Myla said. She produced a pair of climbing axes. "You'll have to climb."

Isiah took one of the axes, and Myla directed them to the tallest spire. It loomed over the surrounding terrain, a pile of craggy rock. Sticks burst from ledges, betraying eagle nests. Several ropes, their ends tied to metal poles, protruded from the summit.

"Won't the eagles bite us?" Marie asked.

"They're used to people," Myla said. "It'll be fine."

Isiah approached the base of the spire. Cracks riddled the rock, providing holes to sink his climbing axe into. He gave the rock a tentative strike. "What if we fall?"

"You won't." Myla grabbed a rope and looped it through her belt. "Not if you're careful, that is."

Aron pushed past Isiah and gabbed a rope. "I've always liked the idea of raising an eagle hatchling," he said. "Enrik's Raiders kept me stuck as a Scavenger."

Isiah took one of the ropes and mimicked Myla, tying it to his harness. The wind raced across the cliffs, whipping his hair into his eyes. He swung the climbing axe and it bit into the rock.

They began to climb. With one hand around the rope, Isiah hauled himself up the spire. Tessa climbed beside him, digging her heels into the rock for purchase. Myla gripped the climbing axe between her teeth as she went.

The lake and its town grew smaller. When Isiah looked over his shoulder, the sight made him dizzy. He clung to the rope so as not to fall off. Loose rock dislodged beneath his foot and clattered to the ground below.

"Look at this place," Aron said. His grin stretched ear to ear. "I feel like I'm on top of the world." He took his hand off the climbing axe and extended his arm.

Isiah frowned. "Careful."

"Come on, Isiah," Aron said. "Are you scared of heights? You're a Raider!" He kicked off the rock and swung on the rope like a circus performer. "When we raided ruins, Enrik always sent me down the ropes." He landed with a thump beside Tessa, standing at a near right-angle. Marie laughed.

Isiah put his focus on not falling. The resident eagle peered down at them. The wind ruffled its feathers.

"Come on, Tessa," Aron said. "Lazaro must have shown you how to do this." He kicked off again and sailed around the spire.

Tessa cracked a smile. "Show-off."

Myla made it to the nest and clambered over the ledge. Isiah hastened after her. He clung to the rockface to avoid being swept off. Aron landed next to Isiah and made him jump.

"You've got to learn to live a little more reckless," Aron said. "Face your fears, you know? Isn't that what you did with Aegon?"

Aegon. The word made Isiah's stomach drop. "Do you think Mauriel found her?"

Tessa's smile faded. "I'm sure she's fine." She reached out and put a hand over Isiah's. "Come on. We'll talk about it when we get down."

Myla's head popped over the edge. "Are you coming or what?"

Isiah climbed the last few feet and scrambled into the eagle nest. The bird adjusted its footing and revealed a cluster of tiny, bald hatchlings.

Tessa appeared next to him. When she saw the chicks, her eyes lit up. "They're adorable."

Aron's nose crinkled. "If you can call that *adorable*."

Myla produced a few strips of dried meat and fed the chicks. They scrambled over one another to reach her. Tufts of hair covered their rubbery skin, and their heads were too big for their bodies.

"They eat solid food quickly," Myla said. "Eagles will grab entire gorgons and drop them in their nests." She lowered her voice. "Or people."

Isiah shivered. The cold air whipped over the spires. The eagle stood watch, motionless. As Myla and the others fed the hatchlings, Aegon played on Isiah's mind.

"Do you think I should tell Solomon about Aegon?" he asked Tessa quietly.

"Why would you do that?" she replied.

"He's Marked. What would he say if he knew that I'd bonded with a dragon?"

Tessa hesitated. "If he believes you, that is."

"He'll *have* to believe me." Isiah checked to make sure Myla wasn't paying attention. "Maybe he knows something about the dragons that will help me. And," he added, "you could ask him about your magic, too."

Tessa pulled a face. "What makes you think he'll know anything about that?"

"I don't know," he admitted. "It's just . . . maybe he was right about that whole connection deal. He's been nothing but nice to us."

"He's still from Paradon," she replied. "I'll believe it when I see him kill a Royal Guard."

"That's it . . . the hatchlings are fed," Myla announced, distracting them. She dusted off her hands. "Who wants to climb down?"

* * *

"You can't be serious." Solomon's hands fell to the table. "And you swear you barely touched the oasis?"

Isiah nodded. He stood beside Tessa in a large room. The Raiders' headquarters stood in the shadow of the tower, inside a large building cut into the red rock of the cliffside. After returning from the eagle nest, he'd convinced Tessa to join him and speak to Solomon.

"Go over it one more time," Solomon said.

Isiah recounted his story, from being Marked during his Ceremony in Paradon to his search for the oasis. Solomon listened with an unreadable expression.

"I was destined to be a Royal Guard," he said when Isiah was finished. "I even flew on their dragons with my father a few times. But after the dragons rejected me . . ." He trailed off.

Isiah caught Tessa's expression. He cleared his throat. "Aegon is still in the Badlands somewhere. I need to make sure she's safe."

"Of course," Solomon said. "I'm sure once my people find Lazaro, they can collect your dragon. Leaving the Hidden Citadel on foot is a death sentence, and you've only just arrived." Solomon stood and paced about the room. "If you can bond with a dragon even after being Marked, it gives me hope," he continued. "What if it's a learnable skill? We might never have to fear being attacked by dragons again."

Isiah shifted his footing. "I'm not sure how I did it."

Solomon seemed not to hear him. "Why, with that skill, we could almost return to Paradon!"

Tessa coughed.

"If we wanted to, of course," he added. "It gives Marked people hope, at least. Carrying these scars is no easy burden." He nodded at Isiah. "Right, Isiah?"

"The nobles would never accept us," Isiah said. "They're too set in their ways."

"Indeed." Solomon sank into his seat. "It's an exciting thought, is all."

Silence descended for a moment. Outside, the muffled sound of talking and laughter filtered through the crack in the door.

"I was wondering if you could teach me about the dragons," Isiah said at last.

Solomon leaned forward. "What did you want to know?"

Isiah's mind drew a blank. "I mean, how does it work?"

"It's a psychic connection," Solomon said. "I'm sure you've been told a million times before how dragons and their riders form their bond. How you develop a feel for each other's emotions. How you can learn to direct your dragon with nothing more than a mere thought." Solomon held his hands up as if grasping a ball. "It's a synergy, a symbiosis. One you can only develop through rigorous practice." He let his hands drop. "But it's supposed to only be possible if the dragons accept you. I'm almost jealous of you, Isiah."

Isiah laughed nervously.

"Once we find your dragon, I'm keen on seeing how you fly together," Solomon said. "Was there anything else you wanted help with?"

Isiah exchanged glances with Tessa. "There was one more thing."

Solomon listened as Tessa told him how she found her magic. When she was finished, he clapped his hands together.

"I know a woman who can help you," he said. "She used to be a Raider herself. She was an ardent collector of magic. She might be able to tell you more about whatever power you've picked up."

Solomon gestured to the tower. "She's the archive-keeper living in the tower. She loves company."

Isiah thanked Solomon and they left the building.

"See?" he said once they were out of earshot. "That wasn't so bad. Maybe the people here can help you out."

Tessa rubbed her arms. "I still don't like them. They're too nice."

"You're just not used to it," he replied.

"What do you mean, *not used to it*?" she said accusingly.

"Nothing," he stammered. "It's just, after living in Alcabaza, I think you're used to seeing the bad side of people."

Tessa huffed. "I'm sure Paradon was *so* much better."

"I didn't say that—"

"Okay," Tessa cut him off. "I'll see what this woman has to say." She broke away. "It pays to be cautious."

Isiah started after her, but she melted into the crowd and was gone.

Cheap Trick

LAZARO SCOWLED AS HE SURVEYED THE BADLANDS. The steady wingbeats of his eagle echoed in his ears as the mountain Alcabaza was built into faded into the bluish haze behind him. Darla, Antony, and the rest of his gang flew around him, heading towards the distant spires where Aegon lived.

"What do you suppose we do when we get there?" Lazaro asked.

"There must be a way to convince Aegon to come with us," Darla said. "Isiah said they were smart, didn't he? She must know something is wrong."

"Good luck trying to communicate with it," Lazaro replied. "The sooner we get this over with, the sooner we can look for Tess." The thought of leaving Alcabaza behind made his blood boil. He tightened his grip on his eagle's reins.

"Uh, Lazaro," Antony started. He motioned back the way they had come. Several figures flew across the Badlands after them, low to the ground. Lazaro's nose crinkled.

"Do you think they're following us?" Antony asked.

"It would be exactly like Mauriel to send people after us to make sure we're leaving," Lazaro replied.

"We can't lead them to Aegon," Darla piped up.

Lazaro spurred his eagle and the bird went into a dive. Darla and the others came after him as they realized what he was doing. Lazaro directed his eagle to skim the ground, flying low between the mesas and valleys that scarred the surface of the Badlands. The landscape stole the distant Raiders from view.

Lazaro kept his eyes trained on the Badlands ahead. Their eagles weaved through the broken landscape, past towering buttes and over the remains of long-looted ruins. The wind rushed in Lazaro's ears, the only other sound aside from the steady thump of eagles' wings.

"Do you think we've shaken them?" Antony asked after a few minutes.

"We'd best stay low to be sure," Lazaro replied. "Who's to say Mauriel didn't order them to attack us once we'd left Alcabaza to be rid of us for good?"

The minutes ticked past. They spotted no sign of the tailing Raiders. Soon, the spires that marked Aegon's hidden sanctuary materialized in the distance. Lazaro spurred his eagle onward.

They climbed in altitude as they neared the spires. Around them, the skies were deserted. Cool shadows washed over Lazaro's skin as they passed into the mass of twisted rock and circled Aegon's home.

"What if she doesn't recognize us?" Antony asked.

"She's met us before," Darla replied. "I'm sure she knows who we are." She cupped her hands to her mouth and called Aegon's name.

A serpentine head emerged from the cave in the rock. Lazaro dug his heels into his eagle's side and directed the bird to land. His eagle landed atop a rock formation and Lazaro dismounted.

He dusted off his hands. "Now what?"

Darla shrugged. "I don't know—we talk to it, I guess."

Lazaro took the lead, navigating the narrow trail that snaked up the side of Aegon's spire. The dragon lumbered out as they approached, lowering her head and emitting a hiss of recognition.

Lazaro cleared his throat. "Good morning . . . dragon," he said. He felt stupid talking to it.

Aegon's dark eyes swept over them. Shafts of sunlight bounced off her blue-purple scales.

Lazaro beckoned her. "You need to come with us."

Aegon shifted her weight. A plume of hot breath erupted from her nostrils.

"This is stupid." Lazaro folded his arms. "We're wasting our time here. How are we supposed to communicate with a dragon?"

"Isiah said it was something about intuition," Darla replied. She beckoned the dragon. "Come on, Aegon. We've got to find Isiah."

Aegon tilted her head at the mention of Isiah's name.

"That's all well and good if you're from Paradon," he said. "We're Raiders. Dragons are our natural-born enemies."

Aegon took a lumbering step toward Darla. The dragon's neck extended and her scales rippled.

"Even if we do convince it to follow us—"

"Her," Darla corrected.

"Even if we convince *her* to follow us, what are we going to do? Fly across the Badlands with a dragon in tow? Every Raider in the Badlands will be after us."

Darla ignored him. She ran her hand down Aegon's neck. "She doesn't seem so bad, you know."

"Mauriel's hunting party won't be far off," Antony cut in. "We ought to move fast."

Lazaro grunted. "If you have any ideas, I'd love to hear them."

"As a matter of fact, I do," he replied. "What if we lay a trap?"

Lazaro cocked his head. The thought of revenge made the corner of his mouth upturn. "For Mauriel?"

"With her hunting party scouting the area around Keegan's ruin, they're bound to stumble onto this place. What if we found a way to make enough chaos to cause the Raiders to scatter?"

Darla wrapped her arms around Aegon's neck. "How do we do that?"

"The Raiders are still on edge after the attacks. If we wrapped ourselves in black to hide our features . . ."

"We could trick them into thinking we're the killers," Lazaro finished.

Antony clicked his fingers. "Exactly. If the hunting party is attacked by both Aegon *and* the mysterious killers they're all so afraid of, who wouldn't turn tail and flee?"

Lazaro rubbed his hands together. "A chance at a bit of revenge, ey? I like the sound of that."

"We still have time to organize everything," Antony said. "And there's a merchant route nearby. I'll bet we can find everything we're looking for there." He and Darla broke away to run back down the trail.

Lazaro matched Aegon's gaze. "If you can take down Mauriel," he said to her, "then you're alright in my book."

* * *

Lazaro sat with his back against a rock. The late afternoon sun painted the spires in long shadows, making the rock glow a deep red. An overhang shielded him from its heat, and his position gave him a clear view of Aegon and her cave.

"How close is the hunting party?" Antony called.

Helen stood on a precipice, holding a spyglass to her eye. Their eagles were nearby, resting in the shade of several scraggy acacia trees.

"They're heading this way," she replied. She scurried down from her post. "They'll be here in minutes."

"Good. I'm getting tired of waiting." Lazaro stood and stretched his back. His legs had gone numb from sitting on the hard stone. Black material covered his robes, and strips covered his face to protect him from the sun's glare. Helen and the others wore similar outfits.

"This had better work," he said. "You bartered the last of our money."

"We need to protect Aegon," Darla replied. She adjusted her sabre and beckoned her eagle. "As soon as Mauriel sees her, we'll swoop in from behind and spook the Raiders."

Lazaro jogged to his eagle. The bird chirped a greeting as he scrambled onto the saddle and took the reins. He spurred his eagle into motion and they climbed in altitude, keeping to the cover of the many spires. Darla, Antony, and the others flew in tight formation, soaring between the rocky crags and melting into the lengthening shadows.

"As soon as the chaos breaks out, that's when we attack," Lazaro ordered. His hand itched to draw his sabre. "The dragon will keep the Raiders busy, and we'll force them to scatter."

Minutes ticked past. An eerie silence fell upon the Badlands. The eagles stretched out their wings and glided on the air currents. Their tails twitched restlessly. Their claws flexed and unflexed as they sensed the tension in the air. Lazaro's muscles coiled like a spring as he waited for the fight to begin.

A piercing shriek split the air.

Lazaro dug his heels into his eagle's flanks and they erupted into motion. A deep, guttural roar echoed off the spires. Battle cries answered it, the voices climbing to a deafening chorus.

Lazaro's eagle lowered its head and fanned out its tail. Darla and Antony flew either side of him in formation. The ground rushed past below. They rounded a spire and the battle materialized.

A flock of eagles swept around the spires, fighting to avoid crashing into one another. Their shrieks of rage and terror made Lazaro's ears ring. A group of Raiders spiralled away as a fireball flashed through the air. Aegon stood on the ledge outside her cave. Her brilliant, purple-streaked wings were outstretched, and her neck was poised like a serpent about to strike.

Lazaro drew his sabre and unleashed a battle cry. The nearest Raiders turned to look as he descended upon them. His eagle threw out its wings and swooped over their heads.

The chaos swallowed Lazaro in its folds. Eagles flashed past left and right, circling Aegon as she launched herself into the air. A second fireball arced to his right. It struck an eagle and the bird reeled away, engulfed in flame. A frenzy rippled through the hunting party as they spotted Lazaro and his black-clad friends.

Lazaro hunched low to his eagle's saddle, gripping the reins with one white-knuckled hand. Eagles surrounded him, diving to his left and right. He narrowed his eyes. *Where's Mauriel?*

The Raiders darted in to attack Aegon, eagles flashing their claws before pulling away to avoid the dragon's jaws. Aegon's wings whipped up the air around her, creating a swirling vortex and bombarding the eagles with stinging sand. Her chest flashed deep red and a stream of fire cut through the hunting party.

Some of the Raiders faltered and broke away. A man screamed as Helen's eagle crashed into him and ripped him from his saddle. Lazaro raised his sabre and bellowed.

An eruption of amber-coloured light washed across the battlefield. Aegon lurched away with a hiss. Lazaro locked eyes with Mauriel. She held aloft a pulsing crystal. As she closed in, Aegon dropped to the ledge and shrank away.

Lazaro swore. He'd seen that crystal before, when Enrik had . . .

Something slammed into his side. His eagle screeched in panic and flailed its wings in a desperate attempt to remain airborne. Lazaro clung to the saddle as they spiralled downward and crashed into the earth. His eagle stumbled a few steps and he was catapulted into the air.

Lazaro slammed into the earth. The air exploded from his lungs and his sabre clattered away. He shielded his face as an eagle landed beside him with a plume of dust. Its dark, hooked talons gleamed inches from his face.

Boots thudded beside him. "I've got you now!" a gruff voice snarled.

Lazaro groaned and clutched his aching side. Each breath sent a stab of pain through his ribs. The boots approached and a Raider grabbed his collar. The man yanked Lazaro to his feet and tore the black material off his face.

"Lazaro," he spat. His lips pulled back to reveal yellowed teeth. "I should have known you were behind the killings."

Mauriel's eagle landed on the ledge outside Aegon's cave. She passed the amber crystal to one of her companions. Aegon huddled in the back of the cave, snarling at them.

As the rest of the hunting party recovered their senses, they landed their eagles in the valley in front of Aegon's spire. Lazaro's captor pinned his arms behind his back and marched him over to the Raiders.

Lazaro struggled to free himself, but the impact had knocked the fight out of him. His heart sank when he noticed Darla and his friends held captive among the hunting party.

"I'm sorry, Lazaro," Darla called. "They forced us to land."

Mauriel flew down from Aegon's cave and landed her eagle in front of Lazaro. She swung herself off and put her hands on her hips. "Thought you could pull one last trick on us, did you?" she taunted.

"Lazaro's the killer," his captor said. "It was him all along. We should execute him."

Mauriel waved him away. "Nonsense—as if Lazaro's gang had the skill to hunt Raiders. No, this is nothing more than a cheap trick designed to scare us."

Lazaro gritted his teeth. "What are you going to do with the dragon?"

Mauriel nodded in the direction of the crystal her companion was using to hold Aegon at bay. "Do you like it? I'm sure you've seen them before. There's something about them that dragons hate." She gave him a predatory grin. "We *were* going to kill it, but our arena has been awfully empty since the last dragon escaped."

"What do we do with Lazaro?" his captor cut in.

"We'll take good care of him," Mauriel said with a wink. "Him and the rest of his gang."

"I'll get you for this, Mauriel," Lazaro spat.

Mauriel laughed. "Of course you will. Third time's the charm, isn't that what they say?" Her smile dropped. "The rest of you, set up camp and secure the dragon." She turned on her heel and marched away. "We'll transport it to Alcabaza at dawn."

Edith

THE TOWER LOOMED OVER THE SURROUNDING TOWN, climbing several stories into the air. Tessa hastened toward it, walking into its long shadow and toward the small wooden door in its side.

The top of the tower appeared half-built, with partial walls and wooden scaffolding forming a skeleton of a room. A lone crane for lifting sandstone blocks jutted over the side. Tessa reached the door and knocked.

Nothing happened for a moment. She waited in the doorway, studying the knots in the old wood.

This is stupid, she thought. *Why am I even doing this?*

As she turned to leave, footsteps sounded inside. A key turned in a lock and the door swung open. Tessa found herself staring into the eyes of a hunched old woman with greying hair and a colourful shawl.

"Have you come to visit?" the woman asked.

Tessa hesitated. "You're the Raider Solomon said lived here?"

The old woman nodded. "I used to be, in my younger days. There's not much use in me flying eagles and looting ruins now, though." She turned and beckoned Tessa. "Do come in."

Tessa stepped into the tower. A narrow hall led past several rooms, all packed with shelves. Piles of books and antiques lined the walls and covered the dusty, creased rugs. Light filtered through narrow windows above Tessa's head.

"I'm the archive-keeper," the woman said. "But really, Solomon offloads whatever junk he finds from the merchants onto me." She chuckled and extended a hand. "My name's Edith."

Tessa shook it and introduced herself. She swallowed. "Solomon said you could help me."

"Come over here and we'll see about that," Edith replied. She stepped over a pile of old scrolls and rounded a corner. Tessa followed her and found a cramped kitchen. She ducked beneath a row of hanging pots. Plants sat on a windowsill, many wilting and stooped over like Edith was.

"Don't mind those," Edith said. "The people here give me plants to nurse back to health." She shuffled over to one and placed her hands on its pot. She closed her eyes and fell still. Tessa's eyes widened as the wilting plant began to straighten up. A lush green shine returned to its leaves.

"You have magic—I mean," she added, "Solomon said you did."

"I have lots of magic," Edith replied with a wink. "Take a seat."

Tessa sat on an old chair beside a leaning table. The cramped room gave her a feeling of claustrophobia. She shoved the sensation away.

"I spent my youth collecting magic," Edith said. "I would loot ruins and save all their artefacts and powers for myself. Sometimes I'd even sneak into other Raider's houses and steal from them." She laughed. "That got me in a lot of trouble."

"Why did you do it?" Tessa asked.

Edith shrugged. "I didn't want it going to waste. There were lots of us collecting magic. Some of us liked feeling we had an extra trick or two up our sleeves. The Badlands isn't a kind place." She leaned forward. "I'm sure you can understand that."

Tessa furrowed her brow.

"You were a labourer, weren't you?" Edith said. "Solomon must have helped you. But you're no stranger to Raiding either."

"Wait," she started, "how do you—"

"I can read people," Edith replied. "It's one of my skills." A sly smile crossed her face. "Or your clothes gave you away."

Tessa looked down at her Raider's robes.

Edith grabbed a kettle from a shelf. "Tea?"

Without waiting for Tessa's reply, she placed it atop a wood stove and clicked her fingers. A burst of sparks fired from her hand and flames crackled to life.

"Being a living fire-starter comes in handy sometimes," Edith said with a sly grin. "Do you have any magic you'd like to share?"

Tessa told the woman the same story she told Solomon—this time including her talk with Helen.

"I can give you a demonstration," Tessa said. She produced a pebble from her pocket and placed it on the table. She focused, channelling the same feeling she'd tapped into when showing Marie. The pebble transformed.

"It's illusion magic, alright," Edith said. "The name alone tells you what you can do. But it's worth much more than mere party tricks."

Tessa exhaled and the pebble returned to its normal form. The cold nausea in her insides persisted for a moment, then faded.

"I've heard stories of the greatest illusionists terrifying entire armies," Edith said. She waved her arm. "Imagine an entire dragon soaring through the sky, spitting fire with a deafening shriek. Or imagine a hillside coming to life with hundreds of skeletal warriors. It's enough to make anybody turn tail and run."

Tessa listened in silence. Her mind buzzed with possibilities.

"The best illusionists can conjure sounds and sensations, too. It's not just the domain of magicians and stage performers." Edith tapped a pile of pages next to her. "I brought my entire archive here when I met Solomon. There must be dozens of scrolls that can teach you."

"How did you meet him?" Tessa asked.

Edith looked out the window. "I found him before we settled here. He was living in a cave with a bunch of other Marked boys and girls. I took them in. I thought maybe I could use my magic to heal them somehow." She shook her head. "No luck yet."

Tessa jumped as Edith's chair scraped back. The woman stood and returned to her plants. "But magic has a funny way of coming with a price," she said. "Yours is no different."

Tessa held her arms to her chest protectively. "What do you mean?"

"If you spend your whole live conjuring illusions, it takes a toll on you," Edith replied. "You might begin to lose your hold on reality. The greatest illusionists had a bad habit of disappearing." Edith caressed one of her plants as it sprang back to life. "They fade away and become illusions themselves."

Tessa shuddered. The magic inside her suddenly felt tainted.

"It's not a power I ever discovered," Edith said. "But I can help you control it if you like."

The image of Enrik and his Raiders popped into Tessa's mind, with the sand vortex they used to dive into combat. If she found a way to use magic too . . . She swallowed. "Maybe it *would* be useful to learn a trick or two."

"You can always use magic for something." Edith returned to the table. "Even if it's in a way you didn't plan for." She cocked her head. "Is there something bothering you?"

"I'm fine," Tessa said.

Edith reached out and took Tessa's hand. "I'm getting a weird feeling from you—and not just because of what I told you." Edith closed her eyes. "You've had it since you arrived at my doorstep—no, since you arrived at the Hidden Citadel."

"I'm just . . . missing my friends," Tessa replied. She tried to pull away.

"It isn't only that." Edith concentrated harder. "I saw a look in your eye when I mentioned Solomon."

"I didn't expect to see anybody Marked."

Edith nodded slowly. "Do you have a problem with it?"

"What?" Tessa slipped out of Edith's grip. "Of course not. Isiah is Marked—"

"I know how Raiders and Royal Guards get along," Edith said. "I was no different. But surely you can't believe Solomon is somehow still connected to them?"

"I never said that," she protested.

"But were you thinking it?" Edith's words hung in the air for a moment.

"I'm still getting used to the idea," Tessa admitted. She turned to leave.

"I'm sorry for accusing you," Edith said quickly. "You can't turn these skills off." She looked absent-mindedly through Tessa. "But your anger *does* seem stronger than it should be. Raiders and Royal Guards are enemies, but I've never felt an anger so . . . personal."

Tessa scowled. "I don't want to talk about it." The memory of her mother's body, head severed and blood staining the earth, flashed into her mind. She buried it back in the furthest reaches of her psyche.

"Solomon's not like that," Edith said, ignoring her. "He and the other Raiders have no ill will toward us. Whatever happened to you—"

"I said I don't want to talk about it."

Edith raised her hands in surrender. "I'm sorry. I get carried away sometimes." She paused as the kettle whistled. "The tea is ready. How about we talk over this some more?"

"No," Tessa said. "I mean, I've got to get going."

Edith put an arm around Tessa and guided her to the door. "You come find me if you need any help with your magic. And you can stay at the Hidden Citadel for as long as you like." They reached the door and Edith swung it open. "Most people love it so much here that they never want to leave."

Tessa thanked the woman and left the tower. She waited until she'd gone a fair distance away, before rubbing the hand Edith had grabbed.

Was that really magic? a voice in her head asked. Their encounter had left her with a lingering feeling of unease.

Tessa shook it off. "Or she's just good at manipulating people."

'Tough Guy'

LAZARO FLEXED HIS WRISTS. ROPES CUT INTO his skin, binding him to a gnarly tree. Several other trees stood on the ridge, overlooking the camp that Mauriel's Raiders had assembled.

Evening shadows cloaked the Badlands, reducing visibility as the twin suns dipped beneath the horizon. Pinpricks of light illuminated the camp from several small campfires. Lazaro's gaze went from the jumble of tents to Aegon's cave. If he squinted, he could make out a handful of Raiders standing guard.

Darla grunted. She was bound to a tree to his left. She wrestled with the ropes, trying to free herself.

"We shouldn't have bothered with the dragon," Lazaro said. "Now look at the mess we've got into."

"Aegon still needs us," Darla replied. She gritted her teeth as the ropes cut into her wrists. "There has to be a way to escape."

Lazaro shifted his weight. The loop of rope binding his wrists was tied around the tree, forcing him to stand in an awkward position. The smooth bark prevented him from sawing away the rope on the trunk.

"Does anybody have a knife?" Lazaro asked.

"I keep one hidden in my boot," Antony replied. "But there's no way I'm getting it like this."

The faint sound of talking and laughter wafted up from the camp below as Raiders celebrated their capture of the dragon. An eagle landed at the base of Aegon's spire and its Raider dismounted, carrying a keg.

"They're having quite the celebration," Helen said. "That'll make our escape easier."

"If we can find a way to untie ourselves," Darla replied.

Lazaro probed his binds again. He placed one foot against the trunk behind him and tried to snap the rope that secured him. It didn't budge.

"What do you think they'll do with us?" Luca asked.

Lazaro scowled. "If Mauriel thinks she can kill us, she's got another thing coming."

"If she wanted to do that, she would have done it already," Helen said. "Maybe she doesn't want to break the Oath . . . what remains of it, at least."

Beyond the spires, a pearly moon climbed into the sky. Shreds of dark cloud obscured the stars as night settled on the Badlands. Lazaro shivered at the chill in the air. On the ledge outside Aegon's cave, the amber glow of the crystal pulsed with its magic light.

Lazaro worked at the ropes, but the thick coils were tough and sinewy. The fires in the camp below grew brighter as the celebrations fell into full swing. The faint sound of fiddles and music echoed across the landscape.

Lazaro tensed as voices grew closer. Footsteps crunched in the dark. A few shadowy figures trudged up to the trees they were bound to.

"So *these* are the midnight killers who murdered Keegan's friends," a Raider slurred. "Not so tough now, are you?"

Lazaro's nose crinkled at the alcohol on the man's breath. Two squat, bald Raiders stood on either side of him. The man prodded Lazaro's chest with a fat finger. "You should be hanged for what you did."

"Stumble back to your camp," Lazaro spat, "else the gorgons will have a feast."

"That attitude's not gonna do you any favours," the man replied. He shoved Lazaro. "Especially when you're so helpless."

One of his companions laughed. "Without their eagles, they've got nothing. Why were we so scared of them, anyway?"

"If you were too dense to hear Mauriel, she doesn't think we're the killers," Lazaro said. He lowered his voice. "But that doesn't mean I wouldn't feed you to our eagles if I got the chance."

"Lazaro . . ." Antony warned.

The drunk man's brow furrowed. He lashed out with a fist. Lazaro grunted as it connected with the side of his face.

"Are you gonna say that to me again?" the man asked.

Lazaro spat a mouthful of blood on the Raider's robes. "Beating a defenceless man? You're shameless."

The man grabbed Lazaro's collar. "You're lucky I don't gut you while you're standing there," he hissed.

Lazaro matched his gaze. "Come on, then. Let's settle this like men."

"What are you—" Antony started.

The Raider beckoned his two companions. They untied Lazaro's binds and dragged him away from the tree. Lazaro tensed as they threw him onto the ground.

"You want to fight us, tough guy?" the drunk man slurred. "Then have at it."

A foot slammed into Lazaro's ribs. He gasped as the wind was knocked out of him. He scrambled to his feet as the Raiders closed in. Their leader launched a haymaker at Lazaro's head. He blocked it, but the force knocked him to one knee. Another foot connected with his right shoulder.

Antony swore. Lazaro crumpled under the force of a third kick. He shielded his face with his hands as the drunk man stomped on his head.

"Hey!" Antony called. "You call yourselves Raiders? What scoundrels gang up like that?"

The drunk man's face darkened. He motioned to his companions and they marched over to Antony. Lazaro staggered to his feet as they untied Antony and dragged him over.

"Want to join in, do you?" the drunk man taunted. He grabbed Antony's collar with his burly hands and threw him on the floor beside Lazaro. Antony grabbed his boot and pulled something free as the man kicked him in the ribs.

Antony stood and swung at the drunk Raider. Steel flashed in his hand. The man jolted and gurgled in pain. Antony ripped his knife free and the drunkard collapsed, clutching his throat.

One of the remaining two reached for his sabre, but Lazaro launched into motion. He threw himself at the man and wrestled him to the floor.

The man tried to cry for help, but Lazaro drove a fist into his throat and then yanked his sabre free. Gritting his teeth, Lazaro pressed the blade against the man's throat and sliced.

A spurt of blood splattered Lazaro's robes. He stood and staggered away, chest heaving. The man lay on the floor, clutching his neck. He gave off a pained gurgle, then fell silent. The third Raider turned to run.

Antony pulled his arm back and threw his knife. It struck the man in the back and he stumbled. His knees gave way and he fell onto his front.

"Help!" he yelled. Terror gripped his voice. He attempted to grab the knife, but it was out of his reach.

Lazaro closed the distance and drove the point of his sabre into the small of the Raider's back. He grimaced as he plunged it in and the man's cries ceased. He pulled Antony's knife free and passed it to him.

"That was stupid," Antony said, pocketing the knife. "They could have killed you."

Lazaro rubbed his aching ribs. "But they didn't, did they?"

"You never think before you speak."

"Maybe you're right." Lazaro looted the fallen Raider for his belt and then sheathed his new sabre. "Or maybe you underestimate me."

Before Antony could reply, he hurried to free his friends. He untied Helen and Luca while Antony freed Darla. The woman rubbed her red wrists.

"What about Aegon?" she asked. "We can't leave her."

Lazaro squinted at the camp. "We'll worry about that later. We need to find our eagles."

"My guess is that they'll be with the others," Luca said.

Lazaro beckoned them. "Then keep to the shadows."

They abandoned the ridge with the trees and approached the camp. The fires had begun to burn low as Raiders filed off to sleep in the tents. A few stood guard to watch for gorgon packs. Keeping to the cover of the boulders littering the landscape, Lazaro approached the camp.

"We should split up," Darla said. "Helen and Luca can sneak in and get our eagles ready, while the rest of us free Aegon."

"Good idea," Helen replied. "If we keep our heads down, I bet they'll be too drunk to recognize us."

Lazaro narrowed his eyes. "And if we can take Mauriel out on the way, it's even better."

As Helen and Luca slipped into the Raider camp, Lazaro led Antony and Darla away, up the rocky trail that leading to Aegon's cave.

"Watch out for their guards," Darla warned. "If they raise the alarm, we're done for."

As they neared the top of the trail, the Raiders became visible. Several sat on boulders, their heads lolling. One clutched the amber crystal that kept Aegon pacified. Lazaro's jaw clenched as he made out Mauriel.

His hand went to his sabre. Mauriel sat with her back against a rock, the crystal in her lap. She was only a few dozen feet away. If he moved fast . . .

Antony cleared his throat. Lazaro hesitated, then tore his eyes away from her. Treading lightly, he slipped past the half-asleep guards and into the relative safety of the cave. Darla's breath tickled the back of his neck. He squinted in the shadows, trying to make out Aegon.

Deep, huffing breaths met his ears. Aegon lay huddled in the back of the cave, a heavy net draped over her shoulders. Ropes tied to stakes secured her to the ground, and her jaws were fastened shut.

Darla glanced over her shoulder at the guards. "We need to be quick."

Lazaro unsheathed his sabre and got to work sawing through the ropes and nets that bound Aegon. The dragon rumbled and one eye slid open.

"Quiet," he whispered.

One of the guards stirred. "Are you sure you're keeping an eye on the dragon?" he asked. "They're crafty ones. I could take over from you if you like."

"Relax," Mauriel replied. "I've got this." She patted the crystal. "The magic will protect us."

Lazaro's sabre sliced through the ropes binding Aegon. Darla and Antony worked alongside him. They grabbed an armful of netting and threw it off. Aegon shifted her weight.

"I said be quiet," Lazaro hissed.

Darla stroked Aegon's flank to calm her. One by one, the ropes came loose. Antony used his knife to free Aegon's jaws and they pulled the weighed net off her flank. Aegon unfurled her wings and stretched out her tail.

"I thought you said it was asleep," the Raider from before said. Lazaro caught the unease in his voice.

"I told you we're fine," Mauriel replied. "Don't be a coward." She stood and marched over to the cave mouth. Lazaro froze. She raised the crystal and flooded the cave with light. "See—"

Mauriel's voice died in her throat as she locked eyes with Lazaro. Aegon puffed herself up and hissed a warning. Lazaro flew into action.

"You!" Mauriel snarled. She fumbled for her sabre.

Lazaro closed the distance between them and lashed out with his sabre. Mauriel screamed and dropped the crystal, clutching her arm. The half-asleep guards snapped awake. The crystal clattered across the ground.

"Get the crystal!" Mauriel cried. Blood streamed down her injured arm.

One of the Raiders made a dive for it. Darla rushed forward and tried to scoop it up. The pair collided and the crystal bounced out of reach. More guards drew their sabres and closed in. Lazaro jumped over Darla and kicked the crystal with all his strength.

The crystal flew off the ledge. The Raiders froze as its light grew fainter, then disappeared. Aegon let out a deafening roar and lurched forward. The Raiders screamed and bolted.

"What are you doing?" Mauriel cried. "Come back here and protect me, you cowards!"

Fire filled Lazaro's veins. He raised his sabre and closed in on Mauriel. She backed away, down the trail.

"You can't chase me, Lazaro," she mocked. "The whole camp will be after you."

"Why won't you face me?" Lazaro replied. "Don't you want to settle the score?"

"Your sister is still out there," Mariel said. She clutched her bloodied arm to her chest. "You can either hunt for her and hope you find her before the merchants sell her, or you can chase me and face my Raider gang."

Lazaro's nostrils flared. He gripped his sabre hilt so hard he thought he'd break it. Part of him urged him to follow her and make her suffer.

Antony caught Lazaro's arm. "Focus. Tessa's more important."

Lazaro let his sabre drop. Mauriel turned and fled, still cradling her bloodied arm. He swore. "I could have had her."

"She's not worth our time," Antony replied. "Where's Helen?"

Below, the camp exploded into motion. The firelight illuminated drunk Raiders as they stumbled out of their tents. Lazaro caught a flash of movement in the sky. "There."

Helen and Luca approached on their eagles. Lazaro's bird flew in tow, alongside Antony and Darla's. Lazaro whistled and waved his arm to attract his bird's attention.

The eagle landed on the ledge, flapping its wings for balance. Lazaro scrambled into the saddle. The disoriented Raiders attempted to give chase, but they fell off their eagles and got in each other's way.

"Let's get out of here," Lazaro said. He spurred his eagle and they took off.

Darla called Aegon's name as her eagle spiralled into the air. Aegon looked between them and the camp, then flew after them.

Luca pumped his fist as they pulled away from the spire and ascended into the dark, cold sky. Aegon's steady, methodical wingbeats swirled in his ears. As the first of Mauriel's hunting party made it into the sky, they had already cleared the spires and were flying across the empty Badlands.

"Where to now?" Helen called.

"We get as far away from here as possible," Antony replied. "Deep into the Badlands where no one will find us."

Lazaro fixed his gaze on the horizon. "I'm coming for you, Tess."

* * *

Lazaro prodded the campfire with a stick. The flames curled into the night sky, emitting a thin trail of smoke that hugged the mesa nearby. Further off, their eagles slept alongside Aegon.

They had stopped to make camp far enough away from the spires that nobody would find them, nestled in a valley to reduce their fire's light and stay hidden from the surrounding wilderness. Fatigue tugged at Lazaro's eyelids, but he forced himself to remain awake.

"In the morning, we'll look for Tess," he said. "I know all the merchant trails that link to Alcabaza. They can't be too far ahead of us." He willed himself to believe it.

Darla put a hand on his shoulder. "We'll find her, I know it."

Lazaro clenched his fist. "I wish I could have finished off Mauriel. It's because of her that Tess is out there."

"She's a smart kid," Helen said. "She'll do fine—and Isiah and Aron, too."

Lazaro's ears twitched. Something crunched out of sight, hidden in the darkness. He stood and grabbed his sabre.

"What do you hear?" Antony asked. He scanned the sky for any sign of eagles above.

Lazaro stepped away from the fire. He peered into the night. Aegon lazily raised her head.

"It could be gorgons," Darla called.

"Then we'd best see them off," Lazaro replied. He strained his ears, listening for the crunch of gorgon claws on the earth. Someone cleared their throat.

Lazaro lashed out with his fist. He caught hold of something and dragged it into the firelight. His sabre flashed into his other hand.

"I don't mean you no harm!" a man yelled. He clutched Lazaro's arm, eyes wide. Behind him, several more figures stepped into the light, their hands raised.

Lazaro scowled. "How did you find us? Who sent you?"

The man swallowed. "We saw your light. When we noticed your dragon, we knew you were the ones."

Lazaro released the man and lowered his sabre. The man stumbled away, rubbing his throat.

"You're Lazaro, right?" he asked.

"Who's asking?"

"We were sent to find you," he explained. "We were told you'd be somewhere this side of Alcabaza."

Darla and the others stood. Aegon climbed to her feet, and her head swivelled between Lazaro and the newcomers. She coiled her muscles as if unsure whether to attack or not.

"A man named Solomon sent us," the newcomer explained. "We're here to take you to him."

Lazaro narrowed his eyes. "And why would we go with you?"

"We found your sister."

Lifeblood

DAYS PASSED AT THE HIDDEN CITADEL. As Isiah and the other freed labourers settled in, Solomon and his Raiders provided food and assigned jobs for them to help keep the town running. Isiah anxiously awaited Lazaro's arrival—and word about Aegon—but Solomon assured him they would have answers soon enough.

Tessa had remained distant. He could tell she still didn't trust Solomon, but part of him hoped it was only her worrying about Lazaro. Aron and Marie had settled in, and they were already helping Myla tend to the hatchlings. As the twin suns dawned, Solomon found Isiah in his tent and called him outside.

Isiah exited the tent and stood alongside Tessa, Aron, and Marie. The other labourers wandered into the town to see to their jobs and collect their day's rations. A few eagles lazily circled the basin—Isiah couldn't tell if they had riders or not.

"I know you've been through a lot," Solomon started. "And not just because of your Mark, Isiah. Aron told me a bit more about your history." He paused. "I'm sorry to hear about the things you all went through."

Isiah remembered Aron's close brush with death at the hands of Enrik. The boy still bore a pale scar from the sabre wound.

"We're used to it," Tessa said. "When you live at the bottom of the city, you see the worst in people."

"I can't change the past," Solomon replied, "but I can make your stay here more comfortable." He lowered his voice so the passing labourers couldn't hear. "There's a swimming hole nearby, one that myself and a few other Raiders know about. I thought you might want to make the trek out there and have some time to yourselves."

Aron rubbed his hands together. "Sounds good to me."

"I often go there to relax and think," Solomon said. "Swimming is banned at our lake here to keep the water pure for drinking, so it's the only nearby place in the Badlands to cool off. I can send Myla to guide you."

"What about Lazaro?" Tessa asked. "Have you heard back from your scouts yet?"

"The Badlands is a big place," Solomon replied. "You have my word that as soon as they return, you'll be the first to know." He gave her a warm smile, but she ignored it. "The lake is a short walk from here," Solomon continued. "If you leave now, you'll easily reach it before midday. It's quite the place, I assure you."

Isiah nudged Tessa. "It beats sitting around waiting, doesn't it?"

Solomon left them to get ready as he went to fetch Myla. She arrived a few minutes later and they set off for the stone archway that marked the entrance to the Hidden Citadel. Isiah fell into a steady pace as they left the basin and then navigated the rocky gullies and passageways of the highlands.

Tessa walked alongside Marie. The girl had spoken little to him in the time that they'd spent in the Hidden Citadel, but she followed Tessa around like a lost puppy.

"I can see why no merchants ever stumbled across this place," Aron said. "It must be so easy to get lost."

"It is," Myla replied. "And the gorgons crawl out of their dens to hunt come nightfall. We have the best natural defences in the whole Badlands."

Myla led them through the bottom of a valley. Sheer, painted cliffs towered either side of them, hemming them in. Scraggly bushes grew out of the cracks. Isiah caught a flash of a vulture as it flew overhead.

"And what do you do if somebody *does* find you?" he asked.

"It's never happened yet," Myla replied. "But Solomon made it clear we have no room for merchants." She kicked the ground. "They're nasty, all of them. I'd like to feed them to the eagles."

Isiah swallowed, remembering the merchants that Solomon had captured.

"And nomads?" Marie asked.

Myla shrugged. "Solomon says he trades with them sometimes. They like him. He respects them."

Isiah smiled. He'd only just come to terms with the reality that so many of Solomon's Raiders were Marked. *Like me,* he thought.

"And what about Raiders?" Tessa's voice distracted him from his daydreaming.

"Solomon says if they're friendly, they can stay," Myla replied. "But we have no time for rivalries and infighting here."

"It sounds so . . . nice," Isiah said. After what Mauriel had done to them, the Hidden Citadel felt like a different world altogether.

They persisted through the rocky, jumbled terrain for over an hour. Myla took them through snaking passageways and cracks in the rock barely wide enough for them to fit through. *Shortcuts*, she called them. Lizards, basking on the warm rocks, scurried out of sight as they passed.

"Here we are," Myla said, squeezing through one last passageway.

Isiah sucked in his stomach and forced himself through the gap. He emerged on a ledge that was surrounded by a circle of rocky cliffs. Ahead, the ground plummeted to a wide, circular pool of turquoise water. Aron let out a low whistle.

Isiah's breath escaped him. "How can something like this exist?" he asked.

Myla pointed to the rim of the cliffs. "Rain falls and collects in the sinkhole here. The water must have carved it out a long time ago." She tapped the rock. "And something in the rocks turns it bright blue."

Tessa and Marie made it through the gap. Isiah hid his smile as Tessa's sullen expression lifted.

"Want to go down?" Myla asked.

She started along a narrow path that snaked to the bottom of the swimming hole. The vibrant blue water lapped against a smooth, pebble-covered beach. Alcoves and ledges surrounded the pool, carved out by time.

Myla put her hands on her hips. "Pretty sweet, huh?" She pulled off her overalls and stripped to her underthings. Isiah hesitated.

"Solomon told me about your Mark," she said. "You don't need to hide it anymore."

Aron pulled off his robes. "I'm gonna jump from the top." He nudged Isiah. "Race you there."

A grin spread across Isiah's face. "You don't stand a chance."

Isiah stripped down and then took off at a sprint. He elbowed Aron aside and clambered to the top of the ledge. The sight of the water so far down made his head spin. He skidded to a halt.

Aron collided with him from behind. Isiah lost his footing and plummeted, arms spinning, into the lake.

He hit the water and plunged beneath its icy surface. Bubbles filled his vision. He floundered and kicked up to the surface. He broke it and gasped for air.

A force slammed into the water beside him, showering him with water. Aron appeared a moment later, laughing like a maniac.

"I'll get you for that one," Isiah said. He rubbed his stinging ribs.

The girls were already in the water. Tessa swam past, her soaked hair trailing behind her.

"I didn't think you could swim," Isiah said.

"Lazaro taught me," she replied. She paused. "But it wasn't somewhere as nice as this."

"Hey Marie," Aron said. "You wanna bet how long I can hold my breath?"

While Aron was fooling around, Isiah swam around the sinkhole. The sunlight reached down to touch the water's surface and illuminate the ripples he made. Its heat warmed the surrounding rock. His feet found a shelf and he stood.

The sun played across his shoulders and torso. He tentatively touched his Mark. The warped, candle-wax skin rippled like a droplet of water in a pond. His brief time with the oasis had cured his burns and blisters, but it had left his body lumpy and pale—a constant reminder of his horrific Ceremony.

"Myla," Aron said. "How much do you want to bet I can swim to the bottom?"

Myla scoffed. "Good luck. I've never found the bottom."

Aron took a deep breath and plunged beneath the surface. Tessa swam around the sinkhole for a while, then pulled herself onto one of the rocks. Isiah watched the water run down her body. She lay in the sun and the light played off her smooth skin.

Maybe Solomon is right, Isiah thought. *Maybe time is a good healer.* His Mark seemed to stare back at him, like a scarred growth. He sank up to his neck in the water so that nobody could see it—including himself.

Isiah kicked off from the rocks and swam to where Tessa was sunbathing like one of the lizards they'd passed. When he reached her side, she raised her head.

"Is your Mark okay?" she asked.

"It's fine," Isiah lied. "Why do you ask?"

"I thought the journey here might have irritated it," she replied. "Not being able to sweat and all."

Isiah rubbed his uneven skin. "Do you think Solomon was telling the truth about his Mark healing?"

"Oh, Isiah." Tessa sat up. "I'm sure he was. You saw what his Mark looked like."

"I guess." Isiah sighed. He felt stupid for bringing it up. "I still think about the oasis sometimes."

"You don't need it, remember?" she said. "You bonded with Aegon without being cured."

It's not the bonding I'm talking about, he thought.

Myla swam over. "Has Aron surfaced yet?"

Isiah looked around the swimming hole. The surface was empty.

"Maybe he came up somewhere else," Marie suggested.

Isiah scanned the surrounding rocks. There was no sign of the boy. A cold dread welled inside him.

"This is bad." Tessa slipped into the water. Myla took a deep breath and plunged in.

Isiah filled his lungs, then went after her. Bubbles filled his vision for a second, then gave way to deep blue water. He kicked, pushing himself further down. He tried to slow his heartbeat.

Aron's probably just taking a while, he told himself. He darted his eyes about, squinting into the depths of the swimming hole. Myla swam off to his right.

Isiah hugged the side of the swimming hole, where the sheer cliff descended into nothingness. The pressure made his ears throb. It felt like a vice squeezing his head. Every second dragged on.

His lungs began to burn. Images of Aron's drowned, lifeless body played on his mind. *What if he got trapped somehow?*

A pair of legs caught his eye. His blood ran cold. Forgetting the ache in his lungs, he powered toward them. Aron's legs protruded from a crack in the rock. Isiah grabbed one and pulled.

Aron kicked. A hand emerged and beckoned him. Isiah grabbed the rock and pulled himself through. His head broke the water and sucked in a mouthful of air.

"Isiah," Aron said. "Look at this."

Isiah waited for his heartbeat to slow. He coughed. "What do you think you're doing?" he said. "We were panicking about you!"

147

The top of Isiah's head pressed against hard rock. A small cavity of air gave them room to breathe. Faint light filtered through from behind them, barely enough to see.

"I found something," Aron said.

Isiah waited for his eyes to adjust. The cavity reached further into the rock. As he peered deeper, he made out a pair of long, thin sticks, then a ribcage. He stifled a gag.

A mummified corpse sat inside the cavity, arms wrapped around its knees. Papery, shrivelled skin stuck to protruding bones. A lifeless face stared at them from empty sockets, mouth hanging open to expose rows of teeth. Rusted manacles were fastened around the corpse's wrists and ankles, the chains broken as if snapped. Tattered clothes hung from its skeletal shoulders.

Isiah looked away. "How did it get here?"

"Maybe he broke the chains and swam down," Aron replied. He pulled a face. "And died sitting there." He took a deep breath and then disappeared beneath the surface. Isiah waited a moment, then went after him.

The pair swam to the surface and broke into the light. Isiah coughed and wiped the hair from his eyes.

"Aron!" Tessa exclaimed. "What sort of sick game are you playing?"

"There's a corpse down there," Aron said in between breaths. "In a cave."

Marie squeaked and scrambled out of the water. Myla frowned. They all climbed onto the rocks and Aron told his story.

"I saw a crevice while diving, so I poked my head in," he said. "I wanted to see what was in there. But there's this dead guy."

"It might be an escaped labourer," Myla said. "Maybe he was running from merchants and had to hide."

Aron shook his head. "Merchants don't use manacles on their labourers."

"Okay, so he might have been a captured merchant," she replied. "One that escaped from Solomon and the Raiders. That would explain the chains."

"And he found his way down there?"

Myla threw up her hands. "I don't know. If he thought the eagles were chasing him, or gorgons were prowling, he might have looked for somewhere to hide. Maybe he suffocated or died of starvation."

Tessa rubbed her arms. "Either way, I don't feel like swimming now."

Isiah grimaced. The idyllic water suddenly felt contaminated. They all navigated around the edge of the swimming hole to the beach where they'd left their things.

Myla slipped on her overalls. "I'll tell Solomon about it when we get back."

"Shame," Aron said. "I was hoping to sunbathe."

Isiah got dressed and they headed up the trail to the exit. They left a trail of dampness behind them. The discovery of the corpse had taken Isiah's mind off his Mark, but the image made his stomach roll. Myla's theories failed to sway him.

"I'm sorry you had to find that," Myla said. "The swimming hole is such a nice place." She sighed. "But I guess you can never tell what's hiding just beneath the surface."

As Isiah slipped through the gap and remerged in the Badlands, one thought played on his mind.

Could the mummified man really have been running from Solomon?

Reunion

"ISIAH!" MYLA'S VOICE RANG THROUGH the camp.

Isiah stirred. He cracked his eyes open. Dawn light filtered through the walls of their tent. He heard Tessa mumble in the room next door.

Isiah swung his legs off the low bed and pulled on his robes. He emerged from the tent, rubbing his bleary eyes, as Myla sprinted toward him. She skidded to a halt and doubled over, panting.

"It's still dawn," he said. "Couldn't you wait until later?"

"Solomon sent me," she replied once she had recovered. "The scouts have returned with your friends."

Isiah stopped rubbing his eyes. Myla pushed past him and called into the tent. "Wake up! Your friends are here."

Tessa shot out of the tent, still fitting her sabre to her belt. Solomon had given them new weapons to replace the ones Mauriel had taken. "Where is he?" she asked.

"They've landed on the cliffs," Myla replied. "I figured you'd want to see them."

Aron and Marie joined them, and they took off at a run. Soft pink and orange coloured the morning sky as the twin suns peered over the rim of the cliffs surrounding the basin. The Hidden Citadel stirred to life, its residents exiting their homes and beginning their daily duties. Eagles circled their nests and departed to hunt for their young.

Isiah ran down the main street and then followed Myla up the narrow cliffside path to the eagle nests. Tessa and Aron fell into excited chatter.

They reached the top and Myla waved. Solomon saw her and pointed. Beside him stood Lazaro and the rest of the Raider gang.

"Lazaro!" Tessa broke into a sprint. She threw herself at her older brother. He wrapped his arms around her and spun her around.

"Tess!" he exclaimed. "Are you alright? What happened to those filthy merchants?"

Tessa buried her face in his chest. "I missed you."

Darla cracked a smile and ruffled Isiah's hair. "See, Lazaro? I told you they'd turn out alright."

Aron gave Luca a high-five. Lazaro released Tessa and she hugged Antony and Helen. Solomon stood off to the side, nodding slowly.

"As I was telling you, welcome to the Hidden Citadel," he said when the reunions had finished. "You can stay here to rest after your journey. Myla will tend to your eagles."

As if on cue, Myla broke off. The gang's eagles stood together, watching the commotion with beady eyes. Tessa laughed when she saw Vyrro among them.

"You found him!" she exclaimed.

"You know I'd never leave him behind," Lazaro said.

Darla nudged Isiah. "We even picked up your dragon."

A bubble of hope welled in Isiah's chest. "Really? Where is she?"

"We left her a mile out," she said. "Solomon's Raiders told us to play it safe."

Solomon shook Lazaro's hand. "I must thank you, Lazaro, for taking in Isiah," he said. "Marked people have few allies out here. I'm glad he could count on you."

"Don't thank me," Lazaro admitted. "It was Tessa's decision."

Isiah stepped forward. "Solomon is Marked too."

A flicker of a frown crossed Lazaro's face. Solomon showed them the scars running down his shoulder and chest. He told Lazaro about the purpose of the Hidden Citadel.

"And your entire Raider group is Marked?" Lazaro asked.

"Indeed it is."

Isiah saw the gears turning in Lazaro's head. He hoped the man wouldn't take issue with the people here.

"What happened after you left Alcabaza?" Tessa asked, distracting them.

"The damn Raiders took our home and threw us out," Lazaro replied. He clenched his fist as he went over the story of rescuing Aegon.

Isiah shifted his footing. "I want to see her."

"That sounds like a grand idea," Solomon replied. "I'm keen on flying out and taking a look myself."

"But your Mark . . ." Isiah started.

"I can keep my distance." He paused. "Unless you think I should stay."

"No," Isiah said quickly. "You can come with me."

"I'll come too," Tessa added. She threw her arms around Vyrro. "Oh, how I've missed you."

While Solomon fetched his eagle, Aron began leading Lazaro and the others to their tent on the edge of town. Marie hovered off to the side, as if unsure of herself.

"Who's this?" Darla asked.

"I found her while we were labourers," Tessa explained. She told Lazaro about their time in the captivity of the merchants. "We took her in because she has nobody else."

Lazaro pulled a face. "We've got no home, Tess. Another mouth to feed isn't an exciting prospect."

"Come on, Lazaro," she said. "She's already staying with us."

"I say we give her a chance," Helen spoke up. "A friend of yours is a friend of ours."

Marie gave the woman a weak smile. Darla put an arm around the girl and guided her after Aron. "You'll fit right in, won't you? My name's Darla. How about I tell you the story of the time I helped Lazaro here break out of prison and beat the strongest Raider in the whole of Alcabaza . . ."

Solomon arrived with his eagle. Isiah climbed onto Vyrro and sat behind Tessa. A third Raider appeared to guide them to where they had left Aegon.

"I look forward to seeing your skills for myself," Solomon said. "Perhaps one day all my Raiders can bond with a dragon of their own."

Tessa spurred Vyrro after the other eagles and he took to the skies. The basin dropped away. Isiah turned his attention to the rugged, labyrinthian terrain ahead.

Aegon was waiting for him.

* * *

The red, arid landscape swept past below. The twin suns climbed higher, casting shadows across the valleys and riverbeds that snaked through it. From Vyrro's back, Isiah watched the highlands stretch into the distance. A few spires and buttes rose into the sky like crooked fingers. Beyond, a line of flat-topped mountains seemed to merge with the clouds.

They flew for several minutes, before their guide's eagle slowed. It spread out its wings and glided toward a mesa. A crevice snaked up its side, the interior awash with shadow. Isiah knew who was waiting for him inside.

Tessa squeezed Vyrro with her legs and he went after. They circled the mesa, then landed on a ridge nearby.

"This is the place," their guide said. He tugged at his collar. "You'd best stay here, Solomon."

"I trust Isiah," Solomon replied. He beckoned the boy. "You lead the way."

Isiah climbed from Vyrro's back and took off toward the cave, Tessa and Solomon in tow. As he drew closer, he made out the silhouette of a dragon. His heart sang as Aegon's head emerged in the light.

Isiah sprinted over to her. The dragon hissed a greeting and lumbered to meet him. Her shimmering wings caught the sunlight like gemstones. Isiah wrapped an arm around her neck and hugged her. Her smooth scales pressed into his cheek. Aegon rumbled and coiled her neck around him.

Solomon let out a low whistle. Aegon's head swivelled in his direction.

"It's okay," Isiah said quickly. "He's a friend."

Aegon surveyed Solomon for a moment, then lost interest. Isiah looked away so that neither Solomon nor Tessa could see the grin on his face.

"That's a beautiful dragon you have there," Solomon said. "It reminds me of the days when I wanted to be a Royal Guard." He stepped forward and outstretched a hand. "Will she mind if I touch her?"

Isiah stroked Aegon's snout. He studied his reflection in her deep eyes. "I think she trusts you."

Solomon touched Aegon's neck. The dragon grumbled for a moment, then fell silent. Isiah shrugged off the familiar ache of his Mark.

"The touch of their magic fire lingers." Solomon scratched his Mark. "We're still cursed."

"But Aegon doesn't care. Maybe the other dragons won't either," Isiah said hopefully.

"That's a bold assumption," Solomon replied. "Even I don't know quite how a Mark works. Paradon would rather pretend we don't exist." He stroked Aegon's wing. Her leathery skin shone with a deep blue and purple hue. "But perhaps you've outgrown whatever made the dragons reject you in the first place."

Isiah hesitated. "Can you teach me more about them?"

Solomon gave him a reassuring smile. "Of course. I still remember my lessons. My dragon-trainer taught me everything he knew." His smile faded. "He was devastated when I failed my Ceremony."

Isiah bit his lip as he remembered Ward. "Mine was too."

"Think of what we could accomplish if we cured ourselves of this curse." Solomon stepped away from Aegon and rubbed his Mark. "I'd put up with the pain if it meant I could fly again."

Tessa folded her arms, but Solomon didn't notice.

"Eagles are great and all, but my heart has always been with dragons." He put a hand on Isiah's shoulder. "I can see you feel the same way."

Aegon nuzzled Isiah. A small scar, still pink where the scales hadn't grown back, studded her neck from the valve the Raiders had inserted into her fire tubes. Aegon looked so different from the vicious, half-starved creature he'd freed from Alcabaza's arena.

"There'll be plenty of time for you to fly with her," Solomon said. "The highlands is a wild, vast place. She'll be safe here from Raiders— and you can fly with her every day."

"What about us?" Tessa asked.

"You can stay at the Hidden Citadel," Solomon replied. "We have enough room for you, and we could use more Raiders with your level of expertise."

A sly smile crossed Tessa's face. "You think we're experienced?"

"You must be," Solomon said. "Myla will be excited to care for your eagles. She always dreamed of becoming a Raider herself."

They broke away from Aegon. Isiah reluctantly left the dragon's side.

"I—I'll be back," he said. "You stay here." He wondered how much she understood.

"Dragons are fast learners," Solomon replied as if reading his mind. "Some call it intuition. They pick up on things." He chuckled. "My dragon-trainer would often joke about the things they'd say if they could talk back to us." He shook Isiah's hand. "I must thank you for the memories you're bringing back."

Isiah's chest swelled with pride. "It's just like you said. We have a connection, don't we?"

"Indeed we do," he replied. "And I hope you and your friends will stick around so we can nurture it."

Storeroom

"AND THIS ONE GOES OVER THERE." EDITH pointed to a shelf on the far side of the room.

Tessa carried an armful of boxes. She picked her way over the floor, stepping over piles of books and around pieces of furniture. The sound of something hitting the floor rang out as Marie bumped into a bookshelf.

"Sorry!" she called.

"Don't worry about it," Edith replied with a laugh. "We'll have this place sorted in no time."

Several days had passed at the Hidden Citadel. Lazaro and his gang had been given a tent next to Tessa's, and despite his initial hostility to Solomon and his Raiders, he seemed to be settling in. Edith had arrived the previous morning to offer Tessa and Marie a job organizing the archives. *To make a bit of pocket money*, the woman had said.

Tessa plonked the box down and began rifling through the books. She spotted a bare patch on the shelf and stacked a few of the threadbare volumes on it.

"I'll start looking through the next level," Edith said. "Today you girls can focus on getting the floor clean. It's been years since I've seen this rug!" She laughed and disappeared up a winding staircase. Tessa coughed and wiped the dust from her eyes as she went through the books.

"She's nice, isn't she?" Marie asked. She was kneeling on the rug, sorting through her own pile.

Tessa shifted her weight. Edith hadn't mentioned anything about their meeting to Marie. She wondered if the woman had forgotten about it.

"I wish the others were here to help, though," Marie continued.

Tessa grunted. Isiah had been gone most days, tending to Aegon. When she woke at dawn, he was already gone, and Aron was spending more and more time with Myla and the eagle hatchlings.

Marie stopped stacking books. "Is there something wrong?"

Tessa sighed. "I'm starting to worry that we're all getting a little too settled in here."

"What do you mean?"

"I mean we're being sucked into life here." Tessa gestured to the shelves. They stood in tight rows, barely wide enough to walk between. "Even we've got a job now."

"Don't you want to stay?" Marie asked.

Tessa lowered her voice in case Edith was listening. "We had a home in Alcabaza. I liked it there."

"I thought you said it was full of bad people?"

"It was," she replied. "But it was *our* home. Lazaro worked really hard to get it. Now we've been thrown out and we're just *accepting* it?"

A knock sounded.

"I'll take care of that," Edith said, hurrying down the stairs.

She stepped around Tessa and picked her way toward the back door. "I had some friends coming over. I'll tell them to reschedule."

Something in the woman's tone made Tessa pause, but she shrugged it off. Her earlier encounter had left a bad taste in her mouth.

Muffled talking sounded in the direction of the back door, then it slammed shut. Edith reappeared with a smile.

"I was wondering how this place works," Tessa asked. The memory of their gruesome discovery at the watering hole played on her mind. "How do you feed the eagles?"

"The highlands are crawling with gorgons," Edith said. "Solomon and his Raiders often hunt them at night to protect us. In the early days, gorgon packs would sneak into tents and carry people off in their sleep."

"Does anyone ever go missing?" Marie asked. "What if they want to leave?"

Edith scrunched up her face. "I don't think anybody has. It's such a long trek to the nearest settlement. And with the highlands so full of gorgons, leaving is a death sentence."

Tessa swallowed her unease. *Stop being so paranoid*, a voice in her head told her.

"But why would anybody want to go?" Edith asked, brightening up. "For so many of us, we have no family out there. Many labourers don't want to risk becoming beggars or being recaptured by merchants. It's so much better to stay here and be safe."

Tessa stood. "I was also wondering why we haven't seen more labourers," she said. "I thought Solomon said you're always freeing people."

"We are," Edith replied. "But we have to wait for merchants to pass through." She sighed. "We can only help so many people. I wish there was a way to extend our reach across the entire Badlands and free all the labourers."

"But there's not enough room here for that," Marie protested.

"I suppose you're right, child," Edith replied. Her face took on a faraway look. "I suppose you're right."

Silence descended. Tessa went back to sorting books. After a moment, Edith excused herself to return upstairs. Tessa found a second box marked *storage.* She picked it up and began hunting for its rightful place.

She waded through the piles of boxes toward the far side of the tower. The bookshelves gave way to a disorganized pile of boxes and furniture, piled high to the ceiling like a hoarder's house. Marie followed her with her own box in tow.

"There must be some kind of storeroom we can use," Tessa said. "There's not enough space to keep everything."

A narrow path led through the mess. She wobbled as she stepped over a loose pile of papers. Thick creases in the rug threatened to trip her, and as she moved forward, she heard Marie cry out as she stumbled.

Tessa tried to catch her, but the girl collided with a pile of boxes and the mountain collapsed. Boxes spilled open and books bounced across the floor. Marie grunted in pain as she slid to the floor.

"Sorry," she said again.

Tessa started to help her up, then paused. Beyond the pile of scattered books, the corner of a door caught her eye. She pulled Marie to her feet and then waded towards it.

As she drew nearer, the creases in the rug grew smaller. *Almost as if someone has stamped them out*, she thought. She stopped in front of a faded tapestry. The bottom was torn and frayed, revealing wood behind. Checking over her shoulder for any sign of Edith, she brushed it aside.

The tapestry swung away to reveal a stout door. Thick iron bolts held it together, and it fit flush against the worn sandstone of the wall.

"Maybe *this* is the storeroom," Marie suggested.

Tessa went for the handle. She paused mid-way. The handle was missing. She searched for any way to open the door.

"That's odd," Marie said. "Has it been abandoned?"

Tessa studied the floor. While dust coated the rug in the rest of the tower, the rug here was clean. Someone had used the door recently.

"Weird . . ." Tessa gave the door a tentative push. It didn't budge. She raised her hand to knock, then footsteps sounded on the floor above. She let the tapestry fall back into place as Edith descended the staircase.

Tessa hurried over. "I'm very sorry," she said, "but Marie had an accident." She pointed out the fallen books.

"Oh, that's quite alright," Edith replied. "You focus on tidying that up and I'll sort you something out in the kitchen."

Tessa searched for any sign of suspicion in the woman's words. Edith shuffled over to the cramped kitchen. Tessa swallowed the lingering sense of unease. Part of her urged her to try the door again. She shook her head to clear it.

"Why didn't you say anything about the door?" Marie whispered.

Tessa watched the kitchen doorway in case Edith returned. "It gives me a funny feeling." With the tapestry covering it, the door gave her the sense that it wasn't supposed to be found.

She instead busied herself in sorting the fallen books. The edge of the door, exposed by the tattered tapestry, beckoned her. She tore her eyes away from it.

It's none of my business, she thought. *It must be a storeroom or something.* She tried to shake the feeling it gave her.

What use was a door with no handle?

'Bad Dream'

TESSA TOSSED IN HER BED. IMAGES PLAYED across her mind's eye, taunting her.

"You're too close to our lands, Raider," a male voice said. A sabre glinted in the sunlight. Her mother lay trapped beneath the carcass of her fallen eagle. A dragon's heavy footsteps made the earth tremble. "We warned you once. Now you've forced our hand."

Her mother spat on him. "I'm not afraid of you."

The seconds dragged on. Each one formed an eternity. Tessa's gut coiled as she anticipated what came next.

"You should be."

A thud sounded, one that shook her to her core. The weight of the dead eagle pressed in on her from all sides, suffocating her. A foul stench invaded Tessa's nostrils, bringing tears to her eyes. Hot air blasted her face as she huddled inside its corpse.

The Royal Guard's boots thundered. Each one rang out in her head like the pounding of a drum. She awaited the thundering wings of the dragon flying away.

The boots stopped in front of the eagle's corpse. Tessa's throat tightened as a hand gripped the gaping hole in the eagle's front and lifted it. Blinding sunlight flooded inside, illuminating her blood-stained, cowering form.

The Royal Guard stared down at her. Tessa's heart stopped as she met the cold, empty eyes of Solomon.

Tessa jolted awake. She sat up, her heart pounding. She swallowed and held a hand against her chest, trying to slow her breathing.

The tent lay still. A soft chirp reached her ears from the insects outside. Her covers were twisted around her like they were trying to strangle her. Tessa carefully freed herself and then climbed out of bed.

Shadows cloaked the interior of the tent. Tessa steadied herself against the bedside table. The image of Solomon's face was burned into her mind.

I can't go to Lazaro, she thought. She wasn't a little girl anymore. Tessa pushed off the bedside table and wandered through the tent. As she passed Isiah's room, he stirred.

"Tessa," he said groggily. "Are you alright?"

"I'm fine." She brushed him off. "I need some fresh air, is all."

Isiah started to say something else, but she swatted the tent flaps aside and emerged in the cool night air. The Hidden Citadel lay still. A pearly moon hung in the air above the lake, playing across the water. The dark sun hovered over the horizon, burning with a smouldering light.

Tessa sucked in the cold air and started to walk. The sandy soil sapped the heat from her bare toes, but she welcomed the night's chill. It cleared the fogginess of her mind and brought her back to the present.

You've seen that dream a million times before, she told herself. *It's nothing you can't handle.* Her conviction faltered. *But it's never looked like that.*

She passed the lake with its clear, still surface and wandered deeper into the town. Thick wooden shutters barred the windows. Shadows filled the streets. A twinge of unease crept into Tessa's mind at the memory of Edith's warnings about gorgon packs, but she pushed it away. With Vyrro and her eagles safely nestled on the cliffs above, she felt safe.

Tessa passed the sandstone buildings, following the main road toward the tower. She didn't quite know where she was going, or why. She walked until the nightmare receded to the depths of her mind and her eyes grew heavy again. She paused against a doorway and yawned. The wind rustled the bushes and trees around the lake. Another sound broke the stillness.

Tessa frowned. Footsteps crunched on the road. Clinging to the shadow of the doorway, she peered out at the main road. The moonlight washed over it, painting its surface a silvery sheen. Under its light, she clearly made out a cluster of figures.

Tessa gripped the doorway. The sense of unease flooded back. She squinted, trying to make out who it was. Four people marched along the road, with three of them carrying the fourth. Their captive's legs dragged behind them, and a cloak obscured their features.

The figures headed toward the tower.

Tessa risked darting across the street. She crouched behind a market stall and peered over the counter. One of the figures darted their head around. Her breath caught in her throat as she made out Solomon's face.

Solomon and the others dragged their captive to the tower door. It swung open and the figures piled inside, then the door shut behind them and silence descended. Tessa realized she hadn't been breathing.

She sucked in a breath. The cold seeped through her thin nightdress, making her shiver. She rubbed her arms to quell the goosebumps. She watched the door in case anybody re-emerged. A small voice told her to go and check it out.

Alone? she thought. She dreaded to think what would happen if Solomon spotted her. *There must be a rational explanation. Maybe they caught a troublemaker or something.* The words failed to soothe her nerves.

Checking the door one last time, she abandoned the merchant stall and scurried back to her tent. Only after she pushed through the flaps and made it to safety did she let her shoulders drop. She sighed in relief.

"Tessa," Isiah whispered. He sat in the main area. "Are you alright?" He frowned. "Why is your dress covered in dust?"

"It's nothing," she lied. Part of her wanted to tell him about what she saw, but she shrugged it away. She tried to convince herself she'd imagined the whole thing.

"Did you have that nightmare again?" Isiah asked.

Tessa walked over and sat in a chair next to him. "I always do." She paused. "I'm sorry I shrugged you off earlier."

Isiah looked at his hands. "It's alright if you need time to yourself."

A soft wind stirred the fabric of the tent. Faint snoring emanated from the direction of Aron's room. Isiah shifted in his seat. "What do you see? If you don't mind me asking," he added quickly.

"It's okay," she replied. She told him the story of her parents' death. Each word cut into her like a knife. She left out the part about Solomon.

"I never knew it was that bad," Isiah said when she was finished. "I'm sorry I dismissed your feelings toward the Royal Guards. I just thought you were overreacting."

"My parents always used to call me Tess," she said. "They and Lazaro were the only ones who did it."

They both sat in silence. Tessa curled a lock of her hair. On the far side of the tent, Aron grunted in his sleep.

"Tessa," Isiah said after a minute.

"Yeah?"

"I was thinking about when we were captured by the merchants," he said, "about when you used your magic to stop them from discovering my Mark." He hesitated. "Can you do it again?"

Tessa reached out and parted Isiah's cloak. The moonlight, muted by the walls of the tent, cast deep shadows across the bumps and groves in his skin. She let her hand linger on its cold, warped surface.

"I'll try," she said. She cleared her mind and focused, conjuring the image of when she'd transformed Isiah's Mark in the merchant camp. She gritted her teeth against the clammy, nauseating sensation that gripped her innards. It crept up from the pit of her being like a phantom's hand.

Isiah's Mark faded. Smooth, unblemished skin appeared across his chest and shoulders. Isiah's breath escaped him as he studied it with wide eyes. He tentatively touched the conjured skin.

"It even feels real," he whispered.

Tessa held the illusion for as long as she could bear. She slumped in her seat and the illusion dissipated.

Isiah let his arm drop. "Thank you."

Tessa managed a weak smile. Using the magic left her feeling drained. The stories Edith had told her of illusionists losing their grip on reality echoed in her mind.

"Maybe it *will* heal," Isiah said. "Like Solomon's has."

At the mention of Solomon's name, Tessa stiffened.

"He's not a bad person, you know," Isiah insisted. "He's not like the Royal Guards who . . ." He trailed off, but Tessa knew what he was going to say.

She wrung her hands. "I know. But whenever I see someone from Paradon, it just reminds me of what happened."

Isiah placed a hand on her knee. "Does seeing me remind you of it?"

"You're not the same," she replied. "You're an outcast to them. Your family is gone—like mine."

"What about Ward?" Isiah asked. "He was different too. He helped save you. He *died* saving you."

Tessa bowed her head. "I know. I'm sorry about what happened. I know how much he meant to you."

"Just promise you'll give Solomon a chance." Isiah studied her face.

Tessa shrugged off the image of Solomon dragging the cloaked captive into Edith's tower. "Okay."

"It's all I ask." Isiah stood. "I should go back to sleep. Solomon wants to watch me flying Aegon again tomorrow. He says we've got a strong bond." He headed to his room. "Are you going to be okay?"

"I'm good," she replied. She parted the curtain and stepped back into her makeshift bedroom. "Goodnight."

"Night," Isiah replied.

Kinship

AEGON WHEELED THROUGH THE BADLANDS SKY. She caught the air on her massive wings and spiralled, her tail trailing behind her. Isiah clung to her back, the wind whipping his hair. He tossed his head back and let out a whoop.

Aegon tilted her body, adjusting her flight to circle one of the craggy spires that pitted the skyline of the highlands. Isiah settled into the rhythm of the swell of her shoulders as she beat her wings. She cracked open her jaws and bellowed. The sound shook Isiah to his bones.

Isiah put a hand to his forehead to shield his eyes from the glare of the sun. Far below, Solomon and Myla stood beside his eagle, staring up at him. Myla had insisted she come along to their training session. She'd begged to see the dragon for herself.

Isiah spurred Aegon forward. He fixed his eyes on a wide valley between two cliffs, and, on cue, Aegon dipped her serpentine neck and they flew toward it. She tilted her body, soaring through the gap and brushing the sides with her wings. Her flank rippled with colour as she passed through the shade, shimmering like a shoal of fish.

The dragon circled for a minute, then landed. Isiah braced himself in the way Solomon had told him to. Aegon collided with the ground and folded her wings. Isiah swung one leg off and slid down her flank effortlessly.

"Great work, Isiah," Solomon said. He marched over, beaming. "You keep pulling off exactly what I tell you. How did a boy like you ever become Marked?"

Isiah's chest swelled with pride. "Aegon is the only dragon I've ever flown with," he admitted.

"I sense a kinship between you," Solomon said. "Maybe it's because of the trials you both went through. I see that scar you mentioned on her neck." He shook his head. "I like the Raiders, but their approach to dragons is barbaric. They don't understand the beauty and power these creatures hold."

Aegon slithered to a Badlands stream and lowered her head to the water. Isiah pulled his waterskin off his belt. "I wanted to ask you something," he said. He told Solomon about their close call with the Raiders outside Keegan's ruin, and how Aegon had come to help him.

"Dragons can sense when you're in trouble," Solomon said. "Of course, it has its limits. But imagine this—a Royal Guard becomes separated from his dragon in the midst of battle. How can he hope to reunite without some kind of psychic connection?"

Isiah nodded slowly. "It's the magic fire, isn't it? The one they use to bond with us."

"Exactly," Solomon replied. "Only I've never felt *that* kind of magic fire." He waved his hand as if to dismiss the thought. "The stronger your bond is, the further you can extend your psychic reach. I

173

suppose the reason you managed it outside the ruin is because she was so close."

Isiah tried to suppress his excitement. "Do you think I could reach her from the Hidden Citadel?"

Solomon inhaled sharply. "That would take quite the skill," he said. "But," he added when Isiah's face fell, "you've already outdone yourself by bonding while Marked. Who can say how far you can take your connection?"

Solomon excused himself to tend to his eagle. Myla stayed behind, watching Aegon with bright eyes.

"That was some good flying," she said. "Solomon won't let me become a Raider yet. He says I'm too young."

"Nonsense," Isiah replied. He puffed himself up. "I think you've got exactly what it takes."

Myla giggled. "Do you think you could take me for a fly?"

"I don't see why not," he said.

They walked to Aegon's side and Isiah clambered up her wing. The dragon's muscles tensed, anticipating the flight to come.

Myla climbed up behind him. She looped her arms around his waist and pressed herself against him. "You won't let me fall off, right?"

"It'll be fine," he replied nonchalantly. "You heard what Solomon said."

He spurred Aegon forward and the dragon launched herself into the air. Myla squeaked as the ground fell away. Aegon powered herself into the air with steady, rhythmic wingbeats. Isiah pushed the hair out of his eyes.

"It's so different to flying an eagle," Myla said. "I feel like I could touch the clouds."

Isiah nudged her. "Why don't we?"

As he said the words, Aegon climbed higher. The wind tugged at her wings as she powered them far above the Badlands. The landscape rolled below like a spiderweb of cracks and ravines. The thin air forced Isiah to suck in each breath. Shreds of cloud drifted above them, tantalizingly within reach.

Aegon slowed. Isiah tightened his grip on her scaly neck as she arched her back and burst through the clouds like a whale breaching the ocean. His heart soared as the sunlight danced across the top of the clouds.

Aegon's wings stirred them and whipped them up around her. Myla's excited laughter rang in Isiah's ears as Aegon dropped through the clouds and spiralled back toward the earth.

Aegon threw out her wings and glided over the Badlands. Isiah winced as his ears popped. Myla tightened her grip around his middle as they soared over the rugged Badland terrain.

"Can she really breathe fire?" Myla asked. She had to shout over the roar of the wind.

A smile crossed Isiah's lips. "You bet."

Below, Aegon's presence spooked a gorgon pack. They fled their shallow caves and scattered to escape her. Aegon lowered her neck and a warm orange light welled in her chest. She cracked open her jaws and flames leapt forth, scorching the air above the ravine. The gorgons scrambled for cover as she swooped over them.

"Is she going to hunt them?" Myla asked.

Isiah stroked her neck. "I don't know. I guess that's what she eats, right?"

"Or she's just showing them who's boss."

Aegon tilted her wing and pulled away from the gorgon pack. She glided back toward the mesa where she had made her home. Isiah braced himself as she slowed her descent and stretched out her hind legs. Aegon came to a stop on the mesa's flat table-top surface and Isiah slipped off.

He helped Myla climb down her wing, and she steadied herself against the dragon's flank. Her eyes shone bright with excitement. Isiah turned his attention to the landscape. Beyond the mesa, the landscape rolled around them, a sea of rugged red stone and yellowed earth.

"So," he said, putting his hands on his hips, "how'd you like it?"

"It was incredible." Myla put a hand on her chest. "I can feel my heart racing. You're as much of a show-off as Aron." She sidled toward him. "I like that."

"Maybe one day you can learn to fly," Isiah replied. "I mean, there's no reason that bonding should only be reserved for Paradon's nobles, right?"

"I'd like that too." Myla turned to him. "And you can teach me."

She leaned forward and planted her lips against his. Isiah's heart soared for a moment. Myla broke away and stepped back, curly hair bouncing.

"Let's fly down," she said. "Solomon will be waiting for us."

* * *

The Hidden Citadel materialized ahead. Isiah sat squished between Solomon and Myla atop his eagle. They'd spoken little since leaving Aegon. Isiah still felt the sensation of Myla's lips against his.

176

Solomon's eagle circled the nests, then folded its wings and landed. Handlers hurried over to lead it away. They dismounted and Solomon dusted off his hands.

"Another good day, Isiah," he said. "A few months like this and you'll rival any Royal Guard."

Isiah beamed. "I'm looking forward to it." His gaze dropped to the town. "I should go check on my friends."

"Fair enough," the man replied. "You need time to recover and dwell on what you've learned."

Myla gave Isiah a little wave. "I've got jobs to do," she said. "I'll see you around."

She bounced off. Isiah took the narrow path to the basin and wandered through the town. The twin suns hovered in the sky above, reflecting off the sandstone facades of the many buildings. To his right, the tower climbed into the sky, beside the building Solomon and his Raiders called home.

Isiah left the town and wandered to the outskirts, where the many tents wrapped around the lake. A few builders dragged sandstone blocks to the foundations of a new building. Others tended to a pen full of scrawny chickens. As Isiah's tent came into view, he sped up.

Lazaro stood outside with his gang. Tessa, Aron, and Marie were among them. When Lazaro saw him, he beckoned Isiah over.

"Get your things," Lazaro said. "We're going."

Isiah's stomach dropped. "What?"

"I knew these people were sketchy," he said. "Tess told me all about it. She saw that Solomon guy dragging a prisoner into the tower in the dead of night."

Isiah turned to Tessa, trying to mask his pain. "I thought you said you'd give Solomon a chance!"

"I did," Tessa insisted. "I only told Aron, and he let it slip to the others."

"This place gives me a weird feeling," Lazaro said. "We can get our eagles and head for the nearest settlement. We'll find a tavern to stay at until I work out a new house for us."

Isiah folded his arms. "It's because they're Marked, isn't it?"

"It's because they're slinking around at night and dragging prisoners to who-knows-where," Lazaro shot back. "After what happened with Mauriel, I'm not taking chances."

"I don't want to go," Isiah said.

Lazaro paused. Darla and the other Raiders shifted their weight.

"I don't know what stories that Solomon has filled your head with, boy," Lazaro said, "but I'm not taking chances with Tess again."

"Don't you drag me into this!" Tessa cut in.

"See?" Isiah said quickly. "She doesn't want to go either. Solomon gave us a place to stay here. Where else are we going to go?"

Lazaro turned to her. "Is this true, Tess?"

Tessa shifted her footing. "You know how I feel about people from Paradon," she said, "but maybe we're overreacting."

"Yeah." Isiah nodded fervently. "What if he was just apprehending a troublemaker? He said they have no time for criminals here. We're all supposed to get along."

Lazaro scoffed. "Good luck on that one."

Tessa looked at her feet. "Maybe I can ask Edith about it. There must be some rational explanation."

"Solomon has been nothing but nice to us," Isiah said. "Why would you want to trade that for going back to a city?" He added, quieter, "Aegon is safe here, too."

"Is that what this is about?" Lazaro asked. "That dragon of yours?"

Isiah stood his ground. "The Raiders at Alcabaza found her hiding place. I don't want to risk her being hunted anymore." He swallowed. "Even if you go, I'm staying here."

"Isiah . . ." Tessa started.

"Solomon promised to teach me," he said. "I can't let this opportunity go to waste."

Lazaro threw up his hands. "So that's where your loyalty lies? After everything we've done for you—"

"Just give Solomon a chance," he pleaded. "I'm sure what Tessa saw was nothing."

Darla bit her lip. "He has a point," she said. "We don't have a home lined up. The last thing we want is to fly to a city and end up on the streets. We don't even know if their roosts will have room for our eagles."

Lazaro scowled. "Then I'll fly ahead."

Helen stepped forward. "You're a fool if you think we're letting you run off on your own." She put a hand on his shoulder. "Raiders stick together."

"We said that before they broke the Oath," Lazaro replied.

"Just let me talk to Edith," Tessa said. "If you're still worried about this place after that, then we can think about leaving." She shot a look at Isiah. "Even if *some* people still want to stay behind."

Lazaro's expression softened. "Fine. But be careful, Tess. You don't know these people."

Tessa took Marie's hand. "We should get going. Edith will be wondering where we've got to."

Lazaro and the others filed back to their own tent. The man refused to make eye contact with Isiah. As they left, he overheard Helen talking.

"You can't keep Tessa under your watchful eye forever, you know. Sometimes you've got to let them spread their wings." She winked at Isiah. "No matter where that takes them."

The Door

TESSA WATCHED THE TAPESTRY COVERING THE door out of the corner of her eye. She stacked a pile of boxes and sorted dusty books, tracking the faded strip of material with her gaze as she went. A light breeze filtered through the narrow windows above her head, rustling the ragged edge of the tapestry and seeming to beckon her. Edith worked nearby on her own pile of books.

"I must thank you for all the good help you've been," she said. "I would never have been able to organize this alone."

Tessa studied the woman's words, searching for any trace of an ulterior motive. When she and Marie had arrived that morning to begin their work, the woman had been unusually cheerful. Tessa exchanged glances with Marie. The girl wobbled on the spot, as if unsure of herself.

"Everybody gets along so well here," Tessa said innocently. "I was talking to Marie, and we were wondering what you do with trouble-makers."

"Oh, we don't get many of those," Edith replied. "I'm sure Solomon told you that. We understand that as outcasts, we have to look out for one another."

"But what about pickpockets? Thieves? Surely there have been some bad labourers you've rescued."

Edith mulled it over. "Solomon always threatened to cast them out. They know they wouldn't last long beyond the basin with all the gorgons prowling around."

Tessa picked apart the woman's words. She grabbed another box and passed the hidden door. It seemed to draw her toward it with a magnetic pull.

"So you don't have prisons?" she asked.

Edith shrugged. "We never needed them."

"Not even for merchants?"

Edith stopped stacking books. "Solomon deals with them. He says he strips them of their gear and casts them into the highlands."

Tessa remembered the mummified corpse that Aron and Isiah had found in the swimming hole. *Then explain the manacles.*

A knock sounded. Tessa frowned. It didn't come from outside.

"I'll get that," Edith said quickly. "How about you girls go upstairs and take a look at the second floor. I promised I'd help revive a neighbour's sick vegetables."

Tessa forced a smile. "Sure." She took Marie's hand and dragged her up the stairs. As soon as they got out of sight, she stopped.

"What are you doing?" Marie whispered.

"I don't trust her," she replied.

Creeping down to where she could peer into the first floor, Tessa watched Edith put down her books and head to the tapestry. She brushed it aside and gave the door a light tap. A handle clicked and the door swung open from the inside.

Edith disappeared inside and the tapestry fell back into place—but the door remained open a crack. Tessa crept down the stairs and towards the door. When she reached it, she pressed her ear against it. Voices came from inside.

"This had better be quick," Edith grumbled. "I have visitors."

"I apologize." Solomon's calm, smooth voice made Tessa's skin crawl. "It's urgent."

Footsteps sounded. Once they had faded, Tessa brushed the tapestry away and gave the door a tentative push. It swung open. A staircase led into the earth. Marie appeared at Tessa's side.

"Where do you think it leads?" she asked.

Tessa eyed the staircase suspiciously. It descended into darkness. "Wherever Solomon took his captive."

She slipped into the room and tip-toed down the stairs. Dust hung thick in the air. The staircase descended in a straight line, cutting deep into the rock beneath the basin. Marie's shallow breathing echoed behind her.

"We should go tell Lazaro and the others," Marie said. "There's something wrong going on here."

Tessa shook her head. "Isiah still won't believe us. We need more evidence."

The stairs gave way to a sloping tunnel, its edges chipped by hand tools. A thin layer of sand covered the floor. Tessa traced the wall with her hand to keep her bearings. Shadows cloaked the tunnel.

They followed it for several painfully slow minutes. A couple of boarded-off passageways branched away.

"They're tunnels," Marie said. "It looks like a mine."

"Maybe it was," she replied. *But why would they need a mine?*

Tessa's foot collided with something. She stumbled and caught herself. Whatever she'd kicked clattered across the floor. She froze.

Silence hung thick in the air. After a moment, Tessa sighed. She knelt and felt whatever had tripped her. Its worn wooden surface pricked her fingers. She felt the edges of what appeared to be a crate, then pried the lid away and the acrid smell of explosives hit her full in the face.

She coughed and pinched her nose. "It's like the explosives Enrik had."

"It *is* a mine," Marie replied.

They abandoned the crates and pressed deeper into the tunnel. The fear of getting lost played on Tessa's mind. She shrugged it off when she caught sight of light ahead. Crouching low to the ground, they hastened toward it.

A sound met Tessa's ears—pained moaning. Goosebumps sprang up on her arms. With her heart pounding against her ribcage, she reached the end of the tunnel and peered out.

The tunnel was framed by an iron doorway, opening into a wide cavern. Oil lanterns stood on rocks, piercing the darkness. Manacles dangled from the walls, with skeletal bodies hanging from them—some still breathing. Tessa stifled a gag.

Solomon and half a dozen Raiders stood in the room, their torsos exposed. One Raider sat in the centre of the cavern on a metal chair. Blood streamed from his raw skin, painting the earth beneath him a copper-red. Solomon raked a long tool down the man's chest, methodically stripping his Mark away.

A second Raider appeared with a blanket. *No,* Tessa realized. Cold dread welled in her insides as the Raider pressed a sheet of skin against the other man's blood-soaked torso. Solomon poured a bucket of water onto the man's head and Edith stepped forward.

Tessa fought the bile climbing her throat. She heard Marie retch beside her. Edith placed her hands on the sheet of skin and closed her eyes. The skin sprang to life. It wrapped around the man's body and melted into him. He grimaced, clenching the arms of the chair. Solomon poured a second bucket of water over the man to clean the blood.

"I'll prepare the next captive," one of the Raiders said. He produced a long, thin blade from a bench, along with a vial of dark liquid.

Edith stepped away and her patient stood. The glow of the lanterns played across his pale, newly attached skin. A few lumps remained from his Mark. He scowled.

"Let it heal," Edith said. "Another treatment or two and it will be hidden for good."

The moaning Tessa had heard intensified. Chains rattled. Solomon passed the bucket to his comrade and took a seat in the chair. He grimaced and braced himself as his comrade went to work.

Tessa squeezed her eyes shut. The stench of blood invaded her nostrils, making her throat tighten. Marie whimpered and stumbled away.

A muffled scream sounded. Trickles of blood ran down Solomon's shoulders as the tool tore at his skin. He grunted and his nostrils flared.

"How many more treatments?" he asked between clenched teeth.

"Two or three," Edith replied. "We should have enough labourers to cover it."

"Good," he said. "Keep Isiah's friends under close watch."

Tessa's blood ran cold. A wave of nausea washed over her. *We have to go*, a voice in her head told her. *Now.*

A lantern dropped. Tessa's heart flew into her throat as her eyes locked with the partially healed Raider. Solomon and the others raised their heads. Tessa scrambled to her feet, but the Raider leapt to cut them off.

"We have more captives," he called. A cruel smile crossed his lips. "You two should have known not to go snooping around."

His hands darted out to catch Tessa and Marie's wrists. Marie screamed and tried to pull away. The other Raiders closed in to apprehend them. Solomon stood, blood still oozing from his damaged skin.

"I'm sorry you had to discover the truth like this," he said. "I hoped to leave you free for a while longer."

Tessa struggled against her captors. They dragged her into the cavern. She kicked at them, but they held fast.

"Let go of us!" she ordered. She fought the panic in her voice. "What do you think you're doing?"

"You've forced our hand," Solomon said. "I can't let you go now."

"You're sick," Tessa spat. "Once Lazaro and Isiah find out what you're up to—"

"He won't," Solomon said, cutting her off. "By the time the others know what's happened, they'll be joining you." He leaned forward. Blood splattered onto the ground at his feet. "And as for Isiah, he'll be sad to learn from Myla that his friends all flew off to another city without saying goodbye."

"He'll never believe it," she snapped.

"At first, yes," Solomon said, "but after a while, he'll come to accept it. After all, you never liked me anyway, did you? And with Myla to keep him company, he'll soon forget all about you." Solomon returned to the chair. "Take them to one of the cells. They can scream all they want—the mines are so deep that nobody will ever hear them."

Tessa's captives dragged her away.

"You'd better use them first," Solomon called after them. "It's too risky to give them a chance of escaping."

Panic gripped Tessa's chest. She wrestled with her captives, but they were too strong. Edith watched them go, her face expressionless. Tessa's captives threw open a door and the woman disappeared from view.

Payback

Isiah wrung his hands. *Tessa should be back by now.*

He sat on his bed inside the tent. Outside, the twin suns dipped toward the horizon. The shadows lengthened as evening took hold of the Hidden Citadel. Isiah shifted his weight. Tessa never stayed this late with Edith.

Maybe she got held up, he reasoned. He stood and peered out the tent flaps for the hundredth time. The pathway that led into the town stood empty. Isiah sucked in a breath. *I can't sit around and do nothing.*

"I'm going to go and check on Tessa," he said.

Aron poked his head out of his room. "Really? They'll be back any minute, I'm sure."

"What if she got into trouble?"

"With Edith? She's an old woman. How dangerous can she be?"

Isiah pushed out of the tent and hastened down the path. He didn't wait for Aron to catch up. His sabre bobbed against his side as he walked.

He entered the town as the shadows grew longer. The twin suns painted the horizon in a hazy yellow and red. Tired townsfolk returned to their houses and filtered past him on the way to their tents. A twinge of doubt tugged at his chest.

Maybe I am *overreacting*, he thought. He studied the crowd, searching for Tessa.

The tower materialized ahead, looming over the surrounding buildings. Its crane jutted out over the street, pointing towards the lake. A rope dangled from it, leading to a wooden platform with a few sandstone bricks piled on top. Isiah quickened his pace.

He reached the door and knocked. No answer. He knocked louder, then idled for a minute. He pressed his ear against the door, listening for any sign of movement.

Silence.

Isiah jiggled the door handle. To his surprise, the door swung open. The dark, dusty hall greeted him.

"Tessa?" he called. He leaned against the doorway and peered into the house. No answer. With every passing second, his heartbeat quickened. He wiped his clammy palms against his robes and wandered into the house.

The main room stood deserted. Piles of boxes and books were scattered about, evidence of Tessa and Marie's work. Isiah checked the first floor and its cluttered kitchen, then climbed the stairs.

"Tessa . . ." His voice wobbled. "Marie?"

Long rows of bookshelves dominated the second floor. A window let dying sunlight filter into the room. Isiah inspected the halls between each shelf, then proceeded to the third floor. More of the same.

Isiah fought the growing panic. He quickened his pace.

Movement sounded above. Isiah sighed. He cupped his hands to his mouth and called Tessa's name. He found the final staircase and hurried to the fourth floor.

Half-built tower walls surrounded him, and gaps in the wooden scaffolding revealed the town beyond. Bits of loose brick and hand tools lay scattered on the floor. Isiah leaned against the handrail and looked around.

An eagle sat atop one of the walls, pinning him with its beady gaze. Boards creaked as a figure stepped through the scaffolding. Isiah froze.

"Hello, Isiah," Enrik said. A predatory grin slid across his face.

Isiah fumbled for his sabre. Enrik's blade appeared in his hand in a flash. "Don't start a fight you can't win, boy."

"What have you done with Tessa?" Isiah said.

Enrik strolled nonchalantly across the tower floor. "I have nothing to do with it. Why don't you ask Solomon about her?"

Isiah took a step back, but the stairs creaked behind him. He turned to see Raiders climbing up to him.

"There's no need to run off so soon," Enrik said. "We have so much to discuss."

"You lost the oasis," Isiah replied. "I saw you crash. What are you doing here?"

"That's more like it." Enrik's smile dropped. "How about I tell the story of how you killed my eagle and left me to die in that forsaken ravine," he spat. "The days I spent trapped beneath its carcass as the gorgons circled me. How I dragged myself free and staggered, half-dead, to the nearest settlement." Enrik raised his twisted metal hand. "How I lost my hand fighting packs of starving gorgons. Let's talk about *that*, why don't we?" Enrik's snarl dropped and his calm, collected demeanour returned. "Mauriel was one of the few friends I had left in Alcabaza after that lying rat Aron turned them against me."

Isiah found his voice. "You broke the Oath."

"And I broke it again," Enrik replied. "I started killing off the Raiders of Alcabaza to whip you all into a frenzy. All Mauriel had to do was point them in the right direction."

Isiah's eyes widened. "This was your fault?"

"I arranged for her to sell you to merchants. They would unwittingly take you into the highlands, marching to their doom." Enrik turned his sabre over. "As for Lazaro, it was easy enough to assume that he'd come after you."

Isiah puffed himself up. "When Solomon knows who you are, he'll kill you."

Enrik laughed. "I know Solomon from my Raiding days. We're the only Raiders who don't hate him for his Mark. It was simple to call in a favour and have him attack the merchant camp. It was a far bolder move than he'd ever pulled off before."

The Raiders reached the top of the stairs and stood blocking the way. Isiah shot a glance at the town below, searching for any sign of his friends.

"Solomon brought you here at my suggestion," Enrik continued. "I told him that I wouldn't touch you, Isiah. He wanted you to join him. He thought you could teach him so much about your bond with Aegon." Enrik shrugged. "But I'm afraid I have no choice but to double-cross him."

"You're lying," Isiah snapped. A fire burned in his chest. "Where are my friends?"

"You don't know what Solomon does to people? Surely you must have picked something up." Enrik sat on a pile of bricks. "The lack of labourers? The way his Mark is so much closer to healing than yours?"

"You won't fool me," Isiah shot back. "It heals over time."

Enrik laughed. "A Mark is for life, boy. I'll tell you what he does." He leaned in. "He frees these labourers to drag them into his tunnels and harvest them for their skin."

"No." Isiah shook his head. "Solomon would never do that."

"He's doing it right now!" Enrik stood. "And your friends will be among his captives."

Isiah staggered away. A Raider caught him and shoved him away from the staircase. "I don't believe you."

"Come on, Isiah. You didn't honestly think that a few years could heal a Mark so much?"

"What do you want?" Isiah whimpered.

Enrik sheathed his sabre. "I'll tell you what I want. You ruined my life, cast me out of Alcabaza, and left me to slowly die in the Badlands. I want payback." Enrik's expression darkened. "I don't want to kill you. Not quickly, at least. I want you to suffer as I did." He spat the words. "While Solomon slowly mutilates and kills your friends, you'll sit here with the knowledge that it's happening."

Isiah fought the bile climbing his throat. A pair of Enrik's Raiders grabbed his shoulders and forced him to sit on a stone slab. Enrik folded his arms behind his back.

"And once their bloodied corpses roll out, you'll know the meaning of suffering," he said. "I'll rob you of everything you love, and then I'll kill you myself."

"Solomon won't let it happen," Isiah replied weakly. Enrik's words cut into him. Every passing suspicion he'd buried about Solomon came flooding back.

"It's not Solomon's choice anymore," Enrik said. "By the time he's finished with your friends, he won't be useful to me anymore."

'Small Price'

TESSA YANKED ON HER CHAINS. THE MANACLES bit into her wrists, painfully tight. Cold stone pressed against her back. More chains bound her ankles, pinning her to the makeshift table. Marie's soft sobbing emanated from somewhere to her left.

More chains hung from the walls. Bodies, skeletal and mummified, hung from them. Some were more recent. Tessa's nose crinkled at the sickly stench of decay. One of the corpses still had his big, bushy beard and tattered merchant robes.

A single lantern flickered in the corner of the room. To her right, iron bars cut the room in two. Figures sat hunched beyond, the shadows obscuring their features. Tessa fought to quell the terror rising inside her.

She yanked on her chains again. They stretched her out on the table, giving her little room to move. She swallowed the feeling of hopelessness.

"What are they going to do to us?" Marie asked.

Tessa craned her neck to try and look at the girl. "Don't worry. Isiah will come for us. They all know where we went."

The seconds dragged on. Tessa knew that beyond the closed door ahead of her, Solomon and the rest of his Raiders were continuing their sick practice. Fire burned in her chest. She cursed herself for not being more suspicious of Edith.

The door creaked open, and Tessa tried to sit up. The table held her at a slight angle, almost parallel to the ground but tilted enough to see the top of the doorway. Solomon walked through. Her heart skipped a beat.

"Keep away from us," she managed to say. She tried not to let her fear betray her.

"I'm sorry it had to be this way," Solomon said. "I really am."

"You're lying," she spat. "You've been lying this entire time."

Solomon ignored her. "You were good friends to Isiah. Most of your kind kill us on sight." He picked up the lantern. His newly attached patch of skin clung to his body, pale and smooth. "And unless we fix ourselves, we'll be stuck that way forever." He approached the table. "We don't have the luxury of Paradon's healers. We're stuck with a much more . . . crude way of doing things."

Tessa glared at him. "You skinned those merchants."

"Why do you care? They enslaved you!" Solomon walked to the decaying body of the bearded merchant. "We have to get our skin from somewhere. Edith's magic was only good for healing plants—or so I thought. But as it turns out, it has a few more uses too."

"I knew she was a witch," Tessa said through gritted teeth.

Solomon spun away from the body. "She's our salvation!" His spittle hit her forehead. "Without her, we'd be stuck like this." He stopped himself. "Do you want to know how it works?"

He produced a long, thin blade from his robes. "We need living subjects, else the skin loses its usefulness." He grabbed her arm and rolled up the sleeve. "We have potions to make the process go more smoothly, but I can't guarantee it will be painless."

Tessa winced as the cold metal of the knife pressed against her soft inner arm. "Once we've taken everything we can from you, then you're no longer useful to us," he said. "Then you're either left to mummify like these poor lads—" he gestured to the corpses around him "—or you're cut up and fed to our eagles."

Tessa forced her face to stay expressionless. She wouldn't give him the satisfaction of seeing her panic.

"We start with the back," Solomon explained. "The largest areas go first, then we work down. Some captives die before we're finished with them, but Edith's magic will help prolong your usefulness."

Solomon removed the blade and traced a finger down her arm. "You have good skin," he said. "Perhaps I'll save you for myself."

"You can't keep us here," Tessa said. "Our friends know where we are." She fought the tremble in her voice. "Let us go and we promise we won't tell anyone."

"You know I can't do that," Solomon replied. He tucked the knife away. "Isiah is wasting his time with people like you. He belongs with us—with his own people."

Tessa gritted her teeth. "You're monsters."

"Are we?" Solomon stood. "Or are we simply trying to cure ourselves of our curse? These merchants and labourers are worthless. Their deaths are a small price to pay for curing our Marks."

He marched to the door. Tessa let her head fall back as it slammed shut. *Focus*, she thought. She tried to take her mind off the muffled screaming coming from another room.

The door opened again. Tessa lifted her head and locked eyes with Edith. Fire burned in her chest.

"You're evil," she said.

Edith hurried over. She cast a glance over her shoulder at the door. "Keep quiet."

Tessa's scowl faded. "What are you—"

Edith pressed a finger against Tessa's lips. She fished around in her pocket. "You need to listen closely. I can only keep Solomon and the Raiders distracted for so long."

She produced a small key and fit it into one of Tessa's manacles. It popped free and Tessa winced as the blood returned to her hand. Edith freed her other limbs and she sat up, rubbing her ankles. "You mean you're not one of them?"

"I can't stand by and let this happen to you," Edith replied. She moved over to Marie and freed her. "When you get out, follow the left-hand tunnel the whole way. You'll come out inside Solomon's living quarters. If you get your friends, you still have a chance to escape."

Marie wrapped her arms around the woman. "Thank you."

"Don't thank me yet," Edith replied. "You've still got to get out of here without being recaptured. Solomon will know something is wrong when he discovers you missing." She tossed the key onto the stone slab. "Maybe I can convince him you managed to pickpocket him somehow."

Tessa swallowed. "I'm sorry I didn't trust you."

"It's okay," Edith replied quickly. "Wait for your moment to go. I'll keep Solomon distracted."

She shuffled out of the room. Tessa and Marie knelt by the door and waited. Tessa pressed her eye against the crack.

"Where are you going?" Solomon's voice echoed.

"I need to gather more potions," Edith replied. She stood in the entryway of the tunnel Tessa and Marie had taken.

"Now? We have plenty."

"Not if you want to keep the labourers alive long enough to use them."

Solomon shrugged. "We have Isiah's friends now. We don't need any more labourers."

"And his friends won't be any use to us if we run out of supplies mid-operation. You don't want to waste more subjects, do you? I have to visit my brewery."

As the pair argued, Tessa inched open the door. The other Raiders stood with their backs to her, facing Edith. The Raider in the chair bowed his head, eyes squeezed shut and grimacing.

"He'll start to scab soon," Edith replied. "We'll miss our chance."

"Go," the man said. "Hurry up so I can be cured."

Tessa slipped out of the door, sticking to the shadows. Marie came after her. Remembering Edith's advice, Tessa put her left hand on the wall and followed it. A tunnel branched away from the cavern, leading into darkness.

She walked as quickly as she dared. Darkness enveloped her, making it impossible to see. She prayed she wouldn't collide with another crate of explosives. Edith's voice grew fainter.

Minutes ticked past. Other passageways branched off. Tessa held Marie's hand with her free one so they didn't become separated.

"Stick close," she whispered.

Edith's voice faded and silence descended. Blood rushed in Tessa's ears as muffled shouting broke out.

Tessa's heart leapt. Marie stifled a scream. Frenzied talking, too far away to be legible, echoed down the tunnel.

"Where do we go?" Marie asked.

Footsteps sounded. Solomon's voice cut above the fray.

"Find them! They can't have gone far."

Tessa quickened her pace. The uneven tunnel forced her to focus in case she slipped and sprained an ankle. The orange glow of lanterns peeked around the corner behind them.

"They're gonna find us!" Marie squeaked.

Another passageway branched off to their right. Gripping Marie's hand, she dragged the girl toward it.

"Where are we going?" she asked. "Edith said to—"

"Trust me," Tessa replied. She huddled in the tunnel and focused on the dimly lit rectangle ahead of her.

A feeling of cold dread welled inside her. This time, she welcomed it. She imagined the tunnel sealing off, forming an impenetrable wall. Beyond, the glow of lanterns grew brighter.

"Search the tunnels," Solomon called. "They'll be lost."

Marie whimpered and clung to Tessa's arm. Tessa pushed her fear to the back of her mind and focused on the illusion.

The empty space in front of her flickered. Dusty red rock began to materialize. It crept across the opening, knitting to the stone around it. The footsteps grew louder.

Tessa's body shuddered. She fought the urge to vomit. The magic sapped her energy. She completed the illusion and they were plunged into darkness.

The footsteps passed beyond the wall. The steady thud of some-body climbing stairs sounded. A door swung open and then slammed shut. Tessa held the illusion as long as she could bear, then let it drop.

Her breath escaped her in a rush. Her stomach spasmed and she lost her battle with the bile. She was thankful for the darkness so Marie didn't have to see it.

Tessa gagged and pulled herself to her feet. Her legs wobbled. She dragged Marie after her and they left the tunnel.

"What if the Raider comes back?" she asked.

"You heard the door," Tessa replied. "We must be close."

They hugged the wall until they found the staircase. Once Tessa's feet met the first step, they clambered to the surface and she threw her-self at the door. The door swung open and they piled out. She winced as she hit the hard stone. Marie landed on top of her with a grunt.

"We have to warn Lazaro and Isiah," Tessa said. She rolled Marie off her and jumped up.

A force slammed into her side. Marie screamed as a Raider grabbed Tessa's hands.

"You're not warning anybody," he spat. Streaks of blood stained his skin and robes.

Tessa grunted and tried to break free. The man pressed her against the wall. His body trembled from blood loss and shock. Tessa aimed a kick at his knee.

The Raider's face twisted in pain. He swore and wrestled with her. Tessa strained under his grip. Her already weakened body left her wobbly and drained.

"Your skin will look good on me." The Raider's hot breath blasted her face. "How about we head back down to the cavern?"

Marie grabbed the Raider's sabre and yanked it free. The man's eyes widened. He let go of Tessa and spun around to grab it, but it was too late.

Marie swung the sabre and it sliced into the man's skin. He screamed and staggered away, clutching the long red line across his chest. His foot hit the end of Solomon's bed and he tripped. Blood stained everything the man touched.

Tessa took the sabre from Marie. "Let's go. The noise will attract the others."

Marie stared at the man with wide eyes. "Did I really do that?"

"You did." Tessa dragged her out of the room. "Good job."

Still clutching the bloodied sabre, Tessa ran through the Raiders' house until she found the main doors. She threw them open and sprinted into the street. Evening shadows helped mask them from any Raiders who might be out searching. A few townsfolk gasped as they saw her blood-stained sabre. Tessa ignored them.

She put her head down and ran in the direction of their tent.

Bone to Pick

Isiah shifted his weight on the block of sandstone. A pair of Raiders stood on either side of him, arms folded. Enrik paced across the tower floor. He ran a hand across his bald head. A few cuts, still yet to heal, crisscrossed his face.

"I wouldn't make any funny moves," he said. "Every single one of these men and women has a bone to pick with you after you cheated them out of the oasis. Let's not give them any excuse to act out their revenge."

Isiah studied the staircase out of the corner of his eye. A third Raider blocked it. He sat sharpening his sabre, the blade propped against one knee. Isiah's hand itched to fall to his own.

"Solomon should have begun by now," Enrik said. "He'll be stripping your friends' skin from their flesh and plastering it onto his own body. It's a remarkable practice—too barbaric for my own tastes."

Isiah clenched his jaw. The memory of the magnifying glass contraption Enrik had used on him in their hideout beneath Alcabaza played on his mind. He racked his brains for a plan. To his right, a network of wooden poles and platforms formed the scaffolding that wrapped around the outside of the fourth floor. Enrik turned on his heel and paced back the way he had come.

"I don't believe you." Isiah forced himself to say the words. "Solomon would never hurt my friends."

"How many times do I have to tell you, boy?" Enrik replied. "Are you blind to reason?"

Isiah folded his arms. "Solomon is my friend."

Enrik's eye twitched. He collected himself. "No matter. You'll see soon enough."

Silence returned. Isiah swallowed the unease rolling in his gut and kicked his legs absent-mindedly. He forced his face to become expressionless.

"Don't you care about your friends?" Enrik said after a minute. "I at least expected *something* from you, boy. I saw how much losing that Royal Guard friend of yours pained you."

A twinge of emotion tugged at Isiah's heart, but he buried it. He pointed at Enrik's arm. "None of this will bring your hand back."

Enrik lifted his twisted metal replacement. "You're right, but I'll sleep a happy man knowing I took my revenge. Nobody shows up Enrik." He jabbed a finger into his chest. "*I'm* the top dog of Alcabaza."

"Aron turned the entire city against you," Isiah continued. "I guess they must trust him more than they trusted you."

Enrik's eye twitched again. "If I told my side of the story, you'd all be executed. Have you forgotten what the other Raiders would think about your Mark? You're lucky I didn't tell Mauriel to have her eagle rip you apart!"

"Then you wouldn't have got your revenge, would you?" Isiah replied. His hand hovered above his sabre.

Enrik swore under his breath. "You're supposed to be suffering! Where do you think Tessa is? Solomon has her locked away beneath the Hidden Citadel. If only you heard her screams, you'd be begging for us to let you go!" Enrik stepped forward. "But you can't save them."

Isiah forced himself to stay calm. "Do I look like I'm panicking?" he asked innocently.

Enrik swore louder. "That's it." He motioned to the pair of Raiders. "Take him captive. We'll fly back to our camp and I'll see to my revenge *personally*."

The Raiders moved to grab Isiah, but he was faster. He leapt to his feet and his sabre flashed into his hand. He lashed out. One of the Raiders yelled in pain and reeled away as Isiah's sabre bit into his sword arm.

The other Raiders exploded into motion. Isiah spun away, trying to stop them from surrounding him. Behind him, the stone tower floor gave way to the scaffolding.

"Don't kill him!" Enrik roared. "Cut off his hand if you have to." He wrestled his demeanour back under control. "Drop the sabre, Isiah. You have nowhere to run."

Isiah adjusted his grip on the blade. Half a dozen Raiders closed in, their sabres poised to strike. The wind whipped through the scaffolding, stirring their cloaks and ruffling Isiah's hair.

Isiah turned around and bolted to the scaffolding.

The Raiders gave chase. Isiah jumped onto a rickety wooden platform and ducked through a mass of wooden beams. He forced his way through, sucking in his chest to slip through the gaps. The Raiders swore as they tried to give chase.

Isiah emerged on a wooden platform. He searched for somewhere to go as the Raiders wrestled with the scaffolding behind him. The structure wobbled as they cut at the robes holding it together.

Isiah spun around and swung his sabre at them, holding them off. The edge of the platform caught his eye. He swallowed. Dropping his sabre, he swung down and let himself hang from the platform.

The Raiders succeeded in breaking through and their boots thundered above. Isiah grabbed hold of the gaps in the tower's brickwork and began to climb down.

"Where's he gone now?" a Raider yelled.

"He's climbing down!" another replied.

Isiah blocked out their voices. He clung to the masonry, pressing his body flat against the windswept sandstone blocks. His foot found one of the windows and he stood on the narrow sill for balance. The sight of the ground so far below made his head spin.

"Cut him off!" Enrik ordered.

Footsteps pounded on the staircase inside the tower. Raiders flew past the window. Isiah adjusted his grip on the wall. His fingers burned as he jammed them into the gaps between the bricks for purchase.

I'll never out-climb them, he thought. He scanned for anything that could help him. The ground was too far away to jump—he'd break a leg—and the nearest buildings were too distant to reach as well.

The crane caught his eye. It jutted over the street, pointing in the direction of the lake. An idea flashed into his mind.

He began climbing up.

"Changed your mind, have you?" Enrik called. "Did you decide it's not worth breaking your legs?"

Isiah ignored his taunts. He grimaced as he dug his fingers into the masonry. The hard bricks cut his fingers and made his joints feel like they were about to pop out. His shoulders screamed as he began climbing around the outside of the tower.

Enrik walked above him. The boards shook with every step. "Maybe I *should* let you fall," he said slowly. "A slow, agonizing death from shattered legs will give you a glimpse of what I went through in that ravine."

A thud echoed and a sabre tip broke through a board. Isiah flinched and pulled away. Enrik grunted and yanked the blade free. Below, the other Raiders spilled out of the tower. They gathered around, waiting for him to fall.

Another thud sounded. Isiah yelped in fright and pulled his hand away as Enrik's sabre plunged through a gap inches from his knuckles.

"How long do you think you can go?" Enrik taunted. He paced on the boards above. "Or will your muscles give out before I can strike you?"

Isiah's fingers burned. He clenched his jaw against the pain and kept moving. He reached the corner of the tower. The sharp angle stabbed his torso as he carefully manoeuvred around it. The crane jutted out only a few feet away. If he could only reach it . . .

The sabre plunged through another gap. Isiah lurched aside as the tip of the blade stopped where his head had been moments earlier. Enrik laughed. "I'm getting close."

The crane inched closer. Isiah's feet found another windowsill and he shuffled along its length. A mass of scaffolding and beams secured the crane to the side of the tower, forming a makeshift wall between him and Enrik.

"I don't see how the crane will help you," Enrik called. "There's still only one way down."

Isiah reached the crane and threw one arm around it. His shoulders throbbed with agony. He imagined his joints ripping free from their sockets. He kicked away from the tower wall and hauled himself onto the crane.

Enrik pulled his sabre free and stood facing him. He spread out his arms. "Where to now?"

Isiah wobbled as he stood. He stuck his arms out to steady himself. The wind tugged at the edges of his robes, threatening to knock him off and send him plummeting to his doom. Isiah carefully turned around. He fixed his eyes on the surface of the lake far below.

Enrik's face darkened. "No you don't."

He jammed an arm through the scaffolding and tried to force his way through, but he was too late. Isiah took a deep breath and sprinted along the length of the crane. He reached the end and threw himself into the air.

Time slowed. His legs kicked uselessly in empty air. His stomach climbed into his throat as he careened toward the lake. The water grew bigger and bigger until it filled his vision.

He hit the surface and plunged into the icy depths.

Pain shot through his legs. Bubbles filled his vision. The impact knocked the air from his lungs and crushed his chest like a vice. Isiah flailed, desperately trying to swim to the surface.

He broke the water and threw his head back, sucking in a breath. But he didn't allow himself time to recover. He dove back under and kicked with all the strength he could muster.

He cut through the water, eager to get as far away from the tower as possible. Evening shadows masked the surface of the lake, colouring the water below him an inky black. He hoped it was dark enough to obscure him from any observers.

Isiah swam for as long as his aching lungs allowed, then broke the surface to catch another mouthful of air. The far side of the lake approached painfully slow. When he finally made it, he hauled himself into the cover of the foliage and collapsed, panting.

His entire body ached. He tentatively pressed a hand against his ribs and winced. Each breath made his chest throb. He twisted around and checked over his shoulder. He couldn't make out any figures on the far bank.

Isiah collected himself and staggered to his feet, leaning against a tree for balance. He knew what he had to do.

I have to find Solomon, he thought. He had to know the truth. *Enrik's a liar. There's no way he'd do that to my friends.*

Keeping to the cover of the foliage, he limped in the direction of Solomon and the Raiders' house. When he neared the rows of tents, he broke away from the lake and followed them toward the town. He listened for any sign of Enrik or his Raiders, but he heard nothing. Night fell upon the basin, giving him much-needed cover.

He put his head down and hobbled toward Solomon's house. He stuck to the alleyways to skirt around Edith's tower, then slipped through the main doors and found himself in the entry hall.

Footsteps echoed. Solomon marched into view, a bandaged Raider in tow.

"Which way did they go?" he asked.

The bandaged Raider shrugged. "I didn't see."

Before they could say anything else, Isiah called out. "Solomon!"

The man's head snapped around. His eyes lit up. "Isiah." His smile dropped. "You're hurt."

"Enrik found me." Isiah leaned against the wall, holding his ribs. "He's trying to kill me."

"That's not possible," Solomon replied. "He promised me—"

"He lied." Isiah coughed. "He wants revenge on me for what I did to him. He lied about you, too."

Solomon's brow creased. "What did he say?"

Isiah told Solomon the things Enrik had said to him. "But I know you're not like that," he added.

Solomon stood dead still. His gaze seemed to look right through Isiah.

"Right?" Isiah asked. His voice grew more desperate.

"I didn't want you to find out this way," Solomon said at last. "You were supposed to learn the truth later."

Isiah took a shaky step back. "Where are my friends?"

"They didn't care about you," Solomon said. "You're Marked. Nobody cares about us." He threw out his arms. "We're hunted from one end of the Badlands to another."

Icy fear welled in Isiah's insides. His voice trembled. "What were you planning for us? What have you done with Tessa?"

"It doesn't matter what I've done to them. We can't count on anybody but ourselves." His voice grew louder. "We're supposed to stick together! Even Enrik betrayed me. I thought we were friends!"

He slammed his hand against the wall, then collected himself. "You were supposed to join us, Isiah. I found a way to cure us of our

Marks. I thought it would allow us to wander the Badlands free from the fear of being discovered—but after seeing your bond with Aegon, I realized that we could return to Paradon to reclaim our rightful positions."

Solomon pulled his robe down to expose his Mark. Bile climbed in Isiah's throat. A fresh patch of skin covered a chunk of Solomon's Mark, pale and smooth.

"We can cure yours," Solomon continued. "We'll finally be free. We won't have to spend any more time *hiding*."

Isiah backed toward the door. "I thought you liked this place."

"This basin is a prison." Solomon's expression darkened. "And every single person in the Badlands are our guards. Show your Mark in any city and you'll be killed." He sighed. "I was going to tell you that your friends left you to fly to another city."

Isiah shook his head. "They'd never do that."

"You'd have come around to it eventually," Solomon said. "With Myla and the others to keep you company, you'd have forgotten all about them." He extended a hand. "You can still join us, Isiah. We can cure you."

Isiah staggered away. "You—You're sick."

"This is our only hope." Solomon moved to cut him off. "Your friends will never understand what it's like to be Marked. They don't know how it feels to live in constant fear."

Isiah found his voice. "Where's Tessa?"

"It doesn't matter where she is!" Solomon towered over him. "I'll protect you from Enrik. In time, you'll come to understand us, Isiah."

The man made a grab for him. Isiah sidestepped and bolted for the door. Solomon barked an order at his bandaged companion, but

Isiah was already sprinting along the street. He took a sharp turn into an alley and let the darkness consume him. The pain of Solomon's betrayal stung his heart.

I have to find Lazaro, he thought. *Someone must still be at our tents.*

He hoped Solomon's Raiders hadn't got to them first.

No Choice

ISIAH'S BREATH SWIRLED IN HIS EARS. HE RAN along the row of tents, lungs burning with effort. Each movement sent a stab of pain through his ribs, but he forced himself to keep going.

He reached the tent and something slammed into his side. He hit the ground and a force landed on top of him.

"Isiah!" Tessa exclaimed. She scrambled off of him. "Where have you been? I was worried we'd lost you."

Isiah groaned. Tessa and the rest of his friends stood around him. She stooped and helped him to his feet.

"I thought you might have been one of Solomon's Raiders," she said sheepishly. She gave him a brief hug that made his ribs ache even more. "I'm glad we found you."

"Why are you here?" Isiah managed to ask. "I thought Solomon said—"

"We escaped," Tessa replied. She quickly told him about what she'd seen in the tunnels.

Isiah blinked back tears. "I thought they were like me . . ." He trailed off, then collected himself. "We need to go. Enrik is here."

Tessa froze. Aron's jaw dropped.

"Enrik is dead," Lazaro said.

"No, he's not." Isiah told them about his capture and escape from Enrik at Edith's tower. "He was working with Solomon all along."

Lazaro's face darkened. "Wait until I get my hands on him." Antony coughed, and Lazaro hesitated. "I mean, we need to get out of here. These tents are the first place Solomon will look."

"What about our eagles?" Tessa asked. "If we can reach them, we can fly away."

"Solomon's Raiders will be guarding them," Isiah replied, "and Enrik might still be there. The eagles are too predictable."

"Then we leave on foot." Her voice grew faster. "We can sneak out and return when they're not expecting us."

"With all the gorgons prowling out there?" Aron asked. "We'll be lucky if we survive until morning."

"It's worth a shot," Lazaro said. "We're running out of options here." He unsheathed his sabre. "Else we'll have to fight our way out."

Isiah hobbled after them as fast as he could manage. Tessa put an arm around his shoulders to help him walk. With every second they spent near the tents, he felt like Solomon and his Raiders would descend on them at any moment.

"Where's your sabre?" Tessa asked.

"I had to leave it at the tower," he replied. He counted their weapons. Lazaro and the rest of his gang had their blades, along with Aron, and Tessa carried one for both her and Marie. Isiah cursed under his breath. "If only Aegon was here."

"Solomon must have left her so far away on purpose," Tessa said.

"I only wish I could sneak out and find her."

"It's too dangerous." She bit her lip. "Without our eagles, we're helpless."

They stuck to the shadow of the basin wall, keeping to its rocky overhangs to lower their chances of being spotted by any eagles. Several birds soared through the darkness. The only sign of their presence was the flicker of the stars as they blotted them from view.

As they neared the rocky archway that marked the only entrance into the basin, piles of boulders gave them cover. Isiah took shelter behind one and they crept closer to the exit. Lazaro put out a hand to block him.

"Something doesn't feel right," he whispered.

As they crouched and watched, Isiah made out a pair of Solomon's Raiders camouflaged against the rock. He swore under his breath. "It's guarded."

"Can we take them?" Darla asked. "There are only two."

"They'll alert the eagles," Lazaro replied. "Then we'll have every Raider in the sky looking for us."

Aron shook his head. "This is silly. There must be a way to get our eagles. What about Myla?" He nudged Isiah. "She might help us."

"We don't know if she's in on it," Tessa cut in. "She might be helping them."

"You don't know that—" Isiah started.

"I was right about Solomon," she shot back.

Isiah fell silent. Lazaro watched the two guards. "If we're quick, we could take them both down before they raise the alarm."

The rocky path ahead narrowed as it approached the archway. Isiah swallowed. All the Raiders would have to do was turn their heads and they'd be spotted.

"Psst." A whisper sounded back the way they had come. Isiah twisted around to see a hunched-over figure.

"Edith?" Tessa asked. Lazaro raised his sabre, but she caught his arm. "It's okay."

"It might be a trap."

They broke away from the boulders and darted to Edith's side. The woman put her hands on Tessa's shoulders.

"I'm so glad you girls escaped," she said. "Solomon will be turning the basin upside-down looking for you all—but I can hide you."

"And what are we supposed to do after that?" Lazaro asked.

"It'll buy you time," Edith replied. "Solomon is furious at Enrik. Once Enrik and his Raiders are gone, you can take your chance to escape."

The group exchanged glances.

"I say we should go," Tessa said. "She's already helped us before."

"We need to get off the surface," Edith urged. "You won't be able to hide for long out here."

Lazaro sighed. "We don't have a choice, do we?"

"Not if you want to live."

Edith beckoned them and shuffled away. "Don't make any noise. I can get you into my tower. We'll hide right under Solomon's nose."

* * *

Isiah walked in a single file with his friends. Tessa and Lazaro went ahead of him, following Edith as she carefully led them through the deserted alleyways of the Hidden Citadel. Her tower loomed above the rooftops of the buildings around them, painfully close.

Edith paused at the end of the alleyway and peered out. After a moment, she beckoned them. "The coast is clear."

Isiah broke from cover and darted toward the tower. Lazaro reached it first. He drew his sabre and pushed open the door.

"Where are you going to hide us?" Tessa asked.

"There are secrets beneath this basin that even Solomon doesn't know about," Edith replied. She ushered them all inside.

While Lazaro, Darla, and Antony performed a sweep of the tower, Edith locked the door and drew the wooden shutters over the windows. Isiah let his shoulders drop. He leaned against the wall and took a deep breath.

"This way," Edith said. She led them to her kitchen. She patted the table. "Help me move this, will you?"

Isiah and Tessa pushed the table aside, revealing a trapdoor on the floor. Edith knelt and, with their help, lifted it. Dust rained from the edges into the darkness below.

"Why are you helping us?" Tessa asked.

"I never agreed to Solomon's sick operations," Edith replied. "I think he's a monster. But by the time I learned the truth, I couldn't do anything to stop him." She gestured to her body. "I'm not the fighter I used to be. I had no choice but to help him."

Lazaro returned from scouting the tower. "We're clear," he said. He scowled at the trapdoor. "Who's to say you won't lock us in there and sell us out?"

"If I was going to do that, I wouldn't have helped the girls escape in the first place," Edith replied. "Solomon had the perfect plan. If I didn't free them, you'd have been ambushed in your sleep and dragged down there to join them."

Isiah shuddered. "I still can't believe Solomon would do such a thing."

"He's desperate." Edith put a hand on Isiah's shoulder. "He wants so badly to be free of his Mark." Her voice took on a more serious tone. "Solomon suspects me of helping you—but he can't prove anything yet."

"What if he threatens to hurt you?" Tessa asked.

Edith shook her head. "He still needs me. My magic is the only thing that makes his skin grafts work." She gestured to the trapdoor. "Make yourselves at home."

Isiah sat on the edge of the hole and lowered himself inside. The dust tickled his nose. He let himself drop and his feet met the sandstone floor. He stepped aside so that Tessa and the others could follow.

"Once Enrik and his Raiders are gone, you'll stand a chance at escaping," Edith said.

Marie hugged the woman. "Thank you."

"Don't thank me until you're safe." Edith raised her head. "You'd better get in there quickly."

A thud sounded at the door. Isiah's heart leapt into his throat. Lazaro ushered the group into the trapdoor. Isiah pressed himself against the wall as everybody jumped inside. Edith swung the trapdoor shut and they were plunged into darkness. Moments later, the sound of wood grating against floorboards sounded as she pushed the table back into place.

The knock sounded again. Louder. Edith's footsteps shuffled away. Isiah strained his ears to make out what was going on.

The door creaked open. He knew who was on the other side.

"Good evening, Edith," Solomon's calm, smooth voice said. "I'm surprised you're awake so late."

"I couldn't sleep," Edith replied. "Not with those runaways still lurking about."

"We'll find them," Solomon said. His footsteps echoed as he strode into the tower. Several others joined him. "There are only so many places they can hide."

"You're not concerned they're trekking through the highlands as we speak?"

"No." Solomon paused. "Enrik's Raiders are watching the surrounding area, and they don't stand a chance without their eagles."

Isiah shifted his weight. He sat with his knees pressed against his chest, surrounded by his friends. Tessa's breaths tickled his ear. He didn't dare make any noise in fear of alerting Solomon to their presence.

Floorboards creaked as Solomon strolled through the tower. "It was unfortunate those girls escaped in the first place. There's only *one* other person who ever managed to escape—but I doubt he got far enough to spread word of what was going on here."

"They're sly ones," Edith replied. "You know how they found my door. Who's to say one of them didn't grab a key while your Raiders were manhandling them."

Solomon grunted. "They must have—unless they had outside help."

Floorboards creaked above Isiah's head. He held his breath.

"We're so close," Solomon said slowly. "Soon we can finally return to our homeland, outcasts no more."

"Then you'd better keep looking," Edith replied. "I don't see what you expect to find here. This is the last place they would come."

The seconds ticked past. Isiah swallowed. The dust brought tears to his eyes and irritated his nostrils. He fought the urge to sneeze.

"Tell me if you see anything." Solomon's footsteps moved away. He and his Raiders filed out of the tower. Isiah heard Edith shut the door. A few moments later, the table squeaked and the trapdoor swung open. A lantern illuminated Edith's face.

"You should try to sleep," she said. "I'll bring you water at dawn."

Tessa shifted her weight. "This feels wrong. There are still people trapped inside those tunnels." She looked up at Edith. "How many are there?"

"Several dozen, at least," Edith replied.

"What are we supposed to do about it?" Aron said. "We can't save everybody."

"I don't know." Tessa folded her arms. "But I'd feel like such a coward if we ran away and let Solomon keep doing these terrible things."

"He's nearly finished," Aron argued. "You heard him yourself."

Isiah found his voice. "But he needs *your* skin to do it. Who says he won't capture more labourers if we get away?"

Aron fell silent.

"I want to help them," Tessa said. "We can't let Solomon get away with this." She looked around the group. "The labourers down there *need* us."

Isiah swallowed. "I'm with you, Tessa."

"Me too," Marie added.

Lazaro stroked his chin. Isiah waited for the man's rebuttal.

"You know how I feel about this," Lazaro said. "But if you're serious, we have to think smart."

"Wait—you mean you're not going to argue?" Tessa asked.

Lazaro cracked a smile. "Do you think I haven't learned by now that I'd be wasting my breath?" He sighed. "It seems like every time I let myself get carried away, we end up worse."

"That's not true—"

"We lost our home because of me," he said, cutting her off. "Even Enrik hates us because of *my* rivalry with him. Every time I rush into things, I fail. Perhaps it's time I learned to stop being so rash."

Tessa squeezed past Isiah and wrapped her arms around Lazaro. "I know you try your best."

Antony patted Lazaro on the shoulder. "There's the Lazaro I want to see."

"There is a way to stop Solomon," Edith spoke up. Everyone turned to her. "There are still explosives left over from the miners who carved these tunnels. One of the tunnels they built is blocked off because it runs dangerously close to the lake." She bit her lip. "It would be risky, but if you detonated those charges in the right place, you could drain the lake into the tunnels . . ."

". . . and drown Solomon and his Raiders in the process," Tessa finished.

"But what about the people trapped down there?" Marie asked.

"We can free them," Tessa replied. "Right, Edith?"

"If you lay the charge in the tunnel near the lake, you can free the labourers and then somebody can detonate it," Edith said. "The resulting chaos should allow you to slip away undetected. I know Solomon's routine. I'm sure I can convince him to go for another healing session right before you blow the charge."

Tessa stood up. "When do we go?"

"Not yet," Edith said. "Wait until dawn, when the Raiders have finished rooting through the town."

"Who'll be carrying the explosives?" Lazaro cut in.

"I will," Tessa replied. "I know the way, and I know where the labourers are kept."

Marie nodded in determination. "I'll go with you."

"Are you sure, Tess?" Lazaro raised his hands. "If Solomon finds you down there, we can't reach you."

Tessa squeezed his hand. "We'll be careful—and we'll have a better chance of not being spotted if there are fewer of us."

"You girls can carry the charges into the tunnel and connect them to the fuse," Edith said. "Then someone else can be waiting with the detonator." Her voice dropped. "But if you detonate it too early, the tunnels will flood before the girls have time to escape."

Isiah gulped. "Maybe someone else should go."

She put a hand on his leg. "I need to do this. Besides," she added, "I trust you to operate the charge."

Isiah almost choked. "Wait—"

Tessa leaned in and whispered. "There's no one I'd trust with my life more than you. Even if you *are* Marked."

Isiah puffed up his chest. "I'll do it."

"The fuse won't be long enough to reach all the way down the tunnel, so you'll need to go together," Edith explained. "Once you've placed the explosives, you can split up. Tessa and Marie can free the labourers, while Isiah takes another tunnel that comes out on the shores of the lake. When Tessa gives the all-clear and Solomon is inside the tunnels, Isiah detonates the charge."

"What about us?" Lazaro asked.

"We wait for them to return, then you can make a run for the eagles. Stealth is of the utmost importance. We have to avoid a crowd." Edith adjusted her footing. "I don't know if Enrik will still be around."

Isiah and his friends exchanged glances. Edith rubbed her hands together. "You should get some sleep," she said. "I'll wake you before dawn."

"Isiah," Lazaro said. "Keep Tess safe for me."

Isiah's expression hardened. "I will," he managed to say.

Edith swung the trapdoor shut, plunging them into darkness. Isiah tried to make himself as comfortable as possible against the rocky wall. His mind spun as the weight of their mission dawned on him.

Tomorrow, he would kill Solomon.

Myla

MYLA STOOD ON THE EDGE OF THE CLIFF and peered across the basin. Dozens of glowing lanterns split the shadows of the town, illuminating groups of Raiders going door-to-door. Eagles soared across the surrounding terrain, swooping low over the ravines and gullies. Myla tried to shake the feeling of unease.

"What do you think is going on?" one of the handlers asked.

Myla swallowed. "I don't know." She shook her head to clear her thoughts. "Maybe a gorgon pack was spotted nearby."

She hurried away from the edge to tend to the last of the eagles. Handlers scurried about with wheelbarrows of food to hand out before the birds went to sleep. Several already sat in their nests, guarding their hatchlings.

Boots crunched on stone. Myla jogged to the narrow path that led up to the basin to see who it was. Solomon marched up the trail, flanked by four of his Raiders.

"Myla," he said. "You're just the one I wanted to see." He gestured to his four Raiders and they broke away. "Where are Lazaro's eagles?"

"Oh—" Myla tried to hide her surprise. "They're being kept alongside yours." She pointed to one side of the cliff.

"Confiscate their saddles," Solomon ordered. "I want all their gear locked away and the birds secured."

One of his Raiders carried an armful of manacles. They took off toward the birds.

"What are you doing?" Myla asked. "You can't chain them up like that—is something wrong?"

"It's just a precaution," Solomon replied. "Once you finish your rounds, you can go back to our home. My Raiders will take care of things from here." He pushed past her and marched toward the eagles. One of the Raiders fit a manacle around an eagle's leg and secured it to a boulder.

Myla tugged on Solomon's robes. "Is there something wrong with Isiah and his group?" she asked.

"Don't worry about it," Solomon replied, not looking at her. "I've got things under control. Tell me if you spot any sign of them."

Myla frowned. "They're not troublemakers, are they?"

"Let's just say that the stories of them breaking the Raider's Oath aren't entirely fabricated."

Myla caught a hint of something wrong in Solomon's tone, but before she could press it further, an eagle swooped toward the cliffs.

"Run along, Myla." Solomon pushed her. "You've still got saddles to confiscate."

Myla jogged away as the eagle landed and a figure slid off. Several others landed nearby, all carrying their own Raiders. She ducked behind a boulder and peered out at them.

Something is wrong, she thought.

The man in the lead—a bald Raider with a prosthetic metal hand—raised his arms. "The boy's a liar, Solomon."

"You promised me you wouldn't touch him!" Solomon spat. Myla winced at the vitriol in his voice. "I had everything going according to plan and you've spooked him. Who knows where he's run off to now?"

The man put a hand on Solomon's shoulder. "Relax. They can't have gone far." He gestured to Lazaro's eagles. Myla ducked to avoid being spotted. "And without their birds, they're stranded in the high-lands."

"Isiah is *ours*," Solomon snapped. A vein bulged in his neck. "You betrayed my trust."

The man's face darkened. "Give it a rest, Solomon. You've got eve-rything you need to leave the basin and fly wherever you want. What's one boy?"

"He's Marked. That means he's one of us. I won't let you get your hands on him."

"We'll deal with that once we've found him." The man beckoned his Raiders. "My people will watch the cliffs. You search the Hidden Cit-adel. Lazaro and his ilk can't leave the basin unless they want to march to their doom in the highlands." He shrugged. "Either way works for me."

"I still need them," Solomon said.

"Then you'd better start looking."

The man turned and climbed onto his eagle. His Raiders fanned out to guard the cliffs. Myla ducked as the man's eagle erupted into mo-tion and soared over the boulder she was hiding behind. Solomon scowled, then rubbed his temples.

"Search the houses," he ordered, beckoning his Raiders. "And double the guard at the archway. We'll find them before the night's out."

The four Raiders took off at a jog. The handlers pulled the last of the saddles off Lazaro's eagles and carried them away. Myla scurried out of her hiding place and blended in with them. She cast a nervous glance at the basin.

Isiah, she thought, *what have you done?*

Cavern

THE TRAPDOOR CREAKED OPEN. EDITH'S FACE APPEARED, illuminated by a lantern. "Wake up," she said. "It's time."

Tessa groaned and shifted her weight. The hard rock left her legs feeling numb. She dragged herself to her feet, leaning against the wall for balance. "How early is it?"

"The blue sun hasn't risen yet," Edith replied. "You have plenty of time to pull off your plan."

As the others woke, Tessa rubbed her legs to make the bloodflow return, then climbed out through the trapdoor. Shutters still blocked the windows, filling the kitchen with shadows. She knelt and helped Isiah climb out, then Marie.

"The others can wait here for your signal," Edith said. "Once the explosives blow, the whole basin will know about it."

Tessa swallowed. She attached the sabre she'd stolen from one of Solomon's Raiders to her belt. "And if we're discovered?"

"Solomon's Raiders have stopped checking houses," Edith said. "Soon he'll be returning to the cavern to begin his next round of operations. If you move fast, you can catch his entire Raider group in the flood."

Isiah wrung his hands. "What about Aegon?" he asked.

"You can reunite with her once Solomon is dead," Edith replied. "I'd worry more about your own safety right now, if I were you." The woman shuffled out of the kitchen. "I left the hidden door open a crack. You can access the tunnels through it."

Tessa started after her, but Isiah caught her arm.

"We can still find another way out of here, you know," he said. "You don't have to do this."

A flicker of uncertainty welled inside her, but she squashed it. "No. I want to stop Solomon."

Lazaro climbed out of the trapdoor behind them, followed by Aron and the other Raiders.

"Be careful, Tess," he said.

She gave him a brief hug. "I will."

Lazaro returned her embrace. For a moment they were back in the slums of Alcabaza together, hiding in the ruined buildings they used to call home.

"Now go and show Solomon that he's messed with the wrong Raiders."

Tessa broke away. Marie gave her a nervous smile. With her and Isiah in tow, Tessa hastened after Edith.

"I drew a rough map," Edith said as they approached. "It will tell you which tunnel to lay your charges in."

Tessa took it from her. "How will we read it when we're down there?"

Edith passed Marie the oil lantern she was holding. "And here are the keys to the cells Solomon keeps the labourers in." She handed a ring of keys to Tessa. "Good luck."

Tessa took a deep breath, then stepped through the door. Marie held the lantern aloft, casting a weak orange light down the sandstone staircase. Tessa walked beside her, covering her nose with her sleeve to stop the dust from making her sneeze.

They descended into darkness. Each step bounced off the walls. Her pulse quickened as images of Solomon's horrible experiments flashed through her mind. She wiped her sweaty palms against her robes.

The staircase levelled out, forming the long tunnel that led to the cavern with the operation chair. Tessa slowed her pace, straining her eyes in the darkness. After a minute, the explosives came into view.

"Here they are," she said. She stooped and lifted a crate. The acrid smell invaded her airways and brought tears to her eyes. Marie took another, balancing her lantern on top of it.

"Watch the flame," Isiah warned.

Tessa pushed away images of the explosives catching alight and going off in their arms. Several more crates stood behind a boarded-off passageway, alongside a length of fuse. Isiah carefully pulled it out and wound it around his arm like a rope.

"Do you think it will be long enough?" Marie asked.

Tessa swallowed. "It has to be."

Alongside the fuse, Tessa spotted a dusty old detonator. Isiah tucked it under one arm.

"Let's go," he said.

Tessa squinted at the map Edith had given her. Their path led past the cavern, then doubled back to run near the lake. She prayed no Raiders were lurking around.

Marie dimmed her lantern as they drew closer to the cavern. Tessa grunted as she carried the crate. Splinters dug into her clothes, and the size of the crate made it awkward to hold. The cavern materialized, and Tessa stopped. Isiah bumped into her.

"What is it?" he whispered.

"Light."

A faint glow peeked around the corner of the tunnel. Tiptoeing and trying her best to support the weight of the explosives, Tessa crept toward it. Footsteps reached her ears from beyond. Marie killed their lantern and they were plunged into shadow.

The light from inside the cavern became brighter. Clinging to the shadowy doorway, Tessa peered into the space beyond.

A lone Raider stood in the cavern, preparing trays of food. Wooden bowls clattered as he dumped ladles of foul-looking broth into them. He had his back turned to her, engrossed in his work.

Isiah nudged her arm and motioned to her sabre. Tessa bit her lip.

It's too risky, she thought. If there were other Raiders nearby, a fight would bring them all down on her head.

The Raider grabbed a tray of bowls and carried them through one of the doorways. Tessa tensed her muscles.

"Let's go," she whispered.

Doubled over, she hurried along the cavern wall, aiming for the tunnel Edith's map had pointed her to. She kept her eyes on the rocky floor in fear of stumbling. Marie's shallow breaths emanated from behind her.

Tessa rounded the corner and made it to the safety of the shadowy tunnel. She waited as Marie joined her, then Isiah. As soon as he reached her, the echo of a slamming metal door sounded and the Raider re-emerged in the cavern.

Clutching the crate of explosives to her chest, Tessa quickened her pace as they followed the new tunnel, eager to get as far away from the Raider as possible. Once the light from his lantern had faded, Marie turned on hers and Tessa stole another quick look at the map.

"It's not far now," she said. "We go straight, then take a right. There's another tunnel you can carry the charge through, Isiah."

Isiah nodded, but she caught the flicker of concern in his eyes. "What about you? If Solomon's Raider is still in the cavern—"

"He won't be," she said, cutting him off. "He was only feeding them. How long could it take?" She willed herself to believe it.

They hastened onward, through the maze of narrow tunnels and sharp corners. Tessa became aware of the weight of the earth around her, pressing in on all sides. For a second, she imagined the earth closing in like a vice to crush her. They made one final turn and ran into a dead end. Piles of rubble and wooden supports blocked the way.

"Is there something wrong?" Isiah asked. "Has the tunnel collapsed?"

Tessa studied the map. "No. The miners stopped." She placed her hand against the wall. Her fingers came away damp. She almost felt the weight of thousands of gallons of water behind, waiting to burst through. "This is it."

She placed her crate of explosives against the mass of wood and stone. Marie set hers down next to it. They pulled the wooden lids off, revealing the explosives within. Isiah knelt and began attaching the fuse to them.

"This looks like enough to bring the whole tunnel down," Tessa said. "And the lake has enough water to flood these tunnels for good."

"Just make sure you get out before it goes off," Isiah replied. He laughed nervously. "Lazaro would kill me if anything happened to you."

"We'll give you a signal," she said. "We'll be long gone by the time Solomon comes down."

Isiah finished attaching the fuse. He began unrolling the coil.

"We only have one lantern," Marie said. "Do you need it?"

"You take it," Isiah replied. "I can work in the dark. It's only a short climb to the surface, right?"

Tessa wrapped her arms around him. "See you on the outside." She broke away and, with one last look at the explosives, hurried off.

* * *

Tessa crouched and crept toward Solomon's cavern. She strained her ears for any sign of the Raider they'd spotted inside.

"What do we do if he's still there?" Marie asked.

Tessa's hand dropped to her sabre. "We'll do whatever we have to."

Marie turned off her lantern, plunging them into darkness. The cavern beyond was dark. A bubble of hope welled in Tessa's chest. *Has he left?*

She reached the tunnel exit and peered out. Nothing.

"Turn on your light," she said.

Marie did as she was told. The soft glow illuminated the metal chair and the blood-stained floor, then the far walls of the empty cavern.

Tessa stood. "Let's be quick before anyone comes back."

She hurried to the room that she and Marie had been held captive in. She tried the handle. Locked. Fumbling with the ring of keys Edith had given her, she opened it and they piled inside.

The empty stone slabs greeted her. Her nose crinkled at the sight of them. Beside it, a wall of iron bars separated them from the rest of the captured labourers.

"Hey," Tessa whispered. She peered into the darkness. "We're here to help you."

A force slammed into the bars. Tessa jumped away as a labourer grabbed at them, his hands bloodied and forearms a reddish-pink.

"You have to let us out," he gurgled. "Solomon is coming back." His eyes darted about frantically. He jammed a hand through the bars in an attempt to grab her. "Give me your keys!"

One of the other labourers caught him and wrestled him away. "Don't be scared," he said quickly. "Can you open the door?"

Tessa swallowed. "I can," she managed to say.

"Then hurry up before Solomon returns."

Tessa moved to the lock. As she went, more labourers were illuminated under Marie's light. Some sat hunched in the corner, tending to their raw skin. Others were newly captured and had escaped the worst of Solomon's treatment.

"We need to work together," Tessa explained. "I have a plan to get you all out of here."

"There are other rooms," one of the labourers said. "I heard their screams."

Tessa forced herself to slow her breathing. The stench of blood and decay hung thick in the air, making her feel like she was breathing through a straw. She slid the key into the door and pulled it open.

Metal groaned. The labourers staggered to their feet and lurched out of the cage. The healthier ones supported the weak.

"If Solomon arrives, we'll overpower him," Tessa instructed. She ignored the tremble in her voice. "Stick together, okay?"

Marie held the door open while the labourers filed into the main cavern. Tessa broke away to free the others. A second door on the far side of the cavern led to another room, similar to the first. She unlocked the metal bars and more labourers spilled out.

"Give me your sabre," one said, lurching toward her. His bare chest was missing patches of skin. "I know how to fight."

Tessa pulled her arms around herself defensively. She fought the bile climbing her throat. The labourer lunged at her, but she unsheathed her sabre and backed away.

"I think I'll keep it," she said.

The labourer wobbled on the spot, as if he was about to challenge her, but the door caught his attention and he staggered into the cavern outside. Tessa finished herding the labourers, then exited herself. She found the healthiest looking one in the crowd.

"Is this everyone?" Tessa asked.

"I think so," the labourer replied. She ran a hand through her hair. Some of it fell out. "Where do we go now?"

Tessa beckoned them. "Follow Marie."

The labourers lurched into motion. Some hobbled, supported by their companions. Others had to be dragged. Tessa wrung her hands. A voice in her head urged her to tell them to hurry up. She pictured

Solomon and his Raiders marching down the tunnel, preparing for another one of their sick experiments.

A flicker of light caught the corner of her eye. Her heart dropped into her stomach.

"Keep moving," she urged. She waved her arms to hurry the labourers along. The tunnel to Edith's tower was too narrow, slowing their advance to a crawl. Tessa's pulse quickened as the light grew brighter and brighter.

"They're coming!" a labourer cried.

The group dissolved into chaos. The healthy labourers scattered, eyes frantically flitting about. The ones on the floor wailed in panic, latching onto anything nearby in an attempt to move their frail bodies. A chorus of shouting echoed along the tunnel. Tessa aimed her sabre in the direction of the light.

Solomon and his Raiders rushed into view. When he saw them, he skidded to a halt. His face twisted into a snarl. "You."

Tessa bolted toward the tunnel. She joined the crush of bodies and forced her way through. Other labourers scattered down the surrounding tunnels, their cries of terror echoing as they went. Solomon drew his sabre and closed in.

"What are we going to do?" Marie cried. "We can't save everyone!"

"Shut the door," Tessa replied. She raised her voice above the panic. "We have to hold Solomon off."

The door slammed shut, and the healthier labourers joined her in bracing their weight against it. The frantic scratching of labourers trapped on the other side transformed into the furious pounding of fists. Tessa dug her feet into the ground and forced herself against the door as it lurched.

"Open this door!" Solomon barked.

The door lurched again. Tessa gritted her teeth as she fought to hold them off. The labourers surrounded her in a crush of bodies, pinning her against the door. From the other side, she heard Solomon swear.

"Come on, lads," he yelled. "They're just a bunch of labourers!"

Tessa braced herself against their renewed assault. Labourers grunted with effort. The door opened a crack and the tip of a sabre plunged through. Panic flared in Tessa's chest and she pushed harder. The blade withdrew and the door slammed shut.

"How are we going to signal Isiah?" Marie cried.

Tessa racked her brains. "You'll have to go and tell him."

Marie gasped. "But the tunnel will flood and—"

"I know." Tessa cut her off. "Just do it. Lazaro and the others can help us hold Solomon off. Run to the lake and give Isiah the signal."

Marie squirmed through the crush of labourers and bolted up the stairs. Tessa squeezed her eyes shut and hoped Isiah wouldn't be too late.

Troublemakers

ISIAH UNRAVELLED THE FUSE AND PLACED the detonator on the ground. In front of him, a narrow, rocky hole led into the earth. The fuse snaked into it, out of sight. He put his hands on his hips and sighed.

Dawn light peeked over the rim of the basin, illuminating the tops of buildings. The wind rustled the foliage around him. Isiah placed the detonator on the ground and knelt on the shores of the lake. To his left, the deep blue water was still and calm. He knew it wouldn't last long.

He carefully connected the end of the fuse to the detonator. It had a long plunger that, when pushed down, would ignite the charge. Isiah placed it on a flat patch of earth and settled down to wait. A few eagles circled in the air overhead, searching for them.

Isiah gulped. He wondered if Edith was right about Enrik leaving. Seeing the man again had left a deep-seated unease in the pit of his stomach. To think that Enrik had planned their entire capture made his skin crawl.

The cliff bordering the basin wrapped around behind him, and the trees overhead shielded him from the view of the eagles above. Isiah wrung his hands, waiting for the signal from Tessa and Marie.

What if they're caught down there? a small voice in his head asked. *What if something happens to them?*

Isiah forced the thoughts away. He trusted Tessa to know what she was doing. Edith's tower rose above the surrounding town. The dawn light played over the crane that he'd jumped from. Isiah probed his ribs. They were still sore from the fall.

Minutes ticked past. Isiah scanned the town, waiting for the sight of Tessa or Marie. The fuse lay on the earth in front of him, ready to ignite and send a charge into the depths of the basin. He picked up a stone and skimmed it across the surface of the lake beside him.

The sky grew brighter. Pink and orange melted to a soft blue. Still no sign of Tessa.

How long could it take? he thought. A voice urged him to go and check, but he didn't dare leave his position.

Leaves crunched beside him, and Isiah jumped. He hurriedly tucked the detonator into a bush and jumped to his feet.

"Isiah, is that you?" Myla's voice called.

Isiah sighed. The sound of crunching leaves grew closer and Myla appeared on the lakeside.

"How did you find me?" Isiah asked.

"I spotted you from the cliffs," she replied. "I was looking for you." Her tone grew more serious. "What are you doing out here?"

"Oh, I . . ." Isiah searched for an excuse.

"Solomon said you were troublemakers," Myla continued. "But I didn't believe it. What does he want from you?"

Isiah racked his brains for a lie to invent. "Solomon is trying to protect us," he said. "There's another Raider group visiting who wants to kill me."

Myla covered her mouth. "Why would they want to do that?"

"We have history," Isiah replied. "From before I was rescued, you know? But my friends don't trust Solomon."

Myla sat on a nearby rock. "Do you trust him?"

Isiah's gaze dropped to his feet. A voice urged him to tell her the truth, but he shot the idea down. *There's no way she'd believe me.*

"You know, I haven't told many people this," Myla said. She looked at her feet. "But I think I can trust you." She leaned in. "I'm from Paradon too."

Isiah paused. "What?"

"Mm-hmm. I used to live on Paradon's side of the border. But when a group of merchants was passing through, they crossed over and attacked us." Myla's face fell. "That's how I became a labourer. It was only after Solomon freed me that I finally got my life back."

Isiah fought to mask his emotions. He stole a glance at the fuse and the detonator. He sidled over to block them from Myla's view. "I'm sorry that happened to you."

"Most other labourers come from the Badlands," she continued. She stood and waltzed toward him. "But I feel like we share a connec-tion." She stopped in front of him. "Don't you feel the same?"

Isiah hesitated. Her bright eyes studied his face. "Yeah," he stam-mered. "That's what I felt when I met Solomon."

"I almost wish sometimes that I could go back to Paradon and be with my own people." Myla curled a finger around his collar. "But I guess now, I don't need to."

Isiah put a hand around her wrist. Myla stepped away. "What's wrong?"

"I—I have something to do," Isiah said.

"What do you mean?" Myla asked. "Everyone is looking for you and you're hiding in the bushes. I thought you'd tell me what's going on."

Isiah scratched the back of his neck. "Solomon is—he's not what he seems."

Myla gave him a puzzled look. "Solomon took me in. I think I know what he's like."

"No," Isiah started. "I mean, don't you ever wonder why so many labourers go missing?"

"They don't go missing," Myla replied. She gestured to the town. "Look at all the tents that Solomon's building. We're always getting new arrivals."

Isiah cast a glance over his shoulder in the direction of the tower. *Come on, Tessa. Where are you?*

"I think you owe me an explanation," Myla said curtly. "Why *is* Solomon looking for you?"

"I already told you," Isiah protested. He kept himself between Myla and the detonator.

Myla narrowed her eyes. "What are you hiding?"

Before he could stop her, she pushed past him. She gasped when she saw the fuse and detonator. "Does that lead to explosives?"

"Solomon is using people to heal his Mark," Isiah blurted out. He tugged on her arm. "I know it sounds crazy, but it's true."

Myla pulled away. "What are you planning on doing to him?"

"I have to stop him," Isiah said. His voice grew faster with every word. "He wants to skin my friends!"

"Solomon wouldn't do that!" Myla insisted. "Let's talk to him. I'm sure it's a misunderstanding—"

"He admitted it himself, Myla! You have to believe me."

"You're going to blow him up, aren't you?" she said slowly. "You can't do that!"

"Isiah!" Marie's shrill voice erupted from the town. He twisted around to see her bolting toward him. "Blow the charge!"

Isiah started toward the detonator, but Myla grabbed his arm and yanked him back.

"Let go of me," Isiah protested. He tried to wriggle free, but her fingers dug into his arm.

"You can't kill Solomon!" She dug her feet into the ground and pulled him away. "I won't let you do it."

Isiah grabbed her arms and tried to pry her free. She gritted her teeth and wrestled him away from the detonator.

"Hurry up," Marie called. She closed the distance between them, but every second seemed to be an eternity. Isiah struggled to free himself from Myla's arms.

"Think about this," Myla pleaded. "I know what Solomon is like."

"I thought I did too," he said. "But I was wrong. He tricked us all."

Myla tripped and they both went sprawling. The detonator lay on its side, painfully close. Myla's arms were locked around Isiah's waist. With all his strength, Isiah lunged for the detonator.

He slipped free of Myla's grip and jammed the plunger down. The hiss of sparks erupted from the box and the fuse came to life.

"No!" Myla scrambled over the top of him and grabbed the detonator, but it was too late.

The spark snaked into the hole, flickering off the rocky walls before disappearing out of sight. Isiah braced himself against the ground as the seconds ticked past.

A deep boom ripped through the Hidden Citadel. The ground trembled and the sky seemed to crackle with thunder. A plume of dust and rock erupted from the hole, showering him with debris. Marie lost her footing and fell over.

The roar of water filled Isiah's ears. He turned his head to see the lake rolling and swirling like a whirlpool. Myla choked back tears as the water drained into the tunnels far below, churning with the power of a frenzied beast.

Isiah rolled Myla off of him and staggered to his feet. The adrenaline made him light-headed, while his insides turned over with dread.

"I'm sorry," he managed to say.

Tears pricked in Myla's eyes. "What have you done?"

Marie waved. "Come on!"

With one last apologetic look at Myla, Isiah put his head down and ran for the tower.

No More Oath

THE EXPLOSION SHOOK TESSA TO THE CORE. Dust rained onto her head from the tunnel above. If not for the crush of bodies around her, the shockwave would have made her collapse.

The frenzied shouting from Solomon's Raiders ceased. Labourers steadied themselves against the walls and a ripple of panicked whispers went through them.

"That's our cue," Lazaro said. He stood in the tunnel beside her, helping the labourers hold Solomon off. "Let's go."

"Not yet," Tessa replied. "Solomon will escape."

As the rumble of explosives faded, a new sound took its place—roaring water. Tessa's braced her entire body against the door.

The enraged yells from the other side turned into frantic banging. Raider's voices climbed above the growing surge.

"Let us out! Open the door!"

The churning water grew louder until it filled Tessa's senses. She pictured it surging through the tunnels, dashing itself against the narrow walls and growing faster and faster.

Solomon's Raiders screamed. The water exploded into the cavern with a deafening roar. Tessa felt it slam against the door as it swirled around the cavern, ripping through the tunnels and leaving nothing in its wake.

Water seeped beneath the door. It erupted through the cracks in the frame and drenched Tessa's clothes. She prayed they had enough strength to hold the door.

"Keep pushing!" she cried. Water poured from the top of the door, drenching her face. She spat out a mouthful of water and ignored the burning in her arms.

The Raiders' screams echoed down the tunnel, growing fainter as the raging torrent carried them away. The water seeping beneath the door climbed to Tessa's ankles.

"We can't hold it!" one of the labourers yelled. The ones at the back of the crowd turned and fled the tunnel.

The water level climbed to Tessa's calves. It forced its way through the sandstone, wearing it away to rain onto her head. She gasped for air and blinked the water from her eyes. It felt like she was about to drown.

"That's it," Lazaro said. He grabbed Tessa around the middle and pulled her away from the door. "We run!"

The rest of the labourers broke away. The door held for a few seconds, then it slammed open and a wall of water flooded into the tunnel. Lazaro dragged Tessa through the crowd of fleeing labourers. Water surged around their legs and whipped up as it crashed against the tunnel walls. Labourers clambered over one another to escape the surge.

The stairs appeared ahead of them, and Antony and Darla stood on either side, helping the labourers clamber up. Lazaro reached the stairs and dragged Tessa after him. The torrent hit the bottom steps and whipped back on itself, white with foam.

Light shone ahead. Tessa coughed and wiped the water from her eyes as they emerged in the tower. Half-drowned labourers ran through the door, spilling into the town beyond.

Lazaro put Tessa down against the wall. "Are you alright?" he asked.

Tessa hacked up the water in her lungs. Her arms screamed from holding the door shut for so long. "I think so."

Lazaro pulled her into a hug. "Good job down there, sis."

Tessa returned his embrace. Her soaked hair clung to her scalp, and she felt like a drowned rat. "I knew you had my back."

"Is Solomon dead?" Edith asked.

"There's no way he could have survived that," Tessa replied.

Edith nodded. "Good. Now's your chance to escape. Enrik might have heard the explosion."

Tessa shakily stood. Lazaro and the others gathered around.

"What about Isiah and Marie?" she asked.

"We'll pick them up on the way," Lazaro replied. "And Edith . . ." He hesitated. "I'm glad I trusted Tess about you."

Edith waved her hands. "I'll clean up the mess here. You escape while you still can."

Lazaro took the lead and they ran out of the tower. Labourers scattered through the streets. Terrified townsfolk peered out of windows and doorways at the chaos. Spooked eagles circled above.

"It's this way to the roosts," Tessa said. She took off running as fast as her legs would allow.

Lazaro and Aron fell in behind her, along with Helen and the rest of their Raider gang. Tessa ducked through the crowd of labourers, scanning the way ahead for any sign of Isiah.

A waving hand caught her eye. She spotted Marie and Isiah fighting their way through the crowd of labourers toward her. She doubled her pace and ran to their side.

"You did it!" Tessa wrapped her arms around the pair. "Solomon is dead."

"Do we leave now?" Marie asked.

Tessa nodded. "Come on."

Isiah hesitated for a moment.

"What's wrong?"

"I found Myla," he started.

Tessa shifted her weight. "We'll worry about her later." She tugged on his hand. "We don't have time."

Isiah relented and came after her. With the group reunited, they made the mad dash up the cliffside trail to where the eagles were kept. Handlers peered over the edge, trying to make sense of the chaos below. When Tessa reached the top, they bombarded her with questions.

"What's going on? Why is everybody panicking?"

"What happened to the lake?"

Tessa turned to it. The lake was half-empty. Its banks dropped several dozen feet to the new water level. A gaping hole exposed the tunnel that the explosives had blown.

Lazaro grabbed Tessa's arm and pulled her away from the handlers. A smile broke out on her face when Vyrro chirped a welcome. She laughed and ran to his side.

She stopped. "What's this?"

A chain linked Vyrro's leg to a nearby boulder, and his saddle and harness were missing.

Lazaro swore. "Solomon knew we'd try to escape." He pointed at the nearest handler. "You, where are the saddles kept?"

Before the handler could reply, a shadow fell over them. Tessa covered her ears as a deafening screech sounded and an eagle landed on the cliffside. Her blood turned to ice as she saw its rider.

"Morning, Lazaro," Enrik said. "Thought you could give me the slip?"

Lazaro drew his sabre. "Give up, Enrik. Your friend Solomon is dead."

"He was getting on my nerves," Enrik replied. "I was going to have to deal with him sooner or later if I wanted my revenge on Isiah." He swivelled to face the boy. "Jumping off the tower was very rude indeed."

Tessa tensed. She watched Lazaro for his reaction. His eyes flitted between Enrik and the town below.

"I only wish I'd found a way to have you exiled from Alcabaza before you ruined my plans," Enrik said. "It would have saved me a lot of trouble." He stretched out his arms. "But I got my own back. I took away everything you worked for."

Lazaro's nostrils flared. "You're still an exile yourself. You can never show your face in Alcabaza again."

"I've outgrown that city," he replied. "And I guess after taking your home from you and selling your brat of a sister to merchants, we're even on that front."

Lazaro adjusted his grip on his sabre. Enrik's Raiders closed in on their eagles, racing across the highlands. Enrik dismounted his eagle.

"Aren't you going to fight me?" he asked. "Let's settle this like men. No more Oath. Now is the time for blood." He laughed. "After everything I've put you through, you must *hate* me."

"You might have outgrown Alcabaza," Lazaro said. He caught Tessa's eye and nodded to the trail snaking down the cliffside. "But I've outgrown your tricks."

Tessa leapt into motion. Enrik swore as they sprinted off the clifftop and ran toward the town. Enrik's eagle let out a shrill cry and his Raiders fell into pursuit.

"What's the plan?" Tessa asked as she wobbled her arms to keep her balance.

"We fight them in the town," Lazaro replied. "We can't hope to face them directly without our eagles. The buildings will force them to land."

They reached the bottom of the trail and ran across the section of flat, empty ground that stretched between the cliff and the town. Behind them, the first of Enrik's eagles cleared the basin wall and dived after them.

Tessa jumped aside and covered her head with her arms as an eagle blasted overhead. Its talons flashed and its wings kicked up plumes of sand. Tessa blinked the stinging particles out of her eyes and kept going.

A second eagle swooped overhead with a screech. The buildings loomed painfully close. The hanging clotheslines and tarps seemed to beckon them.

"Watch out!"

Lazaro grabbed Tessa and they collapsed as an eagle rushed overhead, its talons snatching the air where they had been moments earlier.

Lazaro helped her up and they made it into the streets. Eagles soared overhead, skimming the tops of buildings. Townsfolk screamed and ran for cover as an eagle flew above the main road. Its Raider spat curses as it fought to avoid crashing into balconies and clotheslines.

One of his companions wasn't so lucky. Her eagle screeched in alarm as it struck a clothesline and became tangled in it. Tessa and her friends ducked as the eagle shot overhead, trailing feathers and clothes like a comet, before crashing into a merchant stall and flinging its Raider into the air.

"The alleys will force them to land," Lazaro said. "Then we can fight them on even terms."

"Watch out for their magic," Tessa warned.

As she said this, another eagle went into a dive. It swooped low over the street and a swirling vortex of sand erupted from its back. It hit the ground and materialized into a Raider.

Antony and Darla closed in. The Raider drew his sabre and began to circle them. The other Raiders abandoned their eagles and appeared on rooftops and in alleyways, blocking off their escape.

Lazaro kicked over a merchant stall and spilled its contents across the ground. Fruit and vegetables bounced across the street. He took up a position beside Helen.

"Where's Enrik?" he asked. "Do you see him?"

Tessa aimed her own sabre at a nearby Raider. "He's probably got these guys to do his dirty work."

One of the Raiders attacked, dissolving into a vortex and spinning toward Lazaro. The Raider became solid and swung his sabre. Lazaro parried it and delivered a kick to the man's stomach. He stumbled back and tripped on the produce covering the floor. Lazaro's blade brushed his robes, but he turned into a vortex and darted away.

"Keep your backs together," Helen said. "That way they can't separate us."

Darla and Antony exchanged blows with a group of Enrik's Raiders. Darla caught a blade with her sabre and batted it away, before slicing a Raider's shoulder. "We're outnumbered."

Tessa spotted an unguarded alleyway. "There's our escape!"

Lazaro dashed toward it. He caught his opponent by surprise, forcing him to dart away. The tip of Lazaro's sabre caught him as he dematerialized. He reappeared off to the side, swearing and clutching his stomach.

Tessa and the others fell in behind Lazaro. Enrik's Raiders gave chase, and their eagles circled in the sky above. Tessa struck the end of a clothesline as she went and it collapsed behind her, tangling the Raiders in pursuit.

"Where to now?" Helen asked. She lifted her blade as a Raider appeared beneath an archway street to her left.

Lazaro took a sharp turn into a doorway. He lowered his shoulder and burst through the door. The townsfolk inside bolted. "We've got to get out of the open. It'll force them to come to us."

They piled into the room. Helen turned on her heel to cover the door, while Darla and Antony took up positions at the windows. Sand whipped around the house as Enrik's Raiders closed in.

"We can't hold them off forever," Darla called.

The floorboards creaked upstairs as Raiders erupted into the house. Luca and Aron took positions by the stairs. Sabres flashed through the doorway and windows as their attackers tried to gain entry.

"Barricade the way in," Lazaro ordered. Blood seeped through the robes covering his shoulder from where he had knocked open the door. Tessa ran to help Isiah and Marie shift furniture to block the open doorway, while Darla and Antony fought the Raiders off long enough to close the wooden shutters.

"Things are going south, Lazaro," Helen warned. She ripped off her sleeve and used it to bandage a cut on her arm.

"This is our best shot," Lazaro replied. "We can't fight them in the open. They have too much mobility."

"We need to stop Enrik," Tessa said. "Maybe I could lure the Raiders away from here."

"Absolutely not," Lazaro replied. "We stand a better chance if we're together."

"This is my fault," Isiah blurted out. "It's me that Enrik's after."

Tessa took his arm. "That's not true. He's after us all."

A crash sounded from the staircase. Aron let out a whoop. "We got one!"

Tessa ran to them. A crumpled body lay at the foot of the stairs, his neck twisted at a weird angle.

"He fell down," Aron said.

Grimacing, Tessa scooped up the dead Raider's sabre and passed it to Isiah. "I have a plan."

She pushed past Aron and ran up the stairs. Isiah hesitated, then went after her.

"Hey!" Aron called. "There are still Raiders up there!"

Tessa clambered to the second story. A Raider flew at her. She instinctively parried and the clash of metal stabbed her eardrums.

Tessa lashed out with her foot and her heel connected with the man's kneecap. He grunted in pain and stumbled away before she could follow up with a cut.

She shoved past him and ran to an open window. The wooden shutters lay broken on the floor. She leaned against the sill and peered out. "The ground isn't that far."

"We're going after Enrik, aren't we?" Isiah asked.

"It's the only way to lure some of his Raiders away," she replied. She slammed the door to the room behind them to block off the injured Raider.

Isiah's expression hardened. "Let's do it."

Sheathing her sabre, Tessa climbed out of the window and jumped. She was weightless for a moment, before her legs hit the ground and a shockwave went through her knees.

She rolled, trying to absorb some of the impact. It still sent a stab of pain surging up her legs. Moments later, Isiah landed beside her with a grunt.

Tessa waved her hands in the air. "Hey! Over here!"

Some of the Raiders turned their heads.

"Tess!" Lazaro yelled. "Go kill Enrik for me!"

Tessa smiled. She grabbed Isiah's hand and took off at a run. The Raiders broke away from the house and gave chase. Vortexes of sand spiralled across the tops of houses.

"I know where Enrik's hiding," Isiah said. "Or at least, I know where we can get his attention." He motioned to Edith's tower.

Tessa took a deep breath. "The tower it is."

Showdown

ISIAH FOUGHT HIS BURNING LUNGS AS THEY SPRINTED toward the tower. Raiders darted through alleyways and leapt across balconies, trying to cut them off. Townsfolk watched them, peering through their shutters at the street below.

The tower appeared at the end of the road. Isiah hopped over the fallen stalls that Lazaro had kicked over. Tessa's heavy breathing emanated from beside him. He shot a nervous glance over his shoulder at their pursuers.

The Raiders were still giving chase. Several broke away and tried to summon their eagles. The birds circled overhead, searching for a clear path to dive. Isiah kept to the safety of overhangs and darted beneath low-slung clotheslines to give him cover.

He reached the end of the street and threw open the door to Edith's tower. He piled inside, followed by Tessa, and they slammed the door shut. He spotted a key hanging on the wall and jammed it into the lock.

"Get the shutters," he said.

Tessa obeyed. The thick wood stole away the morning light, plunging the interior of the tower into shadow. Isiah backed away, lungs heaving. Raiders yelled outside. Fists pounded against the shutters, but the wood held.

"Edith?" Isiah cupped his hands to his mouth.

No response.

"She might be hiding," Tessa replied. "She probably heard the chaos."

Isiah swallowed. Eager to get away from the Raiders lurking outside, he took the staircase to the second level. Tessa hung close behind him. The second floor stood deserted. Below, the Raiders threw themselves at the door, trying to break it open.

They climbed to the third floor. The steady thud of wings echoed as the birds circled outside. As Isiah reached the stairs to the fourth floor, a flurry of wingbeats sounded and something heavy landed above his head. After a moment, floorboards creaked as someone walked slowly across them. Isiah knew who they belonged to.

"It's nice of you to return, Isiah," Enrik's voice wafted down.

Isiah shrank away from the stairs. He drew his sabre and held it at the ready. Tessa grabbed his arm and motioned to the shelves. As Enrik's feet appeared on the top of the staircase, Isiah ducked behind a pile of books.

"Now perhaps we can finish what we started," Enrik said. "Your dragon can't save you now."

Isiah hunched low to the ground and stuck to the cover of one of the many bookshelves. The rows of shelves and cluttered piles of furniture turned the third floor into a labyrinth.

"Aren't you going to throw another accusation at me?" Enrik asked. He reached the bottom of the stairs and strolled along the corridor. "About how I'm an Oath-breaker, how I deserved what I got?"

Isiah held his tongue. A board creaked beneath his foot as he adjusted his weight. Tessa crouched beside him, her sabre drawn.

"It must have destroyed you to learn that the only other Marked people you've ever met are monsters," Enrik continued. "You must have thought you'd found your kin. Now you've killed them."

Books tumbled as Enrik's sabre bit into wood. Isiah shuffled away from the noise.

"You can't hide from me forever, boy," Enrik snarled. More books collapsed. "Even if I have to tear this entire place apart."

Isiah paused by a gap in a bookshelf. Enrik walked through the maze, sabre in hand. The man's cold, calculating gaze swept across the room. Isiah ducked before he could be spotted.

"I don't know why you keep fighting." Enrik stepped around a corner and swung his sabre. The impact echoed across the room. "You'll never be free from your Mark. It's your curse, boy. You're doomed to spend the rest of your life hiding and running."

Tessa's hand slipped around Isiah's. He saw the gears turning in her mind.

"We can trick him," she whispered. She narrowed her eyes and concentrated, and a flicker of colour appeared. Isiah's eyes widened as an illusion of himself began to materialize.

"You've given up your only other chance of being free," Enrik called. "Solomon gave you an opportunity, and how did you repay him? By drowning him."

Isiah backed away as Tessa formed the illusion. She put her fingers against her temples and her face twisted in pain. The illusion solidified into a fuzzy replica of himself, with smudged robes and blurry characteristics. Isiah hoped it would be convincing enough.

"Solomon was evil," Isiah said.

Floorboards creaked as Enrik changed direction.

"We're all monsters out here, Isiah. The Badlands doesn't leave anyone unscathed. Solomon did what he had to do."

Tessa grunted. The illusion flickered again. She sank to her knees and squeezed her eyes shut.

"You used him," Isiah replied, louder. He prayed Tessa could hold the illusion long enough.

The footsteps grew closer. "If you had taken his offer, you could by flying to Paradon right now." Isiah almost heard the grin spread across Enrik's face. "But now you'll die instead."

A blast of sand whipped toward the illusion. Enrik materialized and his sabre flashed through the air. It sliced the illusion in two and bit into the bookshelf beside it. Enrik's eyes widened.

Tessa gasped and collapsed against a bookshelf. The illusion disintegrated, and Isiah seized his chance.

He leapt from cover and swung his sabre. Enrik wrenched his sabre free, but not fast enough. Isiah's blade powered through his defence and sliced across his chest.

Enrik swore and staggered away. His robes hung loosely from where they had been cut, and blood began bathing the material a deep red. Enrik's face twisted into a snarl. He recovered and swung at Isiah.

Isiah parried the blow and Enrik's sabre glanced off it. Enrik tried to follow up, but the tight shelving restricted their movements. Isiah aimed a thrust at Enrik to build distance between them.

"I don't know what kind of magic you discovered while I was gone," Enrik said, "but it won't help you."

He darted forward with a flurry of cuts. Isiah stumbled away. He jammed his arm into one of the shelves and lobbed its contents onto the floor between them. Behind him, Tessa shakily stood.

"Where's your fight gone, Tessa?" Enrik asked. "You're a sitting duck." He leapt towards Isiah.

Isiah raised his arms to defend himself, but Enrik exploded into a sand vortex and rushed past him. Isiah coughed and shielded his stinging eyes. The sand whipped his face and invaded his airways. He spun around as Enrik materialized and attacked.

The clash of steel rang out. Isiah's arm trembled under the force of Enrik's blow. Tessa recovered herself and aimed a swing at Enrik's sword arm. The blade glanced off his shoulder armour uselessly.

"You're losing your touch," Enrik mocked. He grabbed her arm and planted a foot against her stomach.

Tessa gasped in pain and collapsed against a shelf. Panic flared in Isiah's chest.

"Maybe I *will* kill her first," Enrik said. He stood between them, his sabre tip poised to strike Isiah's throat. "Letting you watch her die will sweeten my revenge."

Isiah launched a desperate flurry of attacks. Enrik caught them on his blade and deflected them away. He twisted his wrist and his sabre flashed around. Isiah gasped as it sliced his forearm.

"The penalty of foolish attacks," Enrik snapped.

Blood oozed from the cut on Isiah's arm. He gritted his teeth. It hadn't cut deep, but the sight of it made his stomach turn over. He swung at Enrik again. The man transformed into a vortex and darted backwards.

"You can't fight me," Enrik mocked. "My magic makes me *unkilla-ble.*"

Isiah held his free hand to the cut on his forearm. Warm blood seeped between his fingers as the initial shock faded to hot, throbbing pain.

Another round of Enrik's blows weakened his defences. The sabre felt heavier in his hand. Each parry was slower, clumsier. Isiah stumbled on the books scattered on the floor and his elbows bumped against the shelves. He jerked aside and Enrik's blade brushed past his robes.

"I thought I might cut off your hand and keep you alive to suffer for a while," Enrik said. "But you disappoint me, Isiah."

Isiah's muscles ached and his shoulder burned. The heavy, dust-laden air made each breath a struggle. He wiped the sweat off his forehead and left a smear of red from his blood-stained hand in its place. The cut on his arm leeched his strength away.

Enrik transformed into another vortex and dashed towards him. Isiah stumbled away and raised a hand to shield his eyes from the stinging sand. He yelled a strangled battle cry and blindly lashed out with his sabre.

His arm jerked as it hit something solid.

Enrik let out a pained gasp. Isiah opened his eyes to see his sabre impaled in the man's chest. Enrik looked down at it and the colour drained from his face. He wobbled and his sabre clattered to the floor.

Isiah recovered himself. With a yell, he ripped the blade free. Enrik collapsed onto his knees, clutching the hole in his chest. A wave of blood oozed between his fingers. He sucked at the air in an attempt to draw breath, before collapsing against a bookshelf and sliding to the floor.

Isiah stared at Enrik's face-down corpse, panting. The adrenaline gave way to a rush of pain and nausea. With shaking hands, he sheathed his sabre and then clutched his injured arm to his chest.

Tessa hobbled over. "Is he really dead?"

Isiah steadied his breathing. "I think so."

Tessa crouched beside him. She tentatively put a hand on his shoulder. "Let me see."

Isiah extended his arm. Tessa carefully peeled away the material, exposing the long cut down his inner arm.

"You'll live," she said. She grabbed a handful of her sleeve and ripped it away, then bound the material around his cut. As she worked, Isiah made out the faint pink line that betrayed her own injury.

Tessa noticed him looking. "It's like old times, huh?"

Isiah managed a smile. She finished binding the wound and he helped her stand.

"Are you going to be okay?" he asked.

Tessa rubbed her shoulders. "The magic took a lot out of me, but I'm starting to feel normal again." She paused. "Thanks for keeping me safe. I wouldn't have been able to fight Enrik on my own."

"Your illusion was good thinking," Isiah replied. "Does this mean you're going to tell Lazaro about it?"

She gave a weak laugh. "Maybe after all this, he won't flip his lid when I tell him we went into a ruin alone."

They walked to the window and saw that the Raiders were still trying to gain entry to the house. In the town, several eagles spiralled into the air.

"They're fleeing," Isiah said.

"Looks like Lazaro showed 'em a thing or two." Tessa leaned out and called to the Raiders below. "Enrik is dead!"

Isiah pumped his fist into the air. Blood still streaked his forehead from the fight. Tessa pried Enrik's sabre out of his hand and tossed it down to them. When they saw whose sabre it was, the Raiders broke form and scattered.

Tessa stepped away from the window. "I'm sorry about Solomon. I know you looked up to him."

Isiah waved her away, trying to mask the turmoil inside him. "I was so excited to see people who were Marked, I let myself get carried away."

"I know he gave you hope." Tessa wrapped her arms around him. "But I don't care about your Mark."

Isiah returned her embrace. "I'd rather stay Marked than turn into a monster like Solomon was."

Tessa looped her hand around his and they made their way down to the ground floor of the tower. The building lay still and silent, pin-pricks of light peering through the half-destroyed shutters. Isiah tried to shake the feeling of unease.

Enrik is dead, he thought. *It's over.* He unlocked the door and they stepped outside.

Solomon stepped around the corner.

"Isiah!" he yelled. His ripped, sodden robes hung from his shoulders like rags. "How could you betray your own people!"

Isiah's heart dropped into his stomach. Solomon clutched a knife against Edith's neck.

"This traitorous wretch stole our future!" Solomon snapped. His eyes almost bulged out of his head. "And then you try to kill me? Why can't you see that they don't care about us?"

Tessa went for her sabre. "You should be dead!"

"I found another exit!" Solomon coughed. "You drowned my Raiders, but you won't get rid of me that easily."

"Put the knife down, Solomon," Isiah said slowly.

"We were supposed to fly to Paradon," Solomon yelled. His voice echoed through the town. "You could have joined us! I would have healed your Mark and you'd get your life back. No more hiding, no more living in fear."

Edith gripped Solomon's muscular arm. The blade hovered inches from her throat. Isiah racked his brains for a plan, but the fight with Enrik had robbed him of the last of his strength.

Movement flickered in an alleyway. When Isiah looked over, he locked eyes with Myla. She stared at Solomon with an empty gaze, gripping a knife.

"You're evil, Solomon," Isiah said. "I'd never cure my Mark if it meant becoming like you."

Solomon snarled. Myla took her chance and darted from the alleyway. Solomon screamed and arched his back as she buried a knife between his ribs.

Edith seized her chance. She wrestled free of Solomon's grip and spun around, firing a shower of sparks into the man's eyes. Solomon whirled away, bellowing and trying to reach the knife lodged in his back. Edith raised her hands and her face darkened.

"You forced me to help you," she said. "Now I'm going to take back what I've done."

Solomon's face twisted as the skin around his shoulders began to wither.

"No!" he grabbed at it, trying to press it back on. "I've worked so hard for this!"

The sheets of skin darkened and peeled off, one after another. The bumps and ridges of his hidden Mark became visible. Solomon fell to his knees. He scooped the withering skin off the ground and desperately tried to reattach it.

Edith took Tessa's sabre and marched over to him. Isiah squeezed his eyes shut as a sickening thud sounded. Solomon's body collapsed.

"No matter what persona he tried to put on," Edith said, dusting off her hands, "I always knew he was a twisted, sick man."

Myla stood over the body, covering her mouth with her hands. Isiah jogged to her side.

"I'm sorry," he started.

"You were right," she said quietly. "I didn't believe you, but when I heard it for myself . . ." She trailed off.

Isiah wobbled on the spot, unsure what to do. Myla leaned against him. "I should have listened to you."

"You couldn't have known," Isiah said. "He tricked me too." He put an arm around her shoulders. "You saved us."

Myla sniffed. "I guess you're right."

"Look!" Tessa called.

Isiah turned to see Lazaro and the gang jogging down the road. With the last of their energy, he and Tessa ran to greet them.

Another Shot

ISIAH REACHED LAZARO'S SIDE AND SKIDDED to a halt. As Tessa approached, Lazaro sheathed his sabre and wrapped his arms around her.

"Is Enrik dead?" he asked.

"Isiah killed him," Tessa replied. "It's over."

Lazaro laughed and clapped Isiah on the shoulder. "I knew you'd do it, boy."

The other Raiders gathered around. Helen and several others sported cuts from the fight, and a bandage was wrapped around Luca's leg.

"The rest of his Raiders fled," Lazaro announced. "We put them on the run. I don't think they'll be back any time soon."

Edith shuffled over. "Solomon's reign is over. The people of the Hidden Citadel are free."

Isiah shifted his footing. "What's going to happen to the place now?"

"I'll take care of it," Edith replied. "It will take a while for the people here to come to terms with what Solomon was doing."

"All we need now are the saddles to our eagles," Lazaro said. He dusted his hands off. "Then we can be rid of this place."

Isiah exchanged glances with Tessa and the others.

"What is it?" Lazaro asked.

"Now that Solomon and Enrik are dead, I was wondering if we should stay for a while," Isiah said.

"We don't have a reason to run away," Tessa added.

Lazaro's nose crinkled. "After everything we've been through?"

"What if the people here need our help?" Isiah asked. He motioned to the ruined stalls and damaged houses that Enrik's Raiders had left in their wake. "If we leave, where are we going to go?"

Lazaro scratched his chin. "We *do* have a roof over our heads here," he said slowly. "Perhaps we can give this place another shot."

Tessa laughed and hugged him. As Darla and Antony dragged Solomon's body away, Isiah walked over to Myla. She was sitting on a rock, looking out across the half-drained lake.

"I'm sorry you had to betray Solomon," Isiah said. "I wish there had been some other way."

"Solomon was the closest thing I had to family," Myla replied. "But I couldn't let him keep hurting people like that." She bowed her head.

Isiah swallowed. "Do you need some time alone?"

"No," she said quickly. "You can stay."

They sat in silence for a moment. Further away, Tessa fell into conversation with Aron and Marie.

"Is it true what you said before," Isiah asked, "about you being from Paradon?"

Myla nodded. "It made me feel like we understood each other." She traced a circle in the dirt with her foot. "Why did you give up your chance at being cured?"

Isiah searched for the words. The weight of everything they'd been through began to settle on his shoulders as the adrenaline faded. It felt like he'd given up the oasis for a second time.

"I don't need to cure it," he said at last. "Aegon doesn't care about it. Tessa doesn't care about it. That's good enough for me."

"And you don't worry that the people in the Badlands will discover it?"

Isiah shrugged. "My Mark is part of me."

Several townsfolk cautiously walked to the edge of the lake and peered down at the water.

"I hope we haven't ruined it here," Isiah said.

"We'll survive," Myla replied. "There's enough water to sustain us, and maybe some of us handlers can learn to fly the eagles and take over from Solomon."

"You should stay with us," Isiah blurted out.

She cocked her head. "Really?"

"I mean, you don't have Solomon anymore. It's the least we can do after you helped us."

Myla sidled closer. "I'd like that."

"I'm sure Lazaro will be okay with it," Isiah said. He nudged her. "And if we're not going anywhere any time soon, I could even teach you how to fly Aegon."

Myla beamed. "She can live inside the basin with us." She paused. "I hope Tessa won't mind that I'm from Paradon."

"She knows we're not all bad," Isiah replied. "Even if she doesn't show it much."

Aron waved them over. Isiah slipped off the rock and jogged to his side.

"Edith says we can take over Solomon's house," Aron said.

"So no more living in tents?"

"Nope." Aron grinned. "Tessa thinks it's weird, but *I* for one like the idea of becoming the Hidden Citadel's new Raiders."

"Woah," Isiah said with a laugh, "slow down there. Let's not get ahead of ourselves."

"Why not?" Aron said. "*Someone* needs to take the job." He rubbed his hands together. "I might be able to fly my own eagle, too. Myla," he added, "how many eagle hatchlings do you have?"

As Aron fell into conversation with Myla, Isiah broke away. Tessa stood with Lazaro, watching Helen apply bandages to his cuts.

"We're going to have *so* many repairs to do," Helen said, gesturing to his sliced-up robes. "You'd better learn how to sew."

Tessa looked up as Isiah approached.

"How about we go and free our eagles," Isiah asked. He nudged her. "We could even go flying if you like."

Tessa's eyes lit up. "Sounds good to me."

"Hunting the last of Enrik's Raiders, are you?" Helen asked.

Isiah exchanged glances with Tessa. "I had something else in mind."

* * *

Aegon roared as she swept across the highlands. Crags of rock and scraggly trees rushed past below. The basin loomed ahead of them, a pocket of blue and green amid a sea of red rock. Isiah threw back his head and let out a whoop as they cleared the basin wall and soared over the Hidden Citadel.

Aegon's scales glistened deep purple and blue. She turned on her wing and spiralled over the lake, her wingbeats rustling the foliage that hugged its shores. Townsfolk clustered together and gazed up at them as they soared through the sky.

Tessa perched on Vyrro's shoulders nearby. The wind ruffled the mighty eagle's feathers and made his tail twitch as he balanced on the air currents. Isiah braced himself as Aegon descended and landed in the basin on the shores of the lake.

"What are you going to do with her now?" Tessa asked, sliding off Vyrro's saddle.

Isiah patted Aegon's flank. The dragon curled herself around a large tree and watched over the town, her serpentine neck shimmering like an opal in the sunlight. Twin plumes of smoke curled from her nostrils.

"We'll strengthen our bond," Isiah said.

Tessa put her hands on her hips. "She'll be safe here—for real, this time."

The sight of Aegon, so majestic and powerful, filled Isiah with a sense of awe. He remembered when he used to watch the dragons wheel in the skies above Paradon. "You're right." He stepped away. "Solomon was going to teach me. For a moment I thought I'd found someone like Ward."

Tessa put an arm around him. "You don't need Solomon. I know you'll figure things out—teacher or not."

Isiah nodded in determination. "It's a long road, but we can do it." He looped a hand around hers. "Solomon was going to trick me into thinking you'd flown away and left me, but I know you'd never do that."

Tessa squeezed his hand. "Raiders stick together." She gave him a warm smile. "Whether you're from Paradon or not."

Isiah broke away. He jogged toward Aegon. "How about we go for another round?"

As Tessa ran to Vyrro, Isiah scrambled up Aegon's flank and, with a beat of her mighty wings, they erupted into the air once more.

Get a Free Book!

He dreamed of killing a dragon. Now he has to save one.

A single dragon pelt could buy Cole a life outside the slums—but when he joins a band of outlaws to seek his fortune, the hunt doesn't go the way he thought.

Because dragons aren't the monsters he believed... and the moment he refuses to kill it, he becomes the prey.

Stuck with a wounded dragon and with rival hunters closing in, Cole has one chance at survival:

Keep it alive long enough to escape the wilds.

Grab your copy now at: www.morganclasperauthor.com

Acknowledgements

I hope you enjoyed reading Raider's Oath! This is the most fun I've had with a book, and, as of writing this, it's my favourite one yet. The funny thing is that it almost turned out very different indeed...

I never quite believed authors when they said that their characters "came to life" and took control of their stories—until it happened to me. You see, Myla was never supposed to exist!

Originally she was supposed to take Isiah and his friends to see the eagles, and that was it. But from the moment I added her in, she forced her way into the story and just kept popping up in chapter after chapter.

Things seemed to work so naturally with her there that I ended up changing my outline and going with the flow—and personally, I think the book turned out much better for it. Characters work in mysterious ways...

I'd like to thank my long-time editor, Darcy Werkman, for his invaluable insights and advice, as well as my cover designer Fabrice Bertolotto for his incredible work on the cover. I'd also like to extend my thanks to my illustrator Marina Baskakova for the beautiful ink illustrations that really capture this story and bring its scenes to life.

I'm also thankful to my family for their continued support, along with every reader who has given my books a go. Isiah and Tessa's adventures are still far from over, so I hope you'll stick with me to see what's in store for them next.

- Morgan

About the Author

Morgan Lee Clasper is a fantasy author and freelance copywriter who has over seven years of experience in the publishing industry. As a copywriter, he's worked with New York Times, Wall Street Journal, and USA Today bestselling authors to craft beautiful book blurbs, engaging author bios, and eye-catching sales copy.

Morgan is the author of the YA fantasy series The Frostwing Quadrilogy and the Chronicles of Alcabaza. When not writing, he enjoys studying philosophy, existential psychology, and Christian and Orthodox theology. For more information (and a free book!) visit: www.morganclasperauthor.com